Praise for

Bundle of Trouble

"A stellar debut . . . Deftly plotted with a winning protagonist and a glorious San Francisco setting, *Bundle of Trouble* is a page-turning read. We will be hearing much more from this talented newcomer. Highly recommended."

—Sheldon Siegel, *New York Times* bestselling author of *Perfect Alibi*

"Anyone who's been a mother or had one will welcome the arrival of this entertaining new sleuth."

—Gillian Roberts, author of the Amanda Pepper Mysteries

"You'll love keeping up with this amazing mother and sleuth in the fun, fast-paced *Bundle of Trouble*."

—Margaret Grace, author of the Miniature Mysteries

"A charming, gutsy, wry character who will make you laugh so hard you'll forget the labor pains. Cigars all around . . . *Bundle of Trouble* is a natural-born winner."

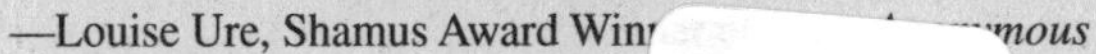

—Louise Ure, Shamus Award Win[...] *[...]mous*

Berkley Prime Crime titles by Diana Orgain

BUNDLE OF TROUBLE
MOTHERHOOD IS MURDER

Motherhood is Murder

Diana Orgain

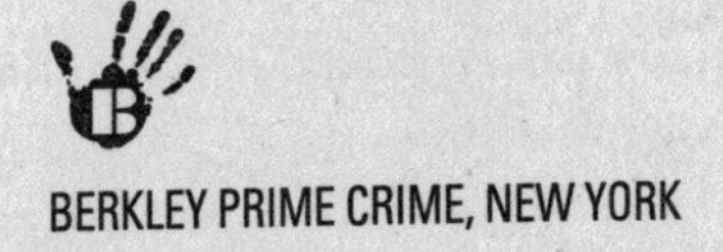

BERKLEY PRIME CRIME, NEW YORK

THE BERKLEY PUBLISHING GROUP
Published by the Penguin Group
Penguin Group (USA) Inc.
375 Hudson Street, New York, New York 10014, USA
Penguin Group (Canada), 90 Eglinton Avenue East, Suite 700, Toronto, Ontario M4P 2Y3, Canada
(a division of Pearson Penguin Canada Inc.)
Penguin Books Ltd., 80 Strand, London WC2R 0RL, England
Penguin Group Ireland, 25 St. Stephen's Green, Dublin 2, Ireland (a division of Penguin Books Ltd.)
Penguin Group (Australia), 250 Camberwell Road, Camberwell, Victoria 3124, Australia
(a division of Pearson Australia Group Pty. Ltd.)
Penguin Books India Pvt. Ltd., 11 Community Centre, Panchsheel Park, New Delhi—110 017, India
Penguin Group (NZ), 67 Apollo Drive, Rosedale, North Shore 0632, New Zealand
(a division of Pearson New Zealand Ltd.)
Penguin Books (South Africa) (Pty.) Ltd., 24 Sturdee Avenue, Rosebank, Johannesburg 2196,
South Africa

Penguin Books Ltd., Registered Offices: 80 Strand, London WC2R 0RL, England

MOTHERHOOD IS MURDER

A Berkley Prime Crime Book / published by arrangement with the author

PRINTING HISTORY
Berkley Prime Crime mass-market edition / March 2010

Cover illustration by Fernando Juarez.
Cover design by Annette Fiore Defex.
Interior text design by Kristin del Rosario.

For information, address: The Berkley Publishing Group,
a division of Penguin Group (USA) Inc.,
375 Hudson Street, New York, New York 10014.

ISBN: 978-0-425-23373-3

BERKLEY® PRIME CRIME
Berkley Prime Crime Books are published by The Berkley Publishing Group,
a division of Penguin Group (USA) Inc.,
375 Hudson Street, New York, New York 10014.
BERKLEY® PRIME CRIME and the PRIME CRIME logo are trademarks of Penguin Group (USA) Inc.

PRINTED IN THE UNITED STATES OF AMERICA

10 9 8 7 6 5 4 3 2 1

This book is dedicated to
Tom, Carmen, Tommy, Jr., and Robert
who always make me smile and feel lucky
to be sharing this wonderful life with them.

ACKNOWLEDGMENTS

Thank you to D. P. Lyle, M.D., and Judy Melinek, M.D., who provided me with details on forensic medicine and poisonings. You were so generous with your time, and patient with my many questions and follow-ups. Thanks to Dave Hardy for providing me with insights into law enforcement, and Kathy Johnson who not only assisted me with law enforcement details but who has always been a source of support and strength for me for so many years. Any errors in forensic or law enforcement procedures are my own.

Thanks to Michelle Vega and Megan Swartz at Berkley Prime Crime and to Lucienne Diver of The Knight Agency—you are all among the very best in the business. Thanks to P. J. Nunn at Breakthrough Promotions for your efforts in promoting my work, and Jeniffer Thompson and Anna Bobro of Monkey C. Media for creating my wonderful website.

Special thanks to my critique group—THAT writing group.

Finally, thanks to my mother, Maria Carmen Noa, and to my loving husband, Tom Orgain.

• CHAPTER ONE •

At Sea

To Do:

1. Buy diapers.
2. Make Laurie's two-month check.
3. Find good "how to" book for PI business.
4. ✓ ~~Find dress for dinner cruise.~~
5. ✓ ~~Ask Mom to babysit.~~
6. Exercise.

I stared into the bathroom mirror and wondered how I'd failed to bring a hairbrush along on the San Francisco Bay dinner cruise. I ran my hands down the length of my mop, trying to tame the frizzies. If I put a little water on the problem, would it help or make it worse?

The door to the restroom flew open. Sara, one of the moms from my new mommy group, appeared. She looked worse than I did. Her lipstick was smudged and her hair had the volume of a lion's mane.

"Oh my God! Kate! I didn't know you were here." She took a step back toward the door, then hesitated, looking like she'd been caught with her hand in the cookie jar.

She was so prim and proper at dinner. Probably doesn't like to be seen looking so rumpled, but hey, if you can't look bad in the ladies' room, then there's no safe haven.

Sara ran her hands along the front of her black cocktail dress, which was wrinkled and wet, then squinted at her reflection. She jumped into action, grabbing a paper towel and fixing the smeared lipstick. "Your husband's been looking everywhere for you. The captain's called an 'all hands on deck.' "

"My hands, too?" I asked, wiggling my fingers under the faucet to activate the automatic water flow.

Sara scrunched her mouth in disapproval.

"I guess I'm not up on ship rules," I said to her reflection.

"Everyone has to go back to their tables, now!" She grabbed another paper towel and frantically scrubbed at the wet section of her dress.

I stopped fussing with my hair and shifted my gaze from Sara's reflection to Sara.

If everyone was supposed to be back to their tables, what was she doing here?

"Why?" I asked.

"There's been an accident."

Goose bumps rose on my arms. "What kind of accident?"

"Helene fell down the back staircase." Sara motioned me toward the door. "Come on, come on."

We made our way through a dimly lit corridor toward the main dining hall. The cruise ship held roughly seventy-five passengers although tonight it was only about half full.

The change in atmosphere was immediately noticeable. Not to mention eerie. The dance floor was empty and the music was off. We crossed the bar area, which moments ago had been packed, and hurried to our dining table.

Most of the passengers were seated at their tables. The chatter that had animated the room was subdued.

I spotted Jim standing alone at our table, gripping the back of his chair. He surveyed the room. When he saw me, his expression relaxed a notch, going from grim to serious.

I hurried to him and reached for his hand.

He embraced me. "Kate! I was worried."

"I need to find my husband," Sara said as she rushed past us and headed for the main stairwell.

"What's happened? Sara said Helene fell down some steps. Is it serious?"

"I'm not sure. The captain asked everyone to return to their dining tables. Didn't you hear him on the microphone? Where've you been?"

Before I could answer, my elbow was jogged by Evelyn, another mommy from our group. She was eight months pregnant with her second child. Her blond hair was pinned neatly back, and her green eyes flashed, enhanced by the lime scarf she wore. The scarf was arranged to draw the eye toward her protruding belly, which she proudly stroked.

"Kate! How awful! Did you hear about Helene?" Her

lips curled a bit, almost as if she were suppressing a smile.

Why was she smiling? Almost gloating.

"Sort of. Is she all right?"

"Ladies and gentlemen," the captain's voice boomed over the microphone. "Please take your seats. We will be a bit delayed in docking in San Francisco due to an unfortunate accident aboard. The U.S. Coast Guard will be joining us shortly. Thank you in advance for your full cooperation."

Evelyn squeezed my elbow and flitted off to gather her husband. Jim pulled my chair out for me.

"Coast Guard? What's going on?" I asked.

Jim's lips formed a line. "I was at the bar getting a Bud, when the brunette—"

"Sara, Miss No-Nonsense?"

"No. The other one, the one with the . . . with the . . ." Jim waved his hands around. "Fluffy dress."

I nodded. "Margaret."

Margaret was wearing a ballet tutu. I wish I could say it looked as ridiculous as it sounded, but the truth was it looked fabulous. Margaret was supertall, pencil thin, and had shapely legs. She looked as if she could have stepped out of a children's book—a cartoon character with spindly spider legs and a ruffle at her waist. But the gold top and shoes added something indescribable to the outfit. Making the cartoon Olive Oyl look glamorous and runway-ish.

"Yeah, Margaret," Jim continued. "She ran up to us, looking a little dazed, and said Helene fell down the back staircase. Said she was unconscious—"

"Unconscious?" I felt a shiver run down my spine.

Jim pulled out my dining chair. "The captain asked if there was a doctor on board."

I sat down and let him push my chair in.

We were the only ones at our table. Earlier, we had dined with all the parents from my new mothers' group: Sara, Helene, Margaret, Evelyn, and their husbands.

We had christened them: Sara was Miss No-Nonsense, Helene was Lean and Mean, Margaret was Tutu, and Evelyn was Preggers. We referred to the husbands as Cardboard Cutout Numbers 1 through 4.

Now, it felt almost irreverent to have given everyone a nickname.

"Where is everybody?" asked Jim.

I shrugged. "Helene, we know about, so her husband is probably with her, right? Wasn't Margaret's husband—"

"Alan?"

"Yeah, Alan, isn't he a doctor?"

Jim frowned. "A podiatrist."

"Okay. Well, med school and all. Maybe she twisted her ankle. Did you see the heels she was wearing?"

Jim tried to hide his smirk by sipping his beer.

I pushed his shoulder. "What's so funny?"

"You. We just heard that Helene may be unconscious and you're worrying about her shoes!"

"I'm not worried about her shoes! I'm wondering what happened to her and where everybody is. I mean, the woman practically kills herself wearing some ungodly high heels, just to please some man, who probably laughed at her—"

Margaret descended the main staircase and closed the distance on our table. I cut myself off despite Jim's snickers into his beer. She raised her hand in acknowledgment and sat down grim-faced.

"Where's Alan?" I asked.

"With Helene," she answered.

I shot Jim a smug look, which he ignored.

"How is she?" Jim asked.

Margaret's eyes clouded over and she shrugged helplessly. "I don't know."

We sat in awkward silence. I perused the other three tables in the dining room. The parties at each table were as somber as we were. The four-hour dinner cruise on the San Francisco Bay had now been delayed indefinitely and nobody looked pleased about it.

Margaret fiddled with a cocktail glass that lingered beside her half-eaten dessert. She lifted the glass and examined the contents. Only two melting ice cubes remained. She stirred them with her straw, hoping, I suppose, to release any vodka that might be clinging to them. After a moment of disappointing results, she returned the glass to the table. Her eyes flicked toward the bar.

"Can I get you anything?" Jim asked.

Margaret flushed. "No. God, no. Thank you." She picked up her discarded navy cloth napkin and wrung it.

From the main staircase Sara and her husband approached. Behind them Evelyn and her husband were struggling to keep up. Evelyn had one hand on her pregnant belly and the other on her husband's shoulder. They took their places at our table in silence. The men smelled of cigar smoke and looked relaxed. In contrast, both women had pinched expressions.

Now, there were only three vacant spots at our table. Helene's, her husband's, and Alan's. My eyes fell on Helene's empty spot. Sara gave me a tight smile, then put her hand on Margaret's to stop her fidgeting.

"Everything will be fine, you'll see," Sara said to Margaret.

Margaret lowered her eyes and nodded.

Suddenly we felt a bump and the ship jostled back and forth. Everyone in the dining room turned toward the sound.

Through the starboard window we could see the U.S. Coast Guard vessel had arrived. Crew members were roping the smaller craft to our ship.

The Coast Guard quickly boarded our ship and disappeared out of sight with the crew members.

Margaret cleared her throat and eyed Evelyn. "Does anyone know what happened? I mean, did she just slip or what?"

I had noticed that the woman hadn't been very chatty with Evelyn throughout the dinner and now wondered what the look Margaret had flashed her might mean.

Evelyn shrugged and returned Margaret's look evenly. "How would I know? Ask Sara."

Sara pressed her shoulders back and sat a little taller.

"She was really out of it," Evelyn continued, rubbing her extended belly. "How much did she have to drink anyway?"

"I didn't think she had that much, did she?" Margaret asked.

Helene's empty place seemed to dominate the table. Her dessert plate still held the untouched apple turnover. The ice cream had melted and run over the edge of the plate onto the navy and white place mat. Next to the plate, two drained cocktail glasses loomed, and in the tall wineglass only the stain of red wine remained.

A strange hush settled on our table.

Howard, Sara's husband, slouched into his chair and casually slung his arm around the back of Sara's. "Looks like we're going to be here awhile."

Everyone at the table looked at Howard, and then followed his eyes to the starboard window. The night and bay were dark except for a troubling light that was converging upon us.

"Oh good!" Margaret exclaimed. "That must be the hospital boat for Helene."

The craft nudged itself alongside us. Silence descended on the entire dining room as letters on the boat came into view: "SFPD."

• CHAPTER TWO •

Outreach

I waved my cell phone around, counting bars as I moved from window to window. I had five bars showing until I hit the first number on the keypad, then three bars disappeared.

Most of the passengers were now lingering in the lounge area. The captain had announced that we would be further delayed and complimentary hot beverages would be served.

Jim was in line getting me a hot coffee, while I frantically tried to reach my mother, who was babysitting for us.

I moved away from the windows, still focused on the phone, and slammed directly into Nick Dowling, the San Francisco Medical Examiner.

"Mrs. Connolly! What a coincidence."

I swallowed the lump in my throat. If Nick was here, it couldn't be good news for Helene.

"Mr. Dowling. Don't tell me Helene is . . ."

Nick brushed his bangs off his forehead. "Well, I'm not supposed to tell you anything. You know that, Kate."

After giving birth to Laurie just a few short weeks ago, I'd been dragged into a murder investigation. Well, maybe "dragged" wasn't the right word. I had launched a fledgling private investigation business. Maybe "launched" wasn't the right word either. I had solved a missing person's case, and two murders.

Yes, I had *solved* it.

I'd also met the medical examiner.

The ME is called to a scene only when a death has occurred.

I closed my eyes and bowed my head. I felt Nick's hand on my elbow.

"I'm sorry, Kate. Were you close?"

I shook my head. "No, I only met her briefly. She and another mom invited me to join their mommy group. Tonight I met the whole gang."

He sighed. Something buzzed from inside his jacket pocket. "Sorry, I have to get that." He fished out his cell phone and hurried toward the exit.

Nick had reception, why didn't I?

I tried to focus on my phone but there was a tightening in my chest, my eyes teared.

Poor Helene. Dead? What could have happened?

How could a fall down some steps have killed her? Had she broken her neck? Head trauma or what?

One minute she was alive and well, eating dinner with us, then suddenly she was gone.

How many children did she have? They needed their mommy.

I swallowed the lump forming in my throat.

What was behind all the looks exchanged at my table? There seemed to be some animosity between the women.

Could Helene have been murdered?

Maybe someone pushed her down the stairs.

No, that didn't make any sense.

Certainly if anyone was trying to kill her, they wouldn't have done it on a crowded dinner cruise, much less by pushing her down a stairwell. That would have been stupid.

Push her overboard, maybe, but not down some steps.

It had to have been an accident. Or perhaps she'd died of natural causes. But she looked so healthy!

Maybe an aneurysm—those could strike suddenly and take someone's life even if they were young and seemingly healthy.

The medical examiner would figure it out.

Could I help in any way? Maybe there'd be a need for a PI?

Right. What was I thinking? I had no license. No way to land a case on my own. The only way I could fathom landing a case would be to enroll help from Senior PI Albert Galigani.

Galigani had been instrumental on my first case. Maybe he would let me use his license, or work for him. I'd do whatever it took to make myself legit.

I pushed the thought aside. Legitimacy didn't matter. Helping Helene did. Although I hardly knew her, my heart grieved.

I recalled meeting her last week. I was at Angles de la Terre, the ultrachic baby store in downtown San Francisco. It was pricey, but they carried high-end products and had a great selection of items such as cradle cap cream, which I hadn't been able to find at Target. Never mind the fact that there is no Target or Walmart in San Francisco. So after being forced to shop in a neighboring town and striking out, I made the trip downtown.

I was rewarded by the smell of chocolate wafting in from next door to Angles de la Terre. A tiny chocolatier selling only superb candy had been at the same location for ninety years. I stopped in and conducted a quality check. After all, old-time traditions need to be maintained. And who better to taste the chocolate than a San Francisco native?

Wasn't there something about chocolate that had medicinal properties anyway?

As I roamed the aisles of Angles de la Terre, I licked what remained of the truffle off my fingers. Indeed the quality was still superb.

I pushed Laurie's stroller down the organic cotton diapers aisle, which was flanked by signs noting MADE BY FAIR TRADE WORKERS, and felt my shoulders relax to the new age music. The next aisle held the remedies I was looking for, including cradle cap cream.

I grabbed the bottle and examined the ingredients—all natural, of course.

And ooh—aroma-therapeutic properties.

A woman, tall and slender with impeccable posture, rounded the corner of my aisle.

She stopped short of Laurie's stroller and gazed down at her. Laurie was decked out in a frilly little pink dress with matching pink booties and hat.

"She's beautiful," the woman said.

I smiled. "Thank you."

She scrutinized me. "Your first?"

I laughed. "That obvious, huh?"

"All new moms have that same look about them."

"Clueless?"

It was her turn to laugh. "No. Sort of shocked, kinda giddy, and yet . . ."

"Clueless."

The woman chuckled and stuck out her hand. "I'm Margaret Lipe."

I juggled the bottle of cream to my left hand and shook hers. "Kate."

"Magic Moments!" she said. "That's the best product line ever. You only need a little bit and it works like a charm. Have you tried their infant massage oil?" She reached over and picked up a bottle. "It's got lavender and I don't know what else in it." She flipped it over to examine the label. "Well, whatever it is, it just makes your little one snooze away."

"Who wouldn't want that?"

Margaret raised her eyebrows in a knowing response and handed me the bottle. "A few drops and you're set."

"I haven't heard about Magic Moments."

She looked at me like I was from Mars. "Are you local?"

I nodded.

"Don't you belong to a mommy group?" she asked.

"No. Who has the time?"

"You have to make the time. It's important not to lose yourself in the mothering process."

"Yeah. It's easy to get caught up in diapers, milk, and not much else." I shook the bottles in my hand. "Except maybe for cradle cap remedies."

"Well, mommy groups are really good for recommendations and keeping up with the latest scoop on everything! I run one and I'm always on the lookout for what works, what saves time, who's the best nanny, that sort of thing. And it's great to have the support. When I had my second baby, the other moms in the group took turns bringing me homemade dinners. Are you a stay-at-home?"

"Oh, a stay-at-home mom? Yes, I mean, I guess so . . . well, I work, too . . . sort of."

She nodded knowingly. "You haven't decided. Are you on maternity leave?"

"Uh. No . . . I . . . um . . ."

Why was I stuttering like a ninny?

I knew what I was doing. I had quit my job and I was staying at home with Laurie. The fact that I was trying to start my own business didn't change my status. Did it? Was I considered a working mom? Or was I a stay-at-home mom?

"I'm at home but I also work," I blurted. I reached into my diaper bag and proudly presented her with a homemade PI business card I had printed.

Margaret looked at the card curiously. "Ooooh. A private investigator?"

My natural inclination was to shy away from the attention, but I recalled my best friend, Paula, scolding me. "If you want to launch a business, the first thing you have to do is tell *everybody*!"

I simply nodded at Margaret and stood there flat-footed.

Another woman appeared at the head of the aisle. "There you are!"

"Oh, sorry. I was chatting," Margaret said. "This is Helene. We cofounded our mommy group, Roo & You."

Helene, lean and mean, was sporting designer blue jeans and chartreuse high heels. Her tan wool jacket was open slightly, revealing a blouse in the exact same shade as her shoes. She reached out and shook my hand. Hanging from her arm was the matching chartreuse handbag.

"Is Margaret recruiting you?" Helene leaned over the stroller. "She's darling. Pretty in pink and matchy-matchy. Just like me. I love it."

"Next week our group is going on a dinner cruise," Margaret said. "Why don't you join us?"

"A dinner cruise?" I asked.

"We usually meet at my place on Thursday afternoons for a playdate, but since you're working, you might not be able to make afternoons, huh?"

So there it was. I was working. I wasn't a stay-at-home.

Something inside me deflated. I wanted to be a stay-at-home mommy. Why couldn't I be? After all, I wasn't really working. I didn't have a current client. I was free on Thursday afternoons. I could make a playdate, whatever that was.

"Helene caught a cruising bug," Margaret continued. "She scored us tickets for a cruise around the bay. We're all bringing our husbands."

"One thing that happens to new moms is that you practically forget about the dads. They need attention, too." Helene rummaged around her handbag and pulled out a package of Nicorette gum. "Margaret wanted to include our guys. So, Roo & You hired a couple of babysitters to watch the wee ones." She unwrapped a piece of gum and popped it into her mouth. "And we're going sailing!"

A bay dinner cruise.

An evening with Jim and no baby? No nursing, no diapers, no bath time, no crying?

Hmmm. A cruise did sound a little more enticing than a playdate.

What would I wear?

Margaret dug a card out of her purse and handed it to me. It read *Roo & You—President* and had a little graphic of a kangaroo with a baby in its pouch. "You should come along and check out our group," she said.

"It sounds like fun," I replied.

Helene poked Margaret. "We need to go. Marcus is probably hungry by now."

Margaret smiled at me. "He's six months old and I'm vetting a new nanny. Unfortunately, someone stole the one I used with my two-year-old."

A nanny. Must be nice.

Helene chomped on the gum. "This stuff doesn't work. I still want a cigarette."

"You should try those patches." Margaret said, linking her arm through Helene's. She turned to me. "Call or e-mail me. I'll save you two tickets for the cruise."

The boat swayed, the motion brought my mind back to the present.

I still needed to call Mom. How could I find a network? I extended my arm and did a ridiculous dance trying to coax more than two bars out of the phone.

I quickly dialed home. All I could see in my mind's eye was Laurie's pretty round face with her rosy cheeks and toothless grin. Thank God I'd pumped before leaving the house this evening. I only hoped they wouldn't keep us here too much longer. I was missing Laurie like crazy.

I twisted and suddenly saw full bars. Mom answered on the third ring.

"How's Lemon Drop?" I asked.

Samba music blared in the background, then suddenly stopped.

"She fine, dear. Sleeping."

"What are you listening to?"

"Ricky Martin."

"Laurie is sleeping through Ricky Martin?"

"Yes, well, she's really still too young to enjoy the finer things in life."

I filled Mom in on the developments.

She gasped. "Don't worry about Laurie and me, we're fine. Just take care of whatever you need to. We'll be here."

What would I do without Mom?

As I was about to thank her and hang up, I heard a male voice in the background. "Who's that?"

"Oh! That's Hank. He came over to keep me company."

After nearly fifteen years of being single, Mom had recently started dating again. Hank was the man who'd brought her out of hiding.

"What are you, a teenager? You have some guy over as soon as the adults are out of the house?"

Mom laughed. "I needed somebody to samba with and Laurie just wasn't cooperating."

From the main staircase four police officers in uniform descended. They wore solemn expressions and walked in lockstep.

"I gotta go," I said to Mom and hung up.

I returned to our table, where Jim and my, no doubt, cold coffee were waiting.

Upon reaching the bottom of the stairs, the officers dispersed. Each one approached a different table, the divide and conquer method.

The officer that came to our table was Asian-American. He had a strong compact build and a smooth complexion. He leaned forward, his hands resting on the tabletop, and cleared his throat. "Evening, ladies and gentlemen, I'm Officer Lee. Sorry about the delay. The captain wants to dock as soon as possible, but before we can let you all go—I need to get a statement from each of you and some contact information."

"How's Helene?" Margaret asked.

Officer Lee focused on Margaret and sized her up, nodding to himself several times. "The medical staff is with her now."

Medical staff?

He meant the medical examiner, I was sure of it. But I supposed SFPD had a reason for not disclosing that. I hadn't had an opportunity to mention to anyone that I had bumped into the ME. Now, I felt certain I should keep it to myself.

Except, of course, for Jim.

Reflexively my hand reached out to touch Jim's leg. He placed his hand over mine and gave it a reassuring squeeze.

Officer Lee straightened and pulled out a notebook from his breast pocket. "I'd like to begin with you," he said to Margaret. "Please follow me."

Margaret gave the napkin in her lap one final wring, then stood up. Her tutu sprang to attention.

Officer Lee seemed momentarily dazed by Margaret's attire. He gathered himself enough to mumble, "If everyone can please get their identification cards or driver's licenses ready, it'll make this whole process go much smoother."

Margaret followed Lee toward the lounge area, where they carved out a private space to speak. The rest of us at the table exchanged sympathetic looks and began to gather up purses and wallets to prove our identity.

Evelyn craned to look out the starboard windows. "Where's the hospital boat? Why aren't they shuttling her off the boat?"

"Maybe she's not hurt all that bad," Sara offered.

"Then why are the police here?" Evelyn shrieked.

Evelyn's husband put his hand on her shoulder. Evelyn sat up straighter and pushed her belly out.

Sara gave Evelyn the evil eye. "How should I know why the police are here? Maybe all this has something to do with you!"

"Me!" Evelyn said, pressing her hand to her heart.

Sara's husband, Howard, looked stunned. "Sara!" He took hold of her arm.

She shrugged him off. "Why did you even come on this cruise?" she said to Evelyn. "You aren't a member of Roo & You anymore. I'm sure Helene made that clear to you!"

Evelyn's face flushed bright red. A lock of blond hair slipped from her barrette and fell across her face; she fiercely brushed it aside, then jutted her finger out at Sara. "I saw you and Helene arguing at the top of the stairs. I saw you. I saw you fighting!"

Indignation crossed Sara's face, but before she could reply, her husband noisily pushed his chair back from the table and stood. "Come on. We don't need to sit here and listen to this."

Sara seemed torn. She looked as though she wanted to stay and fight with Evelyn, but couldn't find the courage to stand up to her husband.

She pressed her lips together as her husband grabbed her arm. She stood and glared at Evelyn, then walked with him to the lounge area.

Evelyn's husband, Fred, patted her arm. "Honey, don't upset yourself or the baby."

Evelyn huffed an inaudible response.

Our table fell into silence.

A fight?

I remembered Sara, Miss No-Nonsense, in the bathroom and how disheveled she looked. Why had her dress been wet?

I imagined Helene throwing a drink at her and Sara pushing Helene down the stairs.

No.

Too dramatic.

Jim leaned close to me and whispered, "I didn't know we'd get to see fireworks on this cruise."

I elbowed him.

"And we didn't even have to pay extra!" he continued.

One agency or other was always advertising firework displays on the San Francisco Bay, whether it was after a ball game or during a dinner cruise. Usually there was an extra charge at those events.

I shook my head at him, conjuring visions of the medical examiner hovering over a pasty Helene.

Poor thing!

Fred leaned in toward Evelyn. "What did she mean, you aren't a member of Roo & You?"

Evelyn flicked her hand about as though to distract us or at the very least indicate to her husband to move off the topic. "I saw Helene and Sara bickering at the top of the staircase that Helene fell down."

"Over what?" Fred asked.

Margaret and Officer Lee approached our table. Evelyn fanned her hand at Fred, silencing him.

Margaret reached her chair and seated herself, tucking in her tutu around her. Lee scanned the room. I followed his gaze, which settled on Sara and Howard arguing in a corner of the lounge. I turned back to face Officer Lee, only to see him leave our table and head toward Sara.

Margaret's lipstick had faded to nothing and her eyes

looked drawn. I glanced at my watch. It was well past midnight now and I was feeling sapped. With Margaret's return, the table had fallen into silence and I longed to be alone with Jim.

Jim wrapped his arm around my shoulder. "Are you cold, honey? You want me to get you some hot coffee?"

I perked up. "I'll go with you."

We stood to leave and ended up taking orders from our table for hot teas and coffees. As we made our way to the bar, I noticed that several passengers were speaking with officers at strategic locations throughout the dining and lounge area. One silver-haired woman was speaking animatedly with a female officer. She was gesticulating wildly while the officer scribbled notes on a notepad.

I tried to eavesdrop on their conversation, but Jim was walking too fast. At six foot two, Jim has serious long legs, so they don't even have to be moving all that fast to leave me in the dust. I pulled at his arm to slow him down.

He stopped walking and smiled at me. "Sorry, honey." He kissed me. "It's terrible about your friend. I hope she's okay."

"She's not. When I called Mom, I bumped into Nick Dowling," I said.

Jim's eyes narrowed. "Isn't he the coroner?"

"Medical examiner, yeah."

Jim paled. "Does his being here mean Helene is—"

"Dead," I whispered.

"Does anyone else know?" Jim asked.

I shrugged. "Well, I suppose the cops do and I'm sure Margaret's podiatrist husband knows. Right? I mean even though he's—"

"Okay, okay. I know a podiatrist can be a doctor. I meant, do you think anyone at our table knows?"

"I think they all know a podiatrist can be a doctor."

Jim shook his head at my bad joke. "Do they know about Helene?"

"I don't think so."

"Well, don't say anything, all right? It looks bad that the ME is here, but we don't know anything for sure, right? So let's not say anything and get anyone more upset than they already are."

I nodded in agreement. We reached the bar and placed our order. Officer Lee appeared next to me.

"Mrs. Connolly, I'd like to have a word with you next."

• CHAPTER THREE •

Digging

Officer Lee and I situated ourselves in a corner of the bar, each of us in a black lounge chair, a video console game of Pac-Man between us.

I placed my coffee on the video game tabletop and fingered the recycling logo on the Styrofoam cup. "What can I do to help?"

"Tell me about your evening. What were you doing on this dinner cruise?" Lee asked.

I shrugged. "What everyone else was doing, having dinner."

Lee closed his eyes and shook his head slightly, indicating he didn't think my comment was funny.

He placed his notebook on the tabletop. At the moment the game preview was killing off one of the Pac-Mans and the defeat music accompanied Lee as he said, "How well did you know Mrs. Helene Chambers?"

"Not well at all. I met her and Margaret last week. They invited me on this cruise. I was checking out the Roo & You club."

"The mommy club?"

I nodded.

"What about the spouses?" Lee asked.

"What do you mean?"

He looked at me as though I was incredibly naive. "Did you know anyone else at your table? Any of the spouses?"

Was he asking if I'd had an affair with any of them?

I looked down at my red cocktail dress. Certainly some cleavage was showing, but nothing risqué. Why would he suggest anything like that?

I leveled my stare at him. "Only my own spouse."

"Did your husband know anyone?"

I shook my head again.

Lee's expression looked sour. "I don't get it."

"Get what?"

"Why you would go on a dinner cruise with a group of people you don't know."

"Like I said, I met Helene and Margaret, they were funny and smart and invited me to join this mommy support club."

He wrote in his pad and said slowly, "Mom-my support." He finished writing and looked up. "What's that mean?"

Another Pac-Man bit the dust and the music played as the token crumpled into thin air. I was beginning to feel aligned with the little game piece, running and dodging. And from Lee's tone I feared that my end could be the same.

"I wanted to talk to other moms. You know, have a peer

group. Be able to check in with someone and make sure you're not nuts."

He made another note. "So you feel like you're going crazy?"

Was this guy for real?

I reflexively glanced around the room for the woman officer. Surely, she would understand.

I shut my eyes and shook my head. "That's not what I meant."

"I understand that you were away from your table when the accident occurred. Can you tell me your whereabouts around ten thirty P.M.?"

"Well, I didn't look at my watch, but I was in the ladies' room when Sara told me the captain wanted us back at our tables."

Lee nodded. "And prior to that?"

Another Pac-Man warbled to his demise.

"I was on the upper deck, admiring the view of the Golden Gate."

"With whom?" Lee asked.

"By myself."

Lee squinted at me. "Where was your husband?"

"Dancing. Are you with homicide?"

Lee looked surprised. "No. Why would you think the homicide division would be here?"

Oh no! Way to put your foot in it, Kate!

"Sorry. I . . . never mind."

Lee scowled and made another note. "So you were on the upper deck and your husband was on the main. Dancing? Alone?"

"No. We'd been dancing together, but I got tired and wanted to get some air. Margaret had been sitting alone at our table for a while because her husband . . . well, actually, I don't know where her husband was . . . maybe he just doesn't dance. I asked Jim to dance with her because she looked lonely. And I went to the upper deck to get some air and enjoy the view."

"So you left your husband with Margaret?"

I nodded.

Lee narrowed his eyes at me. "Margaret was the one who found Helene at the bottom of the stairs."

"Uh-huh," I answered, not following his train of thought.

Lee pinched his lips together, then said in a condescending tone, "So, how can Margaret be dancing with your husband on the main deck and find her friend on the upper deck at the same time?"

I shrugged. "Oh. Well, maybe she didn't want to dance with Jim . . . I really don't know, I haven't asked him . . ."

Lee shook his head at me. He looked as though he wanted to roll his eyes, but some ounce of professionalism remained because he controlled himself.

"Did you see anyone on the upper deck?" he asked.

"Yeah. There were people around."

"Who?"

I stirred my coffee and thought.

"Take your time," Lee said, tapping his pen against the video glass top.

"I don't know, I wasn't cataloging people. I mean, I don't remember being entirely alone, people were hovering around oohing and aahing at the bridge. But I can't exactly say who I saw."

Lee stopped tapping his pen. "I see. Were you upset with anyone here tonight?"

"No, of course not."

"Did you argue or fight with anyone tonight?"

"No."

"Did you see anyone arguing or overhear anything?"

Evelyn accused Sara of fighting with Helene. Should I tell the officer that? But what did I really know?

I shook my head. "I didn't overhear any fights."

"When was the last time you saw Helene?"

"After dinner. We were served dessert, but she didn't eat hers. She said she needed a cigarette. So, she and Margaret went upstairs."

"Margaret?" Lee looked at his notebook and read back to me my own words. "'Margaret had been sitting alone at our table for a while.'" He gestured with his hand for me to elaborate.

"Yeah, that's right, but it was later in the evening. Margaret did go upstairs with Helene, but then came back alone. At that point, dinner was over, so people were milling about. I didn't keep track of everyone's movements."

Maybe I should have.

How would I ever make a good PI if I wasn't more observant?

"So, Helene said she wasn't feeling well. Was she drunk?"

I shrugged, recalling the empty glasses at her place. "She seemed a little tipsy."

Lee pulled his card from a breast pocket and handed it to me. "Okay, Mrs. Connolly, if you remember anything, call me. Otherwise, if I can see your driver's license for a moment, I think we're done here."

As I pulled my wallet from my purse, several slips of paper rained onto the floor. I grabbed the two by my feet, one a shopping list, the other my to-do list. Officer Lee retrieved the piece of paper near him. One of my homemade PI business cards.

Oh no!

Officer Lee read the card and frowned. "You're an investigator?"

"I . . . um . . . I'm trying to be."

Lee leaned in closer as the Pac-Man machine again killed off a character, the tune underscoring my feeling of consternation. He scratched his chin. "Anything else you can think of that you want to share with me right now?"

"Like what?" I stuttered.

Lee pressed his palms against the video game and closed in on me. "Mrs. Connolly, were you on this cruise for business?"

"What? No. What do you mean?"

Lee evaluated me for a long moment. I sat perfectly still, not even sure what expression I should put on my face.

Finally Lee rested back into the lounge chair. "Okay. We'll be in touch if we need anything else."

• CHAPTER FOUR •

Nurture

To Do:

1. Buy diapers.
2. Make Laurie's two-month check.
3. Find good "how to" book for PI business.
4. Exercise.
5. What happened to Helene? Can I help the police?
6. Is there any way to land this case as a PI?
7. Buy Ricky Martin CD—seems to help Laurie sleep.

Five A.M. and I cradled and nursed Laurie in our favorite spot in the living room. Not able to sleep but still being confined to the bedroom made no sense to me, so I'd gotten used to packing Laurie up in her bassinet and wheeling everything to the living room at first light.

Who was I kidding?

There was no light at 5 A.M.—not in November in San Francisco. The first light usually hit after the entire nursing routine was over and Laurie had a fresh diaper and a full tummy and was down to sleep again—around 6 A.M.

Jim and I had arrived home past two in the morning and found Mom asleep on the couch, apparently tuckered out from sambaing with Hank, Ricky Martin, and Laurie.

By all accounts, I should have been in bed fast asleep, but I'd missed Laurie terribly and was trying to make up for lost time.

I was stunned by last night's events. How could Helene be dead? She had been so alive, so full of energy, only hours ago. How tragic for her life to be cut short.

What about her kids? How many? How old were they? Now they would have to grow up without a mommy.

My heart felt heavy. I clutched Laurie and wept.

Mortality.

I squeezed and nuzzled Laurie into my neck and tried to pull whatever comfort I could from the living. Here I held a brand-new baby in my arms, so much ahead of her. All of life, with challenges, with blessings, ups and downs. And I wanted to be there. I wanted to be next to her to support and love her.

I stroked her soft down-like hair and she closed her eyes appreciatively.

"Mommy loves you," I said. "I'm always going to be here for you."

Her eyes opened and she stared straight up at me. A smile crossed her face, and miraculously, she looked as though she had understood me perfectly. She cooed at me.

"Yes, peanut, Mommy loves you."

She grinned.

"And you love Mommy!" I tickled her tummy.

She giggled.

My heart skipped a beat.

My little peanuty pie was growing up so fast! Only seven weeks old and already we were practically having a conversation!

Laurie lost interest in my face and cried out, rooting for milk.

Okay, so maybe we had a ways to go before we could actually have a conversation.

I held her tiny hand and rubbed it. Between the fingers I found lint.

Lint?

I had bathed her last night; where had the lint come from?

I absently picked at it, my mind drifted back to Helene.

What could have happened to her? I recounted the events of the evening; maybe I could come up with something for Officer Lee.

We'd had dinner, then the server had brought dessert.

Was I the only one who ate it?

Ate? Inhaled was more like it.

I recalled the sweet ice cream perfectly complementing the tart apple turnover . . .

Did we have anything sugary in the fridge? Or in the cupboards? Cookies, cake, anything—5 A.M. wasn't such a bad time for a midnight snack, was it?

In fact, if I stayed up, I could call it breakfast.

Laurie fidgeted in my arms, bringing me back to attention. I burped her, then brought my focus back to Helene.

She hadn't touched her dessert. No wonder she was

lean and mean. Not an ounce of fat on that woman. She'd fidgeted with the dessert fork, then pulled some Nicorette patches off her arm and declared them utterly failed. She'd stood and said she was going upstairs to smoke. I recalled her husband's look of despair—or was it disgust?—when she said that. Margaret went with her to smoke, and her husband had taken off in the opposite direction toward the bar.

That was it.

That was the last time I'd seen Helene.

At 9:00 A.M. Laurie went down for a nap and Jim made us homemade waffles and strong coffee for breakfast. As I cut into the first bite of my waffle, the phone rang.

Jim and I eyed each other, hoping the other would answer the phone. He looked as if he had no intention of making a move. I shoved the bite of waffle into my mouth and jutted my chin toward the phone indicating for him to pick it up.

"You know it's for you," he said.

Jim had long ago stopped answering our home phone, since about 90 percent of the calls were for me. Any of Jim's personal friends called him directly on his cell phone. We had an ongoing joke that he deliberately directed traffic there so I wouldn't know who he was talking to.

I swallowed the waffle, washing it down with coffee, then reached across the table and picked up the cordless phone on the fourth ring. "Hello?"

"Kate? This is Margaret. I was calling to let you know. Uh—" Her voice caught and I heard her sob. "Helene died last night."

My stomach tightened, the coffee I had enjoyed just

moments ago turned bitter. Margaret was confirming information I already suspected, and yet the news, the reality of it, struck me. I had hardly known Helene, but she was this woman's best friend and her pain was palpable even through the phone line.

I pushed my breakfast plate aside. "I'm so sorry, Margaret. What happened?"

"We don't know, Kate. She's still at the . . . medical examiner's . . . Alan told me that by the time he got to her, she was unconscious. It didn't seem to him that she had any broken bones, but her breathing was shallow and . . . well, he gave her CPR but . . ." Margaret sobbed. "By the time the Coast Guard got there, she was already gone."

Jim watched me, then reached for my hand and gave it a sympathetic squeeze.

"I don't know about the services yet. They still have her . . ." Another sob caught up with Margaret. "Sorry. I . . ."

"No problem," I said.

"We're waiting on the ME before we make the arrangements, but I . . . I'll let you know about the services." Panic filled her voice. "You'll come, won't you?"

The church was cold and dark. I sat in the back, waiting for the mourners to file in. I had barely known Helene, so I felt somewhat like a voyeur. What was I doing at the poor woman's funeral? And yet, I felt it essential to be there.

I was inexplicably tied to these women now, this mommy group. I was present the night Helene died and it linked me somehow to them.

I watched as Margaret and her husband, Alan, entered Saints Peter and Paul Church, the light from the stained glass windows casting curious shadows on her face and dress. Margaret had on a black dress that was short in the front while long and flowing in the back. I wouldn't have thought it appropriate for a funeral service, but her graceful movements made the dress soft instead of flashy.

A few moments passed as Margaret and her husband walked down the aisle of the church and seated themselves near the front. Shortly after, Sara entered the church escorted by one of the pallbearers. She was dressed in a J.Crew cashmere sweater and black slacks, her hair pulled back in tight chignon. As her gaze fell on me, she scowled.

Was it a scowl?

At the very least a frown. Maybe she was just wondering what I was doing there.

Others entered the church and were seated by the pallbearers. I watched for Evelyn, but she didn't attend. Losing a member of her mothers' club at this late stage of her pregnancy couldn't be easy on her.

Wait.

What had Sara said? Something about Evelyn not being a part of Roo & You anymore. Why would she be on the cruise if she wasn't a member of the group?

My thoughts were interrupted by the altar boys entering the church; the service was about to begin.

I spotted Helene's husband, Bruce, in the first row next to an older couple. By his resemblance to the older man, I guessed the couple were his parents.

Where was Helene's family? And their children? I didn't see any small children at all. Could they be with her parents?

Bruce gave a moving eulogy about his and Helene's dreams for the future. He described their first meeting and shared a story about their honeymoon. He seemed grieved and shocked by her death.

He didn't mention any children.

Why?

After the service, the casket was carried to the hearse. A woman, with flawless olive-colored skin, handed me a card with directions to the cemetery and the reception at Bruce's parents' house. As I took the card from her, Margaret appeared next to me.

"Kate," Margaret said, clutching at my elbow. "I'm so glad you made it." Mascara filled the lines around her eyes. She dabbed at them furiously with a crumpled handkerchief, making them red and swollen.

The woman with the beautiful olive skin handed Margaret a card. "Do you need directions to the cemetery, Margaret?"

Margaret released her clutch from my elbow and fumbled for the card. "I don't know." She gestured to her husband, who was standing next to the circle of attendees surrounding Bruce. "I'm sure Alan knows the way, but I'll take one just in case. Celia, have you met Kate Connolly?"

Celia appraised me with her dark eyes. "No." She smiled a wide smile and stretched out her hand. "Celia Martin."

I shook her hand. "Nice to meet you."

Margaret resumed her clutch on my arm. "Kate is a private investigator."

I felt myself flush inwardly. Could I really pass myself off as a PI?

Why did I ever give that PI card to Margaret?

Okay, I had somehow fumbled through a case a few weeks ago, but I didn't even have a license.

And yet, the prideful side of me or the incredibly stupid side, if they are even different, found myself nodding and saying, "Yup"—like that was really going to convince anyone of my qualifications! "Yup"! Like an idiot! I didn't say the proper word, "yes," only "yup," which rhymes with "pup," which sounds like "schmuck"—how fitting.

Celia, nevertheless, seemed impressed. "Oh!" She gasped.

Margaret turned to me. "Celia's a midwife. She delivered my second, Marcus." Margaret's eyes teared over again. Celia reached out and squeezed her hand.

Sara approached us. She squinted at me. Not quite a frown, but definitely something.

Maybe the chignon was too tight. It made her look so severe, so no-nonsense!

She embraced Margaret and the two wept.

Celia glanced at me, flashing a sad smile. She indicated the cards in her hand and excused herself. I glanced at my watch. I'd been out of the house almost two hours. I had fed Laurie before leaving but was now starting to feel the familiar burn in my breasts indicating feeding time was approaching.

I needed to leave now.

Margaret and Sara disentangled from each other. Sara gave me a curt nod. "Kate, I didn't think you would be here. Thank you for coming."

"You're coming to the reception, aren't you?" Margaret asked.

I glanced at my watch again.

"She probably needs to get back to her baby. Don't you, Kate?" Sara asked.

Why so much disdain?

I felt a surge of rebellion. The answer of course, was "Yes, *yup*!" I needed to get back to Laurie—that is what any responsible mother would say. It is what any *good* mother would have said. Instead I found myself smiling and saying, "Well, she *is* with her dad and I think there's even some milk reserve . . . I suppose it's okay for me to be out just a little while longer."

Margaret's face visibly relaxed. "Oh, good. Good."

Sara and I exchanged tight smiles.

Margaret's husband, Alan, approached. He offered his arm to Margaret. "Shall we?"

Margaret nodded. Alan's eyes raked me over. They had a glimmer of recognition, but it seemed he couldn't quite place me.

"Kate Connolly," I offered. "We met the other night on the dinner cruise."

His eyes darkened and he looked at me as though I were some kind of stalker. "Of course."

Right.

So now there were two people who didn't want me around.

•CHAPTER FIVE•

Disconnect

On my way out of the church, I noticed Inspector McNearny and Inspector Jones hovering around the back.

Homicide cops.

I had met both of them while working on my first case a few weeks ago. In fact, McNearny was a good friend of Galigani's and through that friendship our tenuous meeting had turned a bit more friendly.

McNearny raised a hand to me and gave me a "*not now*" look.

Okay, maybe we weren't that friendly.

He and Jones seemed to be trying to blend in with the crowd. They had positioned themselves near the exit and were pretending to be absorbed with the items posted on the church bulletin board.

Good Lord, didn't they know that even plainclothes cops still looked like cops?

McNearny's brown sport coat and no-nonsense shoes looked worn and at odds with this more affluent crowd. Jones's blue suit was more compatible with the crowd, but his austere crew cut gave him that military look many San Francisco cops sport. Not to mention that both of them were as stiff and stilted as wooden chess pieces.

At least Jones smiled at me when I passed him.

What are they doing here? And why try to look undercover?

I noticed Celia, the midwife, watching me watching the cops. When we made eye contact, hers flicked over to McNearny. McNearny couldn't even muster a rigid smile; instead he coughed into his hand, which caught Jones's attention. They exited the church.

I glanced back at Celia. She shrugged then handed a card with directions to a pallbearer.

I left the church and crossed the Washington Square Park toward Columbus Street, where I had parked. It was blustery in the park and the trees swayed. I wrapped my scarf over my mouth and nose so as not to breathe in the cold air. As I approached Union Street, I saw McNearny and Jones go into Mario's Bohemian Cigar Store Café.

Oh! Mario's meatball sandwich and eggplant focaccia panini!

My mouth watered. I glanced at my watch.

Did I have time to stop in and grab a bite?

But then I'd have to talk to McNearny. Eating something grilled was completely different from *being* grilled.

While that meatball sandwich might well be worth it— I needed to hurry to my car in order to get into the line for the funeral procession.

I guessed McNearny and Jones weren't going to the reception.

Some investigation they were running. Why had they come to the funeral?

I passed the Bohemian shop, and thankfully, because my face was covered by my scarf, neither McNearny nor Jones noticed me rush past.

Once in my car, I dialed Jim from my cell phone.

"How are you holding up?" I asked.

"Me? Great! Are you on your way home?"

"No. I'm going to the cemetery. How is Laurie?"

"She's asleep in her bouncy chair."

Hmmm. Why was babysitting so easy for him?

"Have you fed her?"

"She's been asleep the entire time."

I recalled the lint I'd found between her fingers the other day. "When she wakes up, give her a bath and then feed her. I left some milk for her in the fridge."

"A bath?"

"Yeah."

"What do you mean, in our tub?"

"No, come on. In her little baby tub. You know how to set up it, right? You need to snap in that green meshy net thing to hold her."

Silence. Followed by a low "*hmmm.*"

Visions of him bathing Laurie flashed through my mind. I saw him either scalding her or getting distracted and leaving her alone in the tub, or not putting the net thing in right so she slipped under the water, or getting soap in her eyes, or—

"Never mind. I'll give her a bath when I get home."

"Okay," Jim said cheerfully.

No wonder babysitting was so easy for him.

* * *

I followed the procession to the cemetery, which was a short drive out of San Francisco. My stomach rumbled and I regretted not buying the panini at Mario's.

I would probably dream about meatballs and focaccia tonight. Certainly, there would be food at the reception, but probably not like Mario's.

What kind of coldhearted person was I?

Thinking of food instead of Helene?

I quickly felt remorse as the procession arrived at the cemetery. At the grave site, the wind was unrelenting, whipping us around as though we were rag dolls. As Helene was lowered into the ground, I glanced over those assembled. No sign of McNearny or Jones. The crowd from church had significantly dwindled and I felt even more conspicuous.

Celia stood next to me during the short ceremony, giving me some comfort as she looked like she felt out of place also.

The priest announced the reception at Bruce's parents' house in Hillsborough. The November wind pushed its way between my hair, and up my sleeves, still managing to make me feel cold despite my winter jacket. I pulled my scarf over my ears and tucked my face into the collar of my coat.

We all quietly trailed up the hillside. Despite my efforts to keep up with the crowd, I seemed to be at the tail end of the pack behind all the other mourners. It wasn't such a big hill. How out of shape was I?

Beeps and lights filled the air as the drivers unlocked their cars from a distance.

"Kate!"

I turned to see Celia rushing toward me. I stopped to wait for her.

"Can I get a ride with you?" she asked. "I came with Margaret and Alan. But I think they already left."

"Sure." I was happy to have the company. She could direct me to Bruce's parents' place, and more important, I might be able to glean some information about Helene from her.

We climbed into my Chevy and buckled ourselves in. Celia held the directions in her lap.

I started the car and headed toward the freeway. There was an awkward silence between us. I reached for the radio dial but decided against it. "Were you close to Helene?" I asked.

Celia rocked back and forth. "We were getting close . . . Margaret and Helene were inseparable, so I saw her every time Margaret had a checkup."

I shook my head. "This is all so terrible, so sudden."

"Do you know what happened? You were on that dinner cruise, weren't you?"

"Yes, but all they really told us was that she fell down some stairs and was unconscious. Then the police showed up and took statements. That's all I know."

"Those men at the funeral. They were cops, weren't they?" Celia asked.

I nodded.

Celia lowered her eyes. "I thought Margaret said it was an accident. "

An accident?

Why would homicide attend the funeral if they thought it was an accident?

That had to be wrong.

Obviously, Celia was thinking the same thing because she said, "Why would the police come to her funeral?"

"I don't know," I admitted.

I felt her eyes on me.

I changed topics. "Were you Helene's midwife?"

She looked at me curiously. "No. Helene didn't have any children."

No children?

"I thought she founded the mommy group with Margaret," I said.

"Did she?" Celia shrugged. "I guess she was very anxious to be a part of the group. I think she really wanted to get pregnant, but well, we don't always get what we want, huh?"

That made no sense. Why hang out with a mommy group if you weren't one?

I had grieved for children who I thought lost their mother last night. Turned out I was wrong.

"What about her family? Parents? Siblings?"

"I think her parents passed away a while ago. I don't know. I don't think she had any siblings either. Maybe that's why she wanted to have kids so bad. It's hard not to have a family." Celia indicated an exit from the freeway. "That's our exit."

We pulled up to Bruce's parents' estate in Hillsborough, a beautiful wooded community just south of San Francisco. As I parked, Margaret emerged from the house. She rushed down the pebbled path toward my car and appeared at my driver side window.

"Oh my goodness! I'm so glad you have Celia! I wasn't thinking back there, Celia. I didn't mean to leave you," Margaret said.

Celia flashed a brilliant smile. "No worries. Kate was kind enough to give me a lift."

"I'll take you home. I promise," Margaret said.

We climbed out of the car and walked in unison on the

path toward the house, then single-filed into the grand entrance. Approximately thirty people mingled about the living room. It was a catered affair—no meatball sandwiches, but still a nice layout.

Celia made her way to a table that was doubling as a bar and spoke with the man serving wine.

Margaret joined her husband and Sara in a corner of the room. The three quietly balanced their plates and picked sparingly at their food.

Witnessing their grief made my appetite vanish.

I spotted Helene's husband, Bruce, hovering near the back door looking like he wanted to escape. His head hung a bit and his shoulders slumped, emanating a deep sadness.

I joined him at the doorway. "Bruce, I am so sorry for your loss."

He studied me a moment, his eyes penetrating and dark, then looked out the window of the back door at the garden. I followed his gaze and watched as the wind bent branches on the willow tree in the garden.

"Thank you for coming," he said.

I nodded, feeling awkward. Another guest joined us and gave her condolences to Bruce. I didn't have any more to add to the conversation, so I slipped away.

My breasts were burning and I longed to be home with Laurie and Jim. I glanced at my watch. I had now been away from home for three hours. Time to go.

I looked around for Celia to make sure she had a ride home. I watched as she sauntered up to Bruce. She held two wineglasses and offered him one. Bruce smiled widely, and when he took the glass, their hands brushed and both flushed.

Bruce looked around the room, then said something to

Celia. They exchanged words in a hushed tense tone. I was out of earshot but their conversation certainly looked intimate. I glanced around. Nobody seemed to be paying any attention to them.

What was going on?

Celia looked away from Bruce. He glanced in my direction. I avoided his gaze by perusing the buffet. He reached for her elbow and drew her in closer. He whispered into her ear and, with a final look over his shoulder, guided her out the back door to the garden.

Hmmm.

Could they be having an affair?

CHAPTER SIX

Batting 100

To Do:

1. ✓ ~~Buy diapers.~~
2. ✓ ~~Make Laurie's two-month check.~~
3. Find good "how to" book for PI business.
4. Exercise.
5. Plan Thanksgiving dinner.
6. What happened to Helene?
7. Exercise!!!

Several days had passed since the funeral, and I spent the time alternately fretting between what had happened to Helene and trying to forget about it. This morning Jim was working in our home office and I was in charge of Laurie, who was being extremely needy. Every time I put her down for a nap, she cried. Now she was overtired and as fussy as could be. I wanted to work out, but it seemed impossible to detangle myself from her.

I decided to put her into the front-facing baby carrier and do squats. Multitasking made me feel good anyway. What better way to live? Be a great mom and get in shape at the same time! Wonderful!

The phone rang, interrupting my second set of squats. Hey, I could add a third thing—mothering, exercising, *and* talking on the phone. I was a multitasker extraordinaire.

I grabbed the cordless receiver and managed a breathless "Hello."

"Kate. This is Margaret."

She sounded as breathless as I did.

"Hi, Margaret. How are you?"

"I need to talk to you. I just spoke with Bruce, you know, Helene's husband?"

"Sure," I said, powering through another set of squats.

"He said the medical examiner hasn't released the final report yet, because they won't have the findings from toxicology for several weeks. But they asked him if Helene was a user."

"Uh-huh." I stopped doing the squats, finding it impossible to concentrate on three things at once.

"A user, Kate. A drug addict!"

"Yeah . . ."

"She wasn't. She didn't use drugs. And they sent her blood, or well, whatever they sent to toxicology. Wouldn't that mean that she died from an overdose or something?"

"It's hard to say. I don't know the procedures at the ME's office. Maybe they send everything to toxicology."

"But they asked Bruce if she was a user."

"Right." I absently rubbed the top of Laurie's head, which was peeking out of the baby carrier. "What else did they tell him? Did she have head trauma, broken bones?"

Margaret took a sharp intake of breath. "Oh. There's Alan's car." She let the breath out in a rush. "Kate, I need to hire you. Can we meet?"

"Uh . . . sure. Where and when?"

"Tomorrow, ten A.M.?"

"Okay. There's a cute café near my house—"

"Alan's home. I gotta go."

She hung up.

I put the phone down and resumed my squats. I hadn't been able to give Margaret directions to the café. She'd rushed off the phone so fast. Strange.

But she wanted to hire me.

Jim entered the living room and observed me doing squats with Laurie in the carrier. "What are you doing?" he asked.

"What does it look like?"

"Looks like you're going to hurt yourself."

He was right. My lower back was feeling a little strained but pride makes you say funny things. "No, I'm not. I'm fine. Laurie's light."

He placed his hands on my arms to stop me, then leaned over Laurie and kissed me. He unstrapped the carrier and took Laurie into his arms. "Why didn't you just give her to me?"

"You were working. I didn't want to disturb you."

"No problem. You do your workout. I'm going to catch up on my sleep."

"What?"

Jim headed down the hallway with Laurie. "I'm going to nap with her."

Nap! At this time of day.

Wait a minute! I needed the nap. I was the one up at all hours of the night with her, but I felt wide awake now.

"Don't you need to work?" I called after him.

"Yeah. But I'm out of ideas right now. I need to generate something. Better refuel. Ah! The beauty of working from home." He disappeared from sight.

Suddenly I felt sad. A little lonely somehow.

I started on a set of lunges.

Funny how I craved alone time, and now that I had it, I felt lonely.

I gave up on the lunges and walked down the hallway to our bedroom. "Margaret called. She wants to hire me," I said.

"Who?" Jim asked.

"Tutu," I said.

Jim laughed. He had already climbed into bed and was cuddling Laurie, who was lying on top of him. "What does she want to hire you as?"

"What do you mean? As a PI."

Jim snorted. "PI? You don't have a license."

"She doesn't know that."

"Did something or *someone* give her the idea you did?"

I hung my head. "Someone might have bragged the other night at dinner."

Jim laughed. "Oh. Someone bragged, huh? Here." He held Laurie up to me. "She needs a diaper change."

"So go ahead and change her," I said from my position in the doorway.

"I'm trying to nap."

"I'm doing my workout!"

Jim frowned. "Yeah. I see that."

Men.

Oh well, it would soon be time to nurse and I knew he couldn't do that. May as well stay on duty. I crossed the room and plucked Laurie off his chest. She was like a little sow bug, all curled into him. Warm and cozy on the front and soaked in the back.

"Poor thing," I said.

Jim nodded then turned over, trying to sleep.

I stayed at the foot of the bed. "Do you think if I take the case to Galigani, he'll take it on?"

"What's in it for you then?"

"Galigani can't work the case. At least, I don't think so. It's too early after his open heart surgery. But I could use his license, right?"

"I guess that's up to him. Call him."

After changing Laurie's diaper, I placed her in her crib and twisted the mobile for her. She gazed up at the dancing bears and tried to bat at them.

I did another set of lunges, rehearsing how to ask Galigani for the use of his license. Pain shot through my lower back.

Nice. Try to do too much and wind up getting nothing done.

Taking advantage of Laurie's temporary calmness in the crib, I dialed Galigani. I was still unsure how to ask him, but figured something would occur to me when he picked up. He answered on the third ring.

"Hi, it's Kate Connolly."

"Ah! Kate! You must have read my mind."

"Really, why's that?"

"I was wondering if you and your husband and, of course, your beautiful daughter might join us for dinner."

Us? Who was 'us'? I thought he was single.

"We'd love to."

"Great, how about six?"

"That works."

"So, what can I do for you?"

Okay, here was my moment. *Just say it, spit it out.*

"Uh . . . well . . . no . . . Uh, we'll see you tonight."

Jim shuffled Laurie in his arms as I rang the bell. We waited a moment for the door to open, enjoying the smell of frying garlic wafting in the air.

Galigani pulled the door open and smiled. "Welcome!"

Jim placed a hand on my waist and guided me inside. I handed the bottle of Chianti to Galigani and spotted a woman sitting on the couch. I froze in my tracks. I must have unconsciously taken a step backward because I bumped directly into Jim and Laurie.

Jim recovered first. "Mom, what are you doing here? What a surprise!"

My mother stood from the couch and laughed. "Hello, darlings!"

I regained my composure somewhat and allowed Galigani to take my coat and usher us into the living room.

"Make yourselves at home," Galigani said. "I'll open the Chianti and stir the sauce. I'll be back in a jiffy."

"What are you doing here?" I asked Mom.

She smiled. "Albert invited me."

My mouth gaped and remained that way probably a tad too long, because Jim stepped forward and whispered urgently, "What about Hank?"

My mother hadn't dated anyone since divorcing my father eons ago. Then recently she'd found a beau online and had seemed quite content. They were even planning a cruise to Mexico.

"Well, darlings. I'm not *married*, you know."

My mouth, still hanging open, dropped an inch farther.

Mother motioned for Jim to hand Laurie to her. Jim passed the baby over then glanced at me and subtly pointed his chin toward the kitchen.

The swinging door to the dining room flung open and Galigani appeared with a tray full of prosciutto-wrapped melon. "Let's start with this. I have a plate of antipasto coming up, and let me grab that Chianti."

He placed the tray on the coffee table.

"Oh, Albert, let me help you." Mom passed Laurie to me and disappeared with Galigani toward the kitchen.

I hit Jim's arm. "Can you believe this?"

Jim eagerly popped a prosciutto-wrapped melon into his mouth. "It's crazy. Can you believe these melons are so sweet out of season? This is delicious!"

I remained standing in the same spot. Too stunned to move, I clutched Laurie to me and inhaled her scent. The new shampoo from Magic Moments smelled like jasmine. I hadn't tried the bath gel with lavender yet, because I was so enamored with the jasmine fragrance.

Mother and Galigani reappeared through the swinging door giggling. Mom carried the wineglasses and bottle on a tray. Galigani brought the antipasto plate.

"This melon stuff is unbelievable," Jim said.

Galigani smiled broadly. "That's one of my favorites. I've had to give up a lot of favorites after the open heart surgery, but thankfully this one's on the list of keepers." He picked one up off the plate and examined it thoughtfully. "I think it's because of the fruit."

"Oh! Fruit is so good for you," Mom piped up. "Tons of antioxidants!"

Galigani nodded, then turned to me. "Why don't you have a seat, Kate?"

I willed my feet to move forward.

How awkward. If Mom and Galigani were on a date, what the hell were Jim, Laurie, and I doing here?

I sank into the high-back chair next to the coffee table. Laurie squirmed in my arms then cried out. I don't know how babies detect when you're sitting or standing, but some alarm must sound as soon as you decide to take a load off.

Mom took Laurie out of my arms. "Have some wine, dear."

She began her elaborate "putting the baby to sleep" dance, which included some deep knee bends, tippy-toe rocking, hip sways, and a scary swooping motion as the grand finale. The entire dance bordered on the ridiculous, except for the fact that it worked. Always.

Galigani watched my mother with an expression somewhere between confusion and awe.

I grabbed my wineglass and drank deeply. A little more than I meant to because the wine burned going down and I almost gagged. I watched Jim shovel some salami into his mouth.

"So, what were you calling about earlier, Kate?"

"Uh . . ." I was happy to have my mind engaged on something other than Mom's dating life and yet words evaded me.

"She's got a gig as a PI," Jim said, crunching on a marinated pepper.

I shook my head. "Ummm. Yeah. Well, sort of. I don't know that you'd call it a gig—"

Jim opened his mouth and stuck his tongue out. "Whew! Hot pepper. Love it!" He grabbed his glass of wine. "Lady wants to hire Kate."

Galigani smiled at me. "Only you don't have a license."

"Well, Albert, you have one, right?" Mom chimed in.

Galigani frowned "Yes, I do."

Talk about awkward. Not only had I unknowingly stepped in on some date, but now Mom and Jim were trying to negotiate my business dealings.

Mom tsked. "Poor woman! Murdered on a dinner cruise. And her little ones, left behind. What a tragedy!"

I took another swig of wine. This time smaller, more sip-like. This was more like it. The Chianti tasted fruity and smooth. "Oh. The victim wasn't a mom."

Galigani and Mom stared at me.

"What do you mean?" Mom asked. "I thought she was running that mommy group you were joining."

"She was but she didn't have any children," I said.

Mom frowned. "What on earth was a woman without kids doing in a mothers' group?"

Dinner turned out to be fabulous. Galigani served fettuccini with a light garlic cream sauce that he claimed had been approved by his cardiologist. We debated back and forth about a woman we didn't know and the potential motivation to be involved in a mommy group when you weren't one.

We came up with a pretty paltry list.

We drank wine and laughed a lot, and thankfully Laurie snoozed in the middle of Galigani's king-size bed, surrounded by giant pillows to prevent her from falling off.

No one seemed to care that Laurie, at only seven weeks, still could not roll over. Somehow, the possibility of her falling off the bed still loomed.

After dinner while getting our coats, I finally summoned my courage. "So, um . . . Galigani, what do you think about my using your license?"

Galigani looked confused. "What do you mean, licenses aren't transferable."

"But I could work under yours, right? Like working for you?"

"No. I'm sorry. I'd have to supervise you, and right now I just don't have the energy for that. Not so soon after my surgery anyway."

• CHAPTER SEVEN •

Protection

To Do:

1. Call Margaret and give her directions to café.
2. Prep contract for her.
3. Figure out how to land her without license.
4. Buy baby keepsake book.
5. ~~Exercise~~ Stretch out lower back.
6. Look up postpartum yoga classes.

I snuggled Laurie into the baby carrier and walked down the street toward the café where Margaret and I had agreed to meet.

As I passed my neighbor's house, their seventeen-year-old son, Kenny, was leaping down the front steps.

"Kate! Let me see the baby!"

Kenny had spiky hair that was dyed green. He'd graduated from the School of the Arts a few months prior and was now auditioning like crazy with his trombone.

I folded down the flap on the baby carrier and let Kenny take a peek.

He peered over the carrier. "She looks exactly like Jim, but she's cute."

"Jim's cute, too."

"Only to you, Kate."

I laughed.

"Whenever you need a babysitter, just let me know," Kenny said.

"Right. When was the last time you washed your hands, Kenny?"

He looked at his hands. "Dunno."

"Are you going to the café?" I asked.

Kenny and I often enjoyed a game of backgammon or chess together at the café. He nodded and fell into step with me. As we walked, he pulled his iPod from his pocket and began to untangle the cord of the earphones.

"How's the auditioning going?" I asked.

He held his hand in the position of a high-five. "You're looking at the new substitute trombonist for the SF Opera."

I whooped and gave him a high-five. "Knew you could do it. I'm so proud. Are you going to dye your hair back?"

Kenny's eyes opened wide and his hand shot up to his hair as though I were threatening to cut it. "Back to what?"

"Your natural color. They're not going to let you play in the orchestra pit like that, are they?"

Kenny laughed. "I'm only a sub. I'm not in the pit yet."

"You will be soon," I said.

We arrived at the café and I paused as Kenny pulled the door open. He made a grand gesture for Laurie and me to enter, then tapped his iPod and wiggled his eyebrows at me. "I'm going to study now." He snagged a table and popped his earphones in.

I saw Margaret at the counter balancing her baby on her hip. Her eyes were bloodshot and swollen. She wore black stretch pants that clung to her skinny legs and an oversized striped shirt. Her hair was disheveled and she looked like she hadn't slept in days.

She greeted me with a half smile and a nod, wrestled her baby into the stroller, and picked a table near the window. I ordered my latte and rocked Laurie back and forth in the carrier.

Poor Margaret. I can't imagine how awful it must be to lose your best friend. Mine was in Paris and I missed her like crazy, but I knew she was coming home soon. Helene never would.

I joined her at the table. She sighed when I sat down.

"I haven't slept since the cruise. I really haven't eaten either. Just surviving off caffeine and sugar," she said, breaking a brownie in half then shoving it into her mouth.

I stirred the foam in my latte and waited. Laurie snoozed, her head nestled in the carrier. Margaret's baby swung his feet up at me and smiled through the pacifier in his mouth.

Margaret crossed her long legs underneath herself in the chair and sipped her coffee. "Helene and I were best friends since college. She'd always been there for me, you know? Through all the parties and good times and then through some pretty terrible times."

"Terrible times?" I asked.

I wanted to drink my latte, but hesitated. What if I spilled it on Laurie? Surely it was unsafe to drink hot coffee over her tiny head. I looked around the café. She was still too small for a high chair. Because I had the baby carrier on and my house was so close, I hadn't thought to bring a stroller, but now I had nowhere to put Laurie.

I stirred the foam again longingly.

Margaret looked over her shoulder. "I think, well, I don't think. I know she and Bruce were having problems. He's an investment banker. You know, they work tons of hours. Out of the house all day, most nights, too. Wining and dining clients. And Helene, well, at first she didn't mind. She liked to shop and travel. She started taking lots of trips to Costa Rica. Loved it there. Wanted me to go, too. But, you know, with two small ones you just figure, later. But Helene didn't have any hang-ups about going alone."

"I understand they didn't have any kids."

"No. Not yet. Helene was getting to that place, you know, tick tock. Like a time bomb in your head. But Bruce didn't give any indication of wanting kids. She was really frustrated with that. I also think that's why she stepped up her travel recently. Probably so discouraged at home that she needed a distraction."

"Why was she a member of Roo & You?"

Margaret frowned. "Why not? She loved to hang out with us. She had the idea of starting a club when Matthew, my two-year old, was born. I was meeting lots of moms, because I was attending this class on breastfeeding and nutrition."

I remembered the way Celia and Bruce had huddled at the service.

"Do you think her husband was having an affair?" I asked.

Margaret looked taken aback. "Bruce? No. I don't think

so. They were having problems, sure, but I don't think he was cheating on her. At least Helene never gave me any indication . . ." She looked miserably at what was left of the brownie on her plate, then shrugged and popped the rest of it in her mouth. "Well, these really are extenuating circumstances, aren't they?"

I nodded. "Go ahead, I promise no nutrition police are going to pop out of the woodworks here."

She motioned toward my latte. "You're not drinking your coffee."

"Uh . . ." I glanced at Laurie.

"Oh!" Margaret said. "I know how protective new moms are. Here, give me the baby. I'll tell you I never, not once, spilled hot liquid on my kid's head. But I know how obsessive the thought can be."

I unstrapped Laurie and handed her to Margaret, who smiled for the first time that afternoon. The smile brought relief to her face while at the same time highlighting her swollen eyes.

She gazed at Laurie. "You forget how tiny they start out. I mean . . ." She gestured to her baby in the stroller, who was now snoozing. "Marcus is only six months old, but he seems gargantuan compared to your little thing. I can't believe that he was this size only a few months ago." Margaret stroked Laurie's hair. "Is she lifting her head ninety degrees during tummy time?"

What? Ninety degrees!

I knew I was slacking on that tummy time!

I sipped my latte. It was ice cold. "I don't know. I don't think so."

Margaret's eyes grew wide. "Oh," she said, rounding her mouth and eyes in an exaggerated way.

Was Laurie supposed to be able to hold her head up ninety degrees?

"I mean, she lifts her head. She certainly lifts her head when we do tummy time."

Margaret nodded sympathetically.

I tried to calm the defensiveness that was swelling inside me. Was my face red? I sipped the cold latte, ignoring the acid flavor. I needed the caffeine anyway.

"When are they supposed to be able to do that?" I asked.

Margaret glanced at her baby and fidgeted slightly. "I don't really remember, but I thought it was around two months."

"Well, Laurie's not quite two months yet. She's only seven weeks."

Margaret smiled. "Of course, she'll be holding her head up in no time. So anyway, I was in this class at the hospital and was becoming very friendly with Evelyn. Helene had the nice idea of forming a group. We would meet at each other's houses and organize events and stuff. It worked really well for a while."

"For a while? What happened?"

"I got pregnant again and my neighbor Sara did, too. We asked her to join our group. This may have been one of the things that set Evelyn off, I don't know. But she seemed different. And we ended up having to ask her to leave the group."

"Is that why there was so much tension with Evelyn on the cruise?"

Margaret looked at me and shrugged.

"What about the fight Evelyn said she overheard between Helene and Sara?"

"I don't know anything about that. I asked Sara about it

at the funeral, but she said Evelyn was exaggerating. Which, knowing Evelyn, is not at all surprising. I have to find out what happened to Helene. I need your help, Kate." At this, her eyes filled with tears.

I handed her a napkin off the table. She dabbed at her eyes.

Here was my moment to tell her I didn't have a license.

It's nothing to be ashamed of—after all, it's true. Say it, say it, say it.

"There's something . . . uh . . . I want—"

"Kate, I have a semiconfession."

I stopped stuttering and focused on Margaret.

"When I met you and you said you were a PI, I knew I needed to hire you."

"Hire me for what?"

She sighed. "I've suspected for a long time that Alan's been having an affair. He's been coming home late and acting distant . . . and . . . well, really the list can go on and on. Point being, I thought I could hire you to follow him. And then maybe, finally, I'd have the truth . . . And . . . Oh God. I feel so guilty." She broke down and sobbed.

Kenny looked over at us from his table. He made a little sad face showing sympathy then ducked his head again to fiddle with his iPod.

"What do you feel guilty about?" I asked.

"Kate." She pressed a hand over her heart. "It's all my fault. I'm scared that it's my fault."

"The affair?"

She shook her head vehemently. "Helene!"

"I'm not following you."

Margaret glanced around the café to see if anyone was listening. At the moment, the only other patron was Kenny, who was vigorously tapping his foot to the beat from his iPod. The barista was refilling the pastry case with chocolate-covered croissants and miniature pumpkin pies. She looked about as interested in our conversation as going to the dentist.

Despite this, Margaret leaned over and whispered, "I think Alan was trying to kill me and instead killed Helene by accident."

•CHAPTER EIGHT•

Safekeeping

I fought to control my shock. "What? Why?" I asked. I was stunned by Margaret's words. "You think your husband is trying to kill you?"

Margaret squeezed her eyes shut and nodded. She was still holding Laurie and subconsciously pulled her closer.

"Why do you think that?"

She uncrossed her legs, leaned forward in the chair, and recounted the evening for me. "While we were getting ready for the cruise, Alan and I kept bickering. Everything was going wrong. Remember we were late? I had confronted him about the affair—well, my suspicions about it, and of course, he denied it. But he got very angry, and even though he denied it . . . I know there's something going on. He didn't want to go on the cruise at all. But we never get any time alone together anymore so I forced the issue."

She shrugged. "I guess I thought if I cooled my heels and just showed him we could have fun together that he would fall in love with me again."

I listened to Margaret in silence. Kenny got up from his table and wiggled his fingers at me and then at the barista on his way out. The barista waved back at Kenny, then looked at our table to see if we needed her. When she noticed we seemed rooted to our chairs, she took off to the back room.

Margaret wiped her eyes. "We left the house, then Alan doubled back saying he forgot something. When I asked him what—he got very upset and started acting so strange—that I dropped it."

"Just because he was mad at you doesn't mean he was trying to kill you," I said.

She put her hand to forehead and rubbed her temple. "There's more. On the cruise we were at the bar—Helene, Bruce, Alan, and I." She glanced around the café. "Alan bought the drinks, he grabbed mine from the bar, and I can't remember exactly—but he seemed to hold on to it for a while, then he sort of made a big deal about which one was mine. Said mine was a double and made a stupid joke about me needing it to loosen up."

I nodded and waited for her to continue.

"Then Sara and her husband came over and the men all started talking about investments or whatever. And Helene and I were chatting and, I don't recall exactly, but we were messing around and I think we got our drinks mixed up. Remember she was so tipsy. I think she drank mine and I think Alan slipped something into it."

"Do you think he went back to the house to get something to put into your drink?"

"He has a lot of prescription stuff at home. He's a podiatrist M.D. and he has . . . well, never mind, let's just say he has access to whatever he wants."

"Margaret, have you spoken to the police?"

Her eyes widened. "Kate, please don't tell anyone about the drug thing or, really, any of this!"

Why doesn't she want me to say anything? That doesn't make sense.

"If you think you're in danger, you have to tell the police."

"I called the ME's office after I spoke with you yesterday. Well, after Alan left. He came home for lunch. Can you believe that? He *never* comes home for lunch. I think he's trying to keep tabs on me or something—find out what I know. Anyway, after he left, I called the ME's office and asked the things you asked me, you know, about broken bones or head trauma and stuff. I pried as much information as I could out of the assistant but she didn't disclose much, just said they were waiting for the toxicology report and that she couldn't release any more information. I asked her if it looked like murder and she said the office wasn't calling it a homicide yet."

"Then why were homicide cops at the funeral?"

Margaret looked surprised. "There were?"

I nodded.

Margaret stroked Laurie's head and looked down at her baby in the stroller. I motioned for her to hand me Laurie. She did, then absently picked up Marcus's hand and stroked it while he slept.

"So why would the assistant medical examiner tell me it wasn't a homicide yet? Do you think she didn't believe me?" she asked.

I shrugged. "They probably have a protocol to follow.

Did you tell her about the drinks and your suspicion on the mix-up?"

Margaret begun to cry. "I don't want him to find out, Kate. I feel like I'm still in danger. I'm a nervous wreck. I'm not eating at home thinking he might poison me somehow. And forget about sleeping next to him."

"You have to tell the police. You can't live like this." I reached across the table for her hand.

"I need to know what happened."

"Is there somewhere you can go for a while?"

Margaret shrugged. "Maybe. My mom lives on the peninsula. I was thinking about taking the kids there for a while."

"That's a good idea, but you need to talk to the police first."

Margaret dropped her baby's hand and looked a little like someone had given her an electrical shock. She nodded then closed her eyes tight, but a tear still escaped. "I never thought I would find myself in this situation."

"There's something I need to tell you. I don't have a PI license."

Her baby started fussing.

She leaned down and grabbed his hand. "What do you mean? A license?"

"You need several years' experience before you can apply for your own license and I don't have that yet."

"Kate, I don't have time to shop this around. I'm scared out of my mind. Please help me."

I marched home excitedly.

I have a case! My career as a PI is taking off.

She didn't care that I didn't have a license; she'd signed my contract without even blinking! I was going to do this with or without Galigani's support. I did a happy dance with Laurie in the carrier then stopped suddenly when I spotted someone on my front steps.

Uh-oh!

It was Inspector McNearny. I froze.

He semifrowned and semiglared at me. "Mrs. Connolly."

I unstuck myself and moved past him on the stairs. I jabbed my key in the front door. "What can I do for you?"

"Does trouble follow you or are you the cause?"

I stopped fussing with the door. "Are you accusing me of something?"

"No." He tapped his foot impatiently. "I'd like to ask you a few questions about the cruise the other night."

"Come on inside." I opened the door and called out to Jim.

There was a note on the dining room table.

Went to watch the game at Jack's. Tried your cell phone, but it rang in the other room. Please carry with you and ANSWER it when I call.

Love you!
P.S. Paula called and your mom, too.

McNearny hovered in my doorway.

"Have a seat," I said, motioning to the living room. "Want anything to drink?"

He stayed in place and pulled out a notebook. "What can you tell me about the dinner cruise the other night?"

"I already told Officer Lee all I know. I told him that night. Is it official now? Was Helene killed?" I asked.

"I ask the questions, Mrs. Connolly," he said straight-faced.

"Where's Jones?" I asked, ignoring his attitude.

He glanced at the baby carrier I was still wearing. "His kid's sick."

"Sorry to hear that," I said, unsnapping the carrier and pulling a sleeping Laurie out.

McNearny shrugged. He looked like he could care less about Jones's kid.

Probably annoyed about Jones missing work.

"I saw you at the funeral." McNearny glanced at his notes. "I thought you told Lee that you barely knew the woman."

"Does that mean I'm not allowed to attend her service?"

"Most people wouldn't. Let's cut to the chase—are you working on anything currently?"

"I'm crocheting Laurie a little cap." I tried to hide my smile and look as serious as he did.

He turned red around the gills. "Mrs. Connolly, if you want to be difficult, I'll just drag you downtown. Makes no difference to me."

I glanced around for a spot to place Laurie and settled on her tummy time playmat. "All right. I'll level with you. I just came from a meeting with Margaret Lipe. She thinks her husband poisoned Helene."

McNearny looked stunned. He reviewed his notebook. "Is this the doctor we're talking about?"

"The podiatrist, yeah," I said.

"And did she happen to mention why he might want to do that?"

"It was an accident."

McNearny squinted. "What?"

"She thinks he was trying to poison her."

McNearny shook his head. "Did she tell you what she thought his motive might be?"

"He's having an affair. At least she suspects that's the case. She confronted him that evening. Supposedly he got very angry."

McNearny chewed on the inside of his cheek. "Had she hired you to follow him prior to the cruise?"

"No. Won't you sit down?"

"No."

"You're making me nervous standing there like that."

"That's the whole point, Mrs. Connolly."

I leaned against my dining room table and exhaled. "Have it your way."

"Okay, out with it. She hired you before the cruise. To follow him, right?"

"No," I repeated firmly. "Why do you keep asking?"

He ignored my question. "Why were you on that cruise?"

"I told Officer Lee that—I was checking out Roo & You."

"The mommy club?"

I nodded.

McNearny frowned. "What's a mommy club doing on a dinner cruise? I mean, isn't the whole point of those things to get the kids to play together or whatever?"

I ignored the way he practically spat the words "those things." "That's one of the purposes, yes."

"What about the spouses?"

"What do you mean?"

McNearny waved his hand around. "You know, aren't these mommy clubs just for women?"

"Are you asking why our spouses were with us on the cruise?"

McNearny nodded.

"It was my first meeting with the club. I don't know all the ins and outs of it. The dinner cruise was supposedly a deviation from their normal meeting. This time they were going to include 'the boys.' It sounded fun to me."

McNearny's expression looked sour. Probably to him, the idea of spending time with a bunch of moms sounded like anything but fun.

"It was an opportunity to meet some new couples that were also parents. Get to know the ladies from the club a little better before joining," I continued. "I also wanted the adult time with my husband. I didn't plan on a murder as part of the date, if you know what I mean."

"That's what I'm getting at."

"I thought you said you weren't here to accuse me of anything."

McNearny looked angry. "I'm not accusing you. Here's what I think—you were hired by Mrs. Lipe to follow her husband and figure out who he was sleeping with and maybe things got out of hand on the cruise."

"Look, I'm telling you that she didn't hire me before today. Why would I lie about that?"

McNearny smiled. A huge grin, one that was intended to ridicule me. "You don't know. Do you?"

"What? What am I suppose to know?"

"Not so smart after all."

What was I missing? What did he know that I didn't know?

"Why are you so hostile to me? I'm the one who helped you solve—"

His face turned beet red. "You think you helped solve that? We had that case blown open."

McNearny and I stared each other down.

He was dead wrong but challenging him wasn't going to get me closer to solving this case.

I swallowed my pride. "Sorry if I stepped on your toes."

He stood straighter. "Glad we understand each other."

I understood all right.

He pointed at me. "You don't have a license and I don't want you poking around in this case. If she hired you to follow her husband, to find out who he's sleeping with, that's one thing, but absolutely no nosing around in this case. You understand?"

I nodded.

He grunted.

Any doubts I'd had about taking the case had just been wiped from my head. I didn't know how I would do it, but I was committed to solving this case before McNearny. He didn't care about the victims, only his reputation with the department.

"So you're okay if I follow the husband, right?" I tested.

McNearny shrugged. "Sure, let me know what you find out."

I do the footwork, he takes the glory.

No problem. I didn't have my ego riding on it. I only wanted the facts.

• CHAPTER NINE •

Playing Catch-Up

To Do:

1. Baby development? Check out L's milestones.
2. Drop off dry cleaning.
3. Shop for shoes.
4. Thanksgiving?
5. What does McNearny know?
6. Call/e-mail Paula.

The first thing I did when McNearny left was jump online. I browsed the library collection and found *The Complete Idiot's Guide to Private Investigating*.

Perfect.

I put it on reserve.

Hoping to find out more about Alan, I googled him. I didn't find much, just that his office was on Sacramento Street. There certainly wasn't a headline on Google results about any affair. I wanted to speak with him, but how could I do that without tipping him off about Margaret's suspicions or my investigation?

Maybe *The Complete Idiot's Guide to Private Investigating* could clue me in.

I called Alan's practice and asked for an appointment. The receptionist scheduled me a month out and told me his latest appointment hour was 4:30 P.M.

Bingo.

While online, I sent my best friend Paula an e-mail. I knew she was coming home soon but didn't exactly know when. I would have loved to talk to her, but by my calculations it was already past midnight in Paris.

Then I dialed both Sara and Evelyn and left messages, hoping that they might have some answers about Alan. As soon as I hung up, Laurie began to cry. I picked her up off the playmat and found her soaked through.

Poor little monkey! What was going on with the leaky diapers?

Was it time for the next size already?

I made my way to the nursery to change her but the ringing phone interrupted my route. Turning from the nursery, I walked back to the living room and picked up the cordless.

"Kate! Where have you been?" Mother shouted on the line.

"I took Laurie to coffee."

"She's not old enough to have coffee!" Mother shrieked.

"Not her. Me. She just came along for the company."

"Oh!" Mom yelled.

"Why are you yelling?"

"I'm not yelling!" Mom shouted.

"Yes, you are," I said, elevating my tone to match hers. This caused Laurie to squirm in my arms.

"Am I? I just want to be sure you can hear me."

Laurie started to whimper.

"Why wouldn't I be able to hear you?"

"I'm on my new cell phone!" Mom said.

"You got a cell? For what?"

I'd been telling my mother for years to get a mobile phone, but her reply was always the same—she didn't need one.

She laughed. "Well, I want Hank and Albert to be able to reach me."

"My mom, the female Casanova!"

"A regular man-eater," Mom giggled. "Oh. I wanted to talk to you about Thanksgiving. Should we have it at my place?"

Normally, we had Thanksgiving at my house. Jim did a mean turkey. He put the effort in to brine it, and it paid off every year. We started hosting as soon as we bought our house because Mom's poor turkey was *always* dry.

"Uh. Your place? No, no! We can do it here, like usual."

"Yes, but Laurie is so small and Thanksgiving is so much work. It might be easier to do it here."

I recalled the last year Mom had hosted, she had barred me from entering the kitchen and in an accusatory manner had said, "You're going to tell me the turkey is dry."

When I had asked, "Why would I say that?"

She had replied, "Because the turkey *is* dry."

I wrestled for an inoffensive way to decline Mom's invite. "I'm sure Jim wants to do it here. He loves hosting Thanksgiving. It's our favorite holiday." And before she could get a word in edgewise, I said, "How are you going to juggle it though with Hank and Albert? Who are you going to invite?"

Mom laughed. "Oh, see I got lucky on that one. Hank is flying back East to join one of his daughters. So I'm free to ask Albert."

"Great. Ask him to join us here, what, around four P.M.?"

Laurie's whimper turned into a howl.

"I have to go, Mom, Laurie is completely soaked."

"Okay. I'll see you when I get back from the Mexican Riviera."

"What? Wait. I thought you weren't going until the fifteenth!"

"I'm not but that's the day after tomorrow and I need to pack and have my beauty rest before I go."

"The fifteenth. Wow. Time flies. My little mongoose will be two months on the nineteenth."

"I'll bring her back some maracas."

Had two months almost passed? I kissed Laurie's soft fuzzy head, then changed her diaper and pulled the child development book off my shelf. I quickly turned to the chapter on the second month. I skimmed through it, realizing I was holding my breath.

A box entitled "May Possibly" stated that holding the head up at a 90-degree angle was something an infant may possibly do at 2 ¼ months. So about 10 weeks.

Yeah. Laurie wasn't behind!

I was a success as a mom!

My squirrel was right on track. I did a little jig with Laurie.

I held her up and positioned her so her face was looking down at me and her legs were tilting up.

"You're right on track, bunny girl. Practically a genius!"

She gave me the "scary eye" look, irises pointing down with the whites of the eyes towering above.

I hugged her to me. "Okay, you're practically a genius but not when you give me that look. Let's go on a stakeout! You can use your supergroovy eyes and help mommy see any monkey business."

It was almost four thirty. I would have to hightail it out of the house in order to catch Alan leaving his office.

I packed Laurie into the car along with plenty of diapers, a change of clothes in case her diaper leaked again, and water for me. I wanted to pack snacks, but how was I ever going to lose any weight doing that?

I parked down the street from Alan's office and waited. It looked as though the building had only one entrance and exit. No attached parking garage that he could sneak out from. After about fifteen minutes I was rewarded by Alan leaving and locking up the storefront. He was accompanied by a woman with short gray hair. They exchanged words and departed in different directions.

I watch Alan walk down the street. I assumed he was heading to his car, but I didn't want to lose track of him. I needed binoculars.

How could I be a legitimate PI without binoculars?

Through the rearview mirror I glanced at Laurie in her car seat. Her tiny face was reflected in the Elmo mirror pinned to the backseat. She was sound asleep. I started the car and nosed out of my spot.

Alan was climbing into a silver Lexus. I hesitated in pulling out of my parking space as I wanted to trail him, but another car was already angling for my spot.

I pulled out then passed Alan's Lexus. He pulled out behind me.

Great.

I sped up and turned right at the next corner. I made a quick U-turn. His Lexus and my car intersected at the corner. I ducked my head so he wouldn't see my face and waited a moment for his car to pass.

Instead he honked for me to cross through the intersection. I didn't want to peek up but what was I supposed to do? He honked again. I stayed tucked out of view. He didn't know my car but he would recognize my face.

I recalled the look he gave me at Helene's funeral. He didn't want me around then and certainly he wouldn't want me following him now.

My phone rang from the depths of the diaper bag.

Shoot.

That was probably Jim.

I pulled the bag close and rummaged around inside. Another car honked from behind me. It seemed that enough time had passed that Alan would be gone by now. I peeked up over the dashboard. No Lexus.

The car behind me honked again and my phone continued to ring.

I dropped the bag, ignoring the phone, and turned right. I spotted Alan's taillights a block and a half ahead of me.

Oh good.

I'm not so bad at this follow-the-leader thing after all!

My phone continued to ring, and just as I reached for the bag again, it stopped.

The Lexus was only slightly ahead of me now so I slowed down. I followed the turns Alan made and ended up right at his and Margaret's home.

No "other woman" tonight.

Dissatisfied, I turned the car around to go home. At least he hadn't spotted me; that was one good thing. I could try again tomorrow.

I found my phone. The voice mail icon was showing. I listened to the message—it was Evelyn returning my call.

Okay. When one door closes, another opens.

• CHAPTER TEN •

Washed-up

To Do:

1. Get binoculars.
2. Talk to other members of Roo & You.
3. Exercise.
4. Pick up PI book from library.
5. Plan menu for Thanksgiving.

After leaving Jim to babysit Laurie, I met Evelyn at Ocean Beach. Her thin blond hair was pulled back in a ponytail and she wore flip-flops. I waved as she approached.

She'd surprised me by suggesting a walk on the beach. With her at eight months pregnant, I figured the last thing she'd want to do would be to shuffle through sand, but I needed to work off the baby weight and she insisted she wanted the exercise.

So, hey, I could kill two birds at once. Work out and investigate—multitasking again!

"Thank you for meeting with me," I said, pulling my baseball cap down a bit to shade my eyes from the glare of the sun.

Why hadn't I brought my sunglasses? It was early November and the sun was low in the sky. The weather was clear and thankfully the gusts of wind seemed to be holding off until a later hour. We walked down the concrete steps from the La Playa Boulevard entrance and stepped onto the sand. Evelyn promptly removed her flip-flops.

She frowned at my cross-trainers. "Walking barefoot in the sand is good for your feet."

"Hmmm," I mumbled, not about to remove my shoes and socks.

Yes, digging your feet in the sand is wonderful, but the Pacific Ocean at this latitude is freezing. One dip in the water and my toes go numb.

We walked toward the water in silence. The sand near La Playa Boulevard is extremely hard to get around in because it's deep and loose. But near the water it's compacted by wave after wave, making it a lot firmer and easier to walk on.

I was silent, doing all I could not to keel over. Good Lord, walking on the beach after having a baby is tough! I glanced at Evelyn, who even at eight months pregnant seemed to be cruising along the sand with no effort. I knew from dinner the other night that she had a two-year-old also.

How was it that she was so fit?

The water splashed against her bare feet, but she didn't seem to mind at all.

"Where's your baby?" Evelyn asked.

"At home with Daddy."

Evelyn raised an eyebrow with interest. "A stay-at-home dad?"

"Well, not . . . Sort of. Not really, he works from home."

She frowned. "Doing what?"

"Consulting, advertising," I said, matching her frown.

What was she frowning at?

"Oh." She swung her flip-flops around as she picked up her pace.

"And yours?" I asked.

She puffed up her chest. "He's an IT manager."

I suppressed a giggle at her competitive nature. Obviously, she liked playing "tit for tat." *Nyah-nyah, my husband has a better job than yours.*

I thought Jim's job was awesome. He was creative and fun and got to come up with all sorts of great campaigns. Maybe to someone like Evelyn, Jim's brainstorms were just doodles.

I changed topics. "And your son? Where is he today?"

"With the nanny."

Of course.

Everyone who is anyone has a nanny. When was I going to get a nanny? Although if you're a stay-at-home mom, what do you do with a nanny? Take a break, I suppose. Go get your nails done. I glanced at Evelyn—she had a matching manicure and pedicure in an unbelievably delicious shade of orange. Sort of tangerine.

When was the last time I had my nails done?

"What about you?" I asked. "Are you working and on maternity leave or are you—"

"I am an attorney," Evelyn said.

I raised an eyebrow. "Oh?"

"Well, I was. Contract law. Not criminal. I haven't practiced since Kyle was born." She eyed me. "I've worked with a lot of PIs . . ."

I waited for her to continue, semicringing to myself.

If she frowned at Jim's being an ad consultant, then PIs must be the scum of the earth, but instead of a snide comment, she simply shrugged then sighed.

"Now, I'm a stay-at-home." She rubbed her belly. "I'm having an at-home birth with Celia—do you know her? She delivered Margaret's baby."

I nodded, taking a deep breath. The air was cold and smelled of fish, yet was refreshing at the same time.

Ah, saltwater.

"We met at Helene's funeral," I said. "In fact, that's what I wanted to talk to you about. Can you tell me about the fight you overheard between Sara and Helene?"

Some seagulls in our path squawked.

Evelyn shooed the seagulls with her hand. They circumvented us by running away from the water, then as we passed, they ran back toward the tide.

"They were fighting about the extension that Sara's husband was going to build for her and Bruce. Helene was saying that it wasn't necessary anymore and they didn't want it built."

"And that upset Sara?"

"It really ticked her off. I think Sara and her husband are having some financial problems. She really wanted that contract." Evelyn laughed, seeming to enjoy the memory and the one-upmanship.

"I take it you and Sara don't get along?"

Evelyn made a face. "Well, you know, I got kicked out of Roo & You."

"I gathered that."

"I shouldn't have gone on the dinner cruise." She threw her shoulders back in defiance. "But I already had tickets and it was Kevin's only night off. He works a lot. From seven in the morning until seven at night. Saturdays, too. It's a lot. And lately, he's been preparing for this big IT contract in Asia. He leaves tomorrow and will be gone for about three months." Her shoulders slumped slightly. "He's going to miss the birth."

Suddenly it wasn't the best job in the world.

The water lapped at our feet. I jumped to move out of the way, but Evelyn let the tide run over her toes.

"I'm alone all day with Kyle," she continued. "Except when the nanny comes over, but she doesn't count."

Did she have any idea how disparaging she sounded?

"I really wanted this date night. I couldn't bring myself to tell Fred what happened with the club."

Boy, if Jim were leaving for three months and going to miss the birth of our child, I couldn't imagine that I'd want our last date night to be with a mothers' group, much less one that I'd gotten kicked out of.

I studied her face. "So what happened? Why'd they boot you?"

Evelyn stopped walking and laughed. "You don't know?"

I paused beside her and shook my head.

"I would have thought they'd blabbed it to you right away," she said.

A small boat on the horizon caught my eye. Sadness zinged through me and the enormity of my task weighed on me. A woman had lost her life and here I was trying to piece together the puzzle in search of justice speaking to someone who was only interested in herself.

"I don't know anything it about it, really."

"A few weeks ago I was at a playdate with the group. It was at Sara's house. And my son bit her baby."

Evelyn began walking again. I followed suit.

"It wasn't that big of a deal. But they got all upset. So I left. Then when I got home, I received this very polite e-mail from Margaret. She's got class. Even though she and Helene were conjoined. But anyway Margaret asked me to . . . well, let's say she 'suggested' I *voluntarily* leave the club."

As Evelyn was recounting the story, she was getting angrier and angrier, causing her pace to accelerate. I was barely keeping up.

"So," Evelyn continued. "I responded in a very civil way, asking her to please show me the bylaws of the club where it stated that biting is forbidden and in fact cause for termination of membership. Ha! Bylaws! She doesn't have any bylaws."

She shook her head furiously, her ponytail starting to loosen and strands of shorter hair escaping the confines of the hair tie. The loose hair whipped around her face as she spoke. "So then Helene jumps in. Of course, Margaret had cc'd her on the e-mail. Apparently, Sara is overprotective of her baby and was all upset that Kyle bit her."

Overprotective?

Was she crazy?

Wouldn't everyone freak out if their baby got bitten by a two-year-old monster? I certainly would.

Wait.

Was Kyle a monster?

Does every two-year-old bite?

My heart stopped. Oh God! What if Laurie was going to be a monster and bite little babies?

Evelyn stopped to repin her hair, sticking her flip-flops into her back pocket. I was glad for the break. Ahead of us, The Cliff House, a San Francisco landmark, sat perched on its rocky bluffs. Seal Rock majestically projected out of the water.

A gust of wind buffeted us and I longed to climb up the hill and sit inside the lounge bar sipping something hot by the fireplace. I glanced at Evelyn's bare feet, now covered in sticky sand.

How could she not be cold?

"I told Helene that I was handling Kyle the way they teach us at our co-op preschool, Little Bears." Evelyn turned to me. "Do you know it?"

"I don't think so."

"Oh!" Evelyn frowned again at me. "It's the best preschool in the city. Fred has a friend who is on the board of Stanford University and he told me to do whatever I could to get Kyle into Little Bears. You should get your daughter on the wait list now."

Was she serious? Laurie wasn't even two months old, for crying out loud.

I supposed my stunned expression said it all because she continued, "I know it can be overwhelming, but really, take my word for it. The city is highly competitive when it comes to preschools. Well, that and swim classes. You are enrolled in swim classes, aren't you?"

I shook my head.

Evelyn gasped. "You're not enrolled at La Petite Grenouille?"

I felt my eyebrows furrow and tried to disguise the fact that I hadn't even heard about La Petite Grenouille by turning my face into the wind and smoothing my hair into place.

"You have to sign up for their water acclimation class. It's the best. You can start as soon as your daughter is two months old—but the wait list is at least six months. So you really should have signed up while you were still pregnant."

I fought to keep my facial expression neutral.

Sign up for swim classes for a baby who's not even born yet!

Evelyn glanced at me. I smiled. She smiled back. "Well, it's never too late. You better sign up right away. You never know, someone might have canceled."

I nodded.

"Honestly, Kyle is practically swimming on his own now. It's amazing."

I felt despair creeping over me.

Late again!

I tried to steer the conversation back to avoid the loser mom feeling overtaking me. "So, you were telling me about Helene."

"Right." Evelyn started walking again. I almost regretted bringing her on track because her pace seemed twice as fast as before.

My calves felt tight and I wanted to stretch them, but no way was I going to admit that I needed a break—before a pregnant women who seemed ready to deliver at any moment!

I glanced at my watch. We had only been walking fifteen minutes.

How could that be?

I felt like it had been an hour at least. When would she want to turn back?

"So anyway," Evelyn continued, "I sent Helene and Margaret a note explaining how I'm teaching Kyle, like I've been taught at his preschool."

"Which is?"

"What?" Evelyn asked, stopping cold in her tracks.

"Sorry. I guess I don't know what you mean. Is it a special instruction—like Montessori or . . ."

A strong gust of wind whipped Evelyn's hair loose from her ponytail and she stopped to fix it again. I took the opportunity to stretch. Hell, at least my stretching might keep her in place for a moment.

"No. But Kyle's school doesn't believe in punishing a child for doing something that he doesn't know is wrong, and neither do I."

I reached down to touch my toes and stretch my hamstrings. Thankfully this hid my face. Not that I'm a big believer in punishing small kids, per se, but how in the world is a child supposed to learn right from wrong if you never correct them?

"So then," Evelyn continued, "Helene replies that they weren't upset with Kyle because, after all, he's only two, but that they were upset with me and the way I handled it. Can you imagine? What was I supposed to do? Fawn all over Sara's silly baby?"

I straightened out of my stretch. "What *did* you do?"

She looked perplexed. Her mouth opened then closed. "I explained to Sara that Kyle didn't understand his actions."

"Did you apologize?"

"Apologize?" Evelyn looked horrified. "Kyle didn't break skin or anything."

He bit a baby!

But I couldn't say it. The words got stuck in my throat.

Evelyn continued, "Sara seemed to understand. And the baby didn't cry all that long."

Note to self: Do not leave Laurie in arm's reach of a vampire two-year-old.

Evelyn scooped up her flip-flops and began to walk again. "The whole situation was blown out of proportion. Really, it wasn't a big deal. But then when I got the e-mails and get this—Helene said, 'Well, if that's what they're teaching at Little Bears, when I have kids, you can be sure I won't send them there.' "

The Cliff House was suddenly suspended above us; we had made it to the end of the beach. I stopped walking and glanced at my watch—thirty minutes had elapsed.

"Want to start back?" I asked.

"All right." Evelyn nodded. But instead of turning around, she plopped down in the sand and was silent.

I listened to the lapping sound as the waves crashed against the sand, the tide breaking a few feet from where I stood. I reluctantly sat next to Evelyn, wondering if I would be able to get back up.

I picked up some sand in my fist then slowly let it trickle out like an hourglass. Evelyn watched me, her face showed strain.

"Are you feeling okay?" I asked.

Evelyn shrugged. "Sure, why not?"

"I mean physically? You're not having contractions or anything, are you?"

Why hadn't I brought my cell phone with me? Jim was right—I needed to make a better habit of it! What if the woman went into labor here on the beach? What was I going to do?

"No, don't worry. I won't go into labor on you." Evelyn picked up a stick and drew a flower in the sand. "I'm not due for another couple weeks and my first was five days late, so I don't think I can get that lucky."

"You never know. And we just had this strenuous walk."

"You think that was strenuous?"

Oh, brother. Now I was going to get into a fitness competition—with a pregnant woman, no less.

She picked up her stick, crossed out the flower. "Celia is having me walk every day. Supposedly it can help induce labor, but I don't know. I did my own research and it's not conclusive. I see her on the fifteenth. Maybe I'll be dilated."

I bit my tongue. I could see how having a home birth might be nice. But what about the pain medication, for God's sake!

Evelyn read my face. "What?"

"Aren't you concerned, you know, what if something goes wrong?"

"If there's any emergency, you just go to the hospital."

"What about—"

"The epidural didn't work on me with Kyle. So I experienced labor firsthand. I'm not afraid of that."

"Wow. You have a lot more courage than me."

Evelyn laughed. "It's all relative. We all have stuff we're afraid of."

"What do you think happened to Helene?" I probed.

Evelyn began to draw steps in the sand. "I went outside to get some fresh air. That's when I heard Helene and Sara arguing, then Sara stormed off.

"Why was Sara's dress wet?"

Evelyn stopped drawing in the sand. "Was it? I don't know."

I watched the little boat out in the ocean, bobbing up

and down with the tide. A seagull showing some moxie cawed at us and approached. Evelyn waved the stick at it and it ran off.

"What about the spouses?" I asked. "Can you tell me anything about Bruce or Alan?"

Evelyn scratched out the steps she had drawn and doodled a heart in the sand. "I don't really know them. It was the first time I met them. I thought they were nice enough but my husband said Alan was kind of keyed up."

"What do you mean?"

She shrugged. "Fred was having a cigar with Howard, Sara's husband, who said Alan was running around like a chicken with his head cut off."

"Do you know anything about an affair Alan might have been having?"

A smile crossed her face. "Was he cheating on Margaret?"

My heart dropped. How could she be happy at someone else's pain?

It's not my job to judge.

"Do you know anything about it?"

She shrugged. "No. You ask Sara, though. They're neighbors. She might know something."

• CHAPTER ELEVEN •

Falling Behind

To Do:

1. Call Sara.
2. Clean the house.
3. What does a nanny cost? Do they clean house, too?
4. Look up swim classes for Laurie!
5. Research preschools!
6. Walk on the beach every day!!! It is pathetic that I get out of breath after a few steps!

When I arrived home, the first thing I did was make straight for the washing machine. I pulled off my sneakers and emptied them directly into the mop sink. I was mesmerized by the amount of sand pouring out.

How could my feet fit in there with all that sand?

I peeled off my socks. What was it about Ocean Beach that made this sand so sticky? It clung to my socks and was even between my toes. I put my socks into the washing machine and dumped the contents of the laundry basket, which was next to the machine, inside it.

I heard the upstairs door creak open.

"Kate?" Jim called from the top of the stairs.

"It's me. I'm doing laundry. I didn't want to track sand upstairs."

Jim descended the stairs. "How was your walk?"

"Good, but it nearly killed me. I'm totally out of shape."

He wrapped his arms around my waist. "Don't be so hard on yourself, you just had a baby."

"That was weeks ago! I can't believe this woman at eight months pregnant outpaced me."

Jim laughed. "Sleep deprivation can do funny things to stamina."

I leaned my head onto his chest and listened to his heartbeat. "That's so nice of you to say, honey, when we both know I need to get my butt in gear and work out."

He kissed my hair. "You'll be ready to run with the bulls by spring."

I pulled away from his chest and looked at his face. "Speaking of bulls or bullies—this woman was a piece of work! No wonder they kicked her out of the club. So mean!"

Jim laughed. "You think everyone is mean, but that's because you're too nice."

"I'm not nice."

Jim looked incredulous.

"Where's Laurie?" I asked.

"Upstairs. I left her unsupervised. I'm sure she's trashed the place by now."

I made a fist and playfully waved it in his face. "Okay, I'm nice, but not that nice."

He laughed. "She's asleep in her crib. And by the way, Dr. Alan Lipe's office called. They said there was a cancellation for tomorrow, wanted to know if you wanted the spot."

I opened the door to the medical office and peered into the waiting room. It was empty except for the receptionist sitting behind a closed-in glass counter. She was dressed in a white lab coat and had thick short gray hair.

She peered at me over her bifocals.

I smiled. "Hi. I'm Kate Connolly. I have an appointment with Dr. Alan Lipe."

She studied the appointment book. "Yes. May I see your referral slip?"

"Ooooh. Um. I forgot that."

She tapped the book with the eraser of her pencil. "And the referring doctor is . . . ?"

Of course, I didn't have one.

Think, Kate, think!

"Dr. Green," I lied.

Dr. Green was my ob-gyn, but was the only name I could come up with.

She frowned. "Which practice is Dr. Green with?"

"Uh. I don't remember."

Her lips pursed, she stared at me sternly. I smiled. She got up from her chair in silence and disappeared down a hallway. I remained standing at the counter.

I'd made the appointment with the intent of grilling Alan, but I didn't really want him to know Margaret was on to him.

What would I say to him?

A few moments later, the receptionist reappeared in the doorway connected to the hallway. "Mrs. Connolly, right this way."

We walked down the hallway and she motioned me into the third door on the left.

The room had only a patient table, a stool, and a small set of drawers. On the wall hung a print of a foot with all the ligaments, joints, and muscles exposed.

I hoisted myself on the table and waited for Alan.

A few minutes passed and then came a knock on the door. It creaked open before I could respond. Alan entered, wearing a blue polo shirt and Dockers. His curly hair was unruly and there were dark circles under his eyes.

He stuck out his hand. "Mrs. Connolly, I'm Dr. Lipe."

"Hello, Alan." I shook his hand. "Do you remember me? From the cruise on the other night—"

"Of course, yes. Of course. Terrible night." He moved his head up and down repeatedly as though trying to sift through some memories. "You're a private investigator, correct?"

I nodded.

"Yes. I recall Margaret saying so. We saw each other again at Helene's service."

"That's right."

He glanced at my feet. "What kind of problems are you having? What can I do you for?"

"Um." I looked at my feet as well. "Uh. I just had a baby—"

"Congratulations! When?"

"She's seven weeks old."

"Wonderful." He smiled, but it did little to light up his face. "And your feet are giving you problems?"

"Yeah. Sort of."

He nodded. "Take off your shoes."

I kicked off my Keds and dangled my feet off the table.

He picked up my left foot and squeezed it gently then rotated my foot. My ankle cracked and popped.

"Margaret is heartbroken about Helene," I said.

He looked at me for a split second. There was surprise on his face, but he quickly adjusted his expression back to blank. "Yes. They were best friends. Tell me about your feet."

"They're swollen all the time and none of my shoes fit."

He nodded. "That's very common following a pregnancy. Do you have pain?"

I didn't. Not really, but not fitting into your shoes didn't seem like a reason to visit a podiatrist, so I said, "Yes."

He dropped my left foot and picked up my right one. He palpated the foot then rotated the ankle. "Your feet aren't swollen now. Would you say you had a lot of swelling during pregnancy?"

"Yes," I said.

He seemed so sincere. So caring. So gentle.

For a murderer.

"With Helene gone, Margaret's probably at a loss. It could put a strain on a marriage," I said.

He dropped my foot as if it had just given him a shock. "Typically after pregnancy, pain can be caused by the edema, which put pressure on the structures of the feet and nerves. Even after the edema leaves, there may be pain."

He pointed to the print on the wall and started to outline some ligaments. "I think you could benefit from a pair of orthotics."

Orthotics?

There was nothing sexy about that. I only wanted to be able to fit into my cute open-toed shoes again.

"Umm, they don't really hurt all that much . . ."

He looked upset.

"Doctor, what do you think happened to Helene the other night? It was all so sudden."

He paled. "I don't know."

"It's strange, though, isn't it? You were with her when she died, weren't you?" I tested.

He took a step back and swallowed. "Unfortunate set of circumstances." He turned his back on me and steadied himself by putting his hands on the small set of drawers. "Shall we schedule you for the prescription orthotics?"

He waited for my reply with his back to me.

He was as uncomfortable speaking to me as I had been with Inspector McNearny.

"What do you think was the cause of death?"

He whipped around, his face set in stone. "I'm not the medical examiner. Look, are you here about your feet or something else?"

I let my feet dangle and furrowed my brows. "What else would I be here about?"

"What are all these questions about? Are you investigating me?"

"Why would I?"

He self-consciously smoothed down his shirt and shifted his eyes around the room. He took a breath. "Right. Have Joan schedule you for a follow-up."

• CHAPTER TWELVE •

Keeping Up

To Do:

1. Talk to Miss No-Nonsense.
2. Get manicure.
3. Order turkey.
4. When's Paula coming home?
5. Build up milk supply—pump, pump, pump!!!

The following day, I decided to pop in on Sara. She hadn't returned my phone calls and I was starting to get antsy about her.

Was she avoiding me?

I packed Laurie into the car and headed to Jordan Park,

which was down the street from California Pacific Hospital, where Laurie was born. This same hospital had also been the initial meeting place for Roo & You members, since they had all given birth to their first children and taken classes there, too. Well, all of them except Helene.

And what about these home births?

I had a hard enough time keeping my place clean; now I imagined the mess of a home birth. Blood, placenta, and goo on the baby. Good Lord. Why on earth would anyone want to do that?

Well, now, no reason to be critical. I'm sure people had their reasons—it just simply wasn't for me.

Jordan Park is a beautiful neighborhood but lacks parking like most of San Francisco. I circled around and was surprised to see Margaret in front of her house watering the lawn. I double-parked, rolled down my window, and called to her.

She looked up, startled, then waved at me to wait a moment. She put down the hose, rushed to her garage to turn off the water, then came over to my car.

She was wearing a slip dress that accentuated her slimness, making her look as if the wind could blow her over. In contrast to the whimsical look of the dress, she had on clunky green mules that seemed to ground her. To combat the weather she had on a wool scarf and hat, although I can never understand how people don't freeze with bare arms and legs.

She rested her hands on my car and leaned in. "Have you found anything out?"

"Not much, Margaret. I followed Alan the other day. He came directly home. Didn't stop anywhere. Do you think he's still having the affair?"

"It's strange. I know. He's been coming home on time lately and is seemingly more interested in me and the kids. I'm not buying it, though. He's only doing that because I confronted him. I think he's trying to get me off my guard. I can't trust him, Kate."

"Are you going to stay with your mom for a while?"

Her face conveyed a sudden sadness. "Yes, I'm leaving with the kids tomorrow. I haven't told Alan, though."

Another car rolled down the street and had to maneuver around me.

"Is it okay if I park in your driveway? I'd like to ask Sara a few things."

Margaret looked annoyed. She crossed her bare arms in front of herself and rubbed them. "Sara? What do you need to see her about?"

"Well, I'm trying to get to the bottom of what happened to Helene."

What did she think I wanted to see her about?

"Well, Sara doesn't know anything."

Another car came down the street. I waved at the driver to go around.

"Okay. Sure, park here." Margaret motioned for me to pull into her driveway.

I parked and got out of the car, then unhitched Laurie's car seat from the back. She was sound asleep. I tucked a knit blanket securely around her to protect her from the wind that threatened to bluster at any moment.

The exchange between us now felt halted and awkward. "I'm going to run across the street and meet Sara."

"Of course." Margaret reached out and patted my arm. "Do you need help with the diaper bag and gear and all?"

I smiled, reassuring her all was fine between us. "No. I got it. Thanks!"

I was a little nervous about meeting with Sara since the last time I'd seen her, at Helene's funeral, she'd given me such an unwelcoming vibe and now wasn't even returning my calls.

She answered the bell on the first ring. She had on a red wool sweater and fitted jeans.

"Oh, hi, Kate." She looked beyond me then back. "Are you here alone?"

I held up Laurie's bucket. "Just me and my monkey."

She smiled. "Right. Yes. I got your messages. I'm sorry I haven't called you back. Busy, busy, busy."

After an awkward moment, she ushered Laurie and me into her enormous living room. A baby play station, complete with swing, rocking chair, colorful balls, and mirrors, dominated the room. In the center of it all sat a beautiful rosy-cheeked little girl, who graced us with a toothless smile as we entered the room.

"This is Amanda. You can put Laurie on the playmat with her when she wakes up. Amanda loves company."

At that moment Amanda squeezed a cow on the play station. A high-pitched rendition of "Old MacDonald" started playing.

I nodded, nestling Laurie's car seat next to my chair as I took a seat by the window. "Great. I'm sure she'll love all the colors and sounds."

If they don't wake her immediately.

"Probably too little for it still. Amanda just started

playing in it a few weeks ago. She's six months now," Sara said.

"Is she your first?"

Sara nodded.

"So you joined Roo & You a few months ago after Amanda was born?"

Sara looked up toward the ceiling as if trying to recall the actual date. "Let's see. I joined, more or less, unofficially before she was born. Because I knew Margaret from across the street, the others were always hanging out at her place. So when I was about six months pregnant and full of baby questions, I started attending the playdates." She indicated my car through the front window. "I see that you spoke with Margaret already."

I turned to look out the window and could plainly see my Chevy parked in Margaret's driveway. "Yeah. I didn't know you two were neighbors until Evelyn mentioned it the other day."

At the mention of Evelyn's name, anger flashed across Sara's eyes and she glanced toward Amanda.

After a moment, she said, "I've lived here about four years. We're a tight group of neighbors. Watch each other's dogs when we vacation and pick up mail. That sort of thing."

I looked around for signs of a dog but didn't see any. Maybe Sara was only a dog watcher.

"Margaret befriended me immediately when I moved in. Which was great, because coming from the East Coast, I didn't know a lot of people and Howard works a lot. He's a general contractor. It was nice to have a friend right away."

"She's very nice. I imagine she's been a good friend to have."

Sara tilted her head and looked across the street thoughtfully. "Margaret is a good friend. Very trusting. She only sees the best in people. When she's talking to you, it's as if you're the only other person in the world. She has a gift for making you feel special. The problem is she can be taken advantage of it and not know it. It's hard for me to stand by and watch."

"Taken advantage of how?"

Sara rolled up the sleeves of her wool sweater. "People use her. Helene was definitely what I would classify a taker. And Margaret is a giver. You can imagine what kind of relationship it was."

"Margaret said Helene was her best friend."

Sara sighed and shook her head in disapproval.

I waited in silence for her to continue, resisting the urge to check on Laurie and focusing only on Miss No-Nonsense. She seemed to like attention and I hoped it would urge her to open up to me.

Amanda played with some knobs on the playmat and squealed. Both Sara and I turned to her.

"She is so cute. I can't wait until Laurie can sit up and play like that," I said.

Sara smiled. "It won't be long. Time flies. Amanda's only been sitting since we started water acclamation class. I had no idea it would help with motor skill development."

It did?

Water acclamation? Weren't infants just getting used to being out of water?

I hated to ask, but I had to know.

"Where do you take classes?"

She looked down her nose at me. "La Petite Grenouille, of course. Aren't you enrolled?"

"Uh. No. Not yet."

I wasn't born with a day timer in my hand, like you, Miss No-Nonsense. I'm sure you aren't ever late for anything!

"They have a free trial class. You should really try and make it. Your daughter will enjoy it," she said.

Eager to switch subjects, I said, "Sara, what can you tell me about that night on the cruise?"

She shrugged. "What's to tell? You were there, too."

"Do you recall being at the bar with Margaret, Helene, and their husbands?"

She frowned. "Well, sure. We were all at the bar."

"Do you remember anything about a drink mix-up?"

"What do you mean? Like the bartender gave us the wrong drinks or something? I don't really remember anything like that," she said.

"No. I mean . . ."

Might as well come right out and ask it.

"Did you notice that maybe Helene and Margaret got their drinks switched? Like perhaps Helene drank Margaret's drink?"

She shook her head. "No. I don't remember anything like that."

Okay, so no smoking gun.

I tried a different tack. "What can you tell me about your final exchange with Helene?"

Sara squinted. "There's not much to tell. We were chatting on the deck then this lady bumped into me and spilled her drink. I left Helene on the deck and went to the restroom."

The timing seemed off.

"Did you stop anywhere on the way?" I asked.

Sara titled her head, her brow furrowing. "I don't remember."

How could she not remember?

"When you got to the ladies' room, you told me that the captain had called an all hands on deck."

She chewed her thumbnail. "That's right."

"But if you came directly to the restroom after leaving Helene on deck, I don't see how there was time for her to fall down the stairs and be found and for the captain—"

She stopped chewing her nail. "Oh. I see what you mean. I think I probably stopped to talk to Howard first. Yeah. That's right. I went to talk to Howard, but he was smoking a cigar with Evelyn's husband." She rolled her eyes, the disdain apparent in her voice. "And I didn't want to be there."

"You really don't care for her."

Sara laughed. "To put it mildly. She's a nightmare. High maintenance. All about her. The husband is boring and her kid's a fiend. Not that it's his fault. She's just so into herself, she lets him run wild. And whenever he gets into trouble, she acts all bothered about having to do something about it."

"I understand she was asked to leave Roo & You."

Sara shrugged. "She wasn't a fit with us."

Who was? It sounded like she hadn't liked anyone in the group, except Margaret.

"Was there anyone else in the group??"

Sara shook her head. "No. Just the four of us. It seemed to really work for a while, but . . ."

I waited again for her to continue. Laurie stirred in the car seat. Amanda tipped over on the playmat and began to cry, unable to sit herself back up.

Sara rose and crossed the room to Amanda. She picked her up and cuddled her. "It's attention time. She needs a change and some food. Are we done?"

I rose. "Actually, I have a couple more questions."

Sara fidgeted and patted her baby on the back. "Okay. Is it all right then if we move this conversation to the kitchen?"

"Of course." I picked up Laurie's car seat and her eyes flew open. "Oops. I think it's attention time for Laurie, too."

"I'll show you Amanda's room. You can use her changing station," Sara said, turning to leave the room.

I unstrapped Laurie and scooped her out of the car seat. I glanced through the front window and spotted a woman pushing a double stroller down the street. A collie was leashed to the stroller. The woman stopped in front of Margaret's house and fished for something in her parka. She pulled out a set of keys.

Must be the nanny coming back from the park.

I picked up the diaper bag and headed in the direction Sara had gone. There was a long hallway connecting to a formal dining room followed by an enormous marble kitchen. Bedrooms were in the back of the house, overlooking a huge fenced-in garden.

Sara was changing Amanda on a white wooden changing table.

A few months ago, my life had been so different. Before having Laurie, the only person I knew with a baby was Paula. Now it seemed that I was surrounded by pregnancies, new moms, infants, diapers, bottles, and nursery rhymes.

Sara picked up her baby from the station and placed a disposable changing pad on the table for me. I laid Laurie down and went through the same routine Sara had just completed.

"We can feed them in the kitchen. Do you need formula or want me to heat water or something?"

"No. I'm nursing."

Sara nodded. "I couldn't do it for very long. I found it so taxing."

"I'm getting the hang of it."

I followed her from the bedroom into the enormous kitchen. She placed Amanda in her highchair and proceeded to heat orange-colored mashed food on the stove.

She smiled. "Homemade baby food."

She was making the baby food? How do you do that? Was I supposed to make Laurie's baby food? Thank God solids weren't for a few more months.

I placed Laurie on my lap and pulled my nursing wrap out of the diaper bag.

"I understand from Margaret that she thinks her husband is cheating on her. Do you know anything about that?"

Sara looked surprised. "I didn't know Margaret knew. She never said anything about it to me."

"But you knew?"

She shrugged. "What can I say? I live across the street. I noticed Alan coming home later and later. Margaret told me some mumbo jumbo about his having to work late. But good Lord, the man is a podiatrist, not a surgeon. He works clinic hours, not the emergency room. But who am I to say anything?"

"Do you know who he's seeing?"

She leveled her gaze at me. "Does it matter? The guy's a two-timer."

I nodded in agreement. "It matters. An affair is hard to prove without knowing who the other party is."

"Why does she need to prove anything? Just dump him."

It didn't feel right to outline Margaret's suspicions to Sara, so I simply said, "Sometimes it's not that easy."

"Well, I know they have kids and all."

Sara put a spoonful of mush to Amanda's mouth. Amanda promptly turned from it.

Maybe she would like Gerber's instead?

"Any idea how long the affair has been going on for?"

"Let's see, Amanda is six months now. I'd say she was probably four months or so when I first noticed him coming home late."

Sara succeeded in stuffing a spoonful of slop into Amanda's mouth, only to have Amanda's little tongue push it back out again. Sara sighed and wiped Amanda's chin.

She stirred the food and made another attempt. Amanda turned her head.

"Guess she's not hungry," she said, pulling the baby from the highchair.

Amanda wailed in protest. Sara sighed. "I don't think she likes my squash pottage." She placed the baby back in the highchair. Amanda kicked her feet in delight. Sara pulled some Cheerios off a shelf and sprinkled a handful in front on the tray. Amanda dug in with relish, wrapping her chubby fingers around each Cheerio and shoving them into her mouth with a giggle.

"What did you and Helene fight about that night?"

Her eyes darted around the room. "We didn't fight."

"I thought there had been a disagreement between you two . . . ?"

"Oh right. Someone with a very big mouth said that at our table, right?"

She poured more cereal onto Amanda's highchair tray. Her hand was slightly shaking and the cereal tumbled in droves over the side. She swore under her breath.

I took the moment to unlatch Laurie and burp her, hoping Sara would fill in some gaps. When she didn't, I said, "Evelyn said Helene was canceling a construction project your husband was working on and you were very upset by that."

The box of Cheerios slipped from Sara's hand and spilled out on the floor. "No. No, she didn't cancel. We're still on. Set to start next week for Bruce."

·CHAPTER THIRTEEN·

Sitting Duck

To Do:

1. ✓ ~~Talk to Miss No-Nonsense.~~
2. Get manicure.
3. Order turkey.
4. Exercise.
5. Figure out how to make homemade baby food.

The next morning I could barely drag myself out of bed. I had been up at 11:00 P.M., at 1:00 A.M., at 3:00 A.M., and at 6:00 A.M. Jim had hardly seemed to notice.

Thankfully he was brewing coffee.

He sauntered into the bedroom. "Honey, do you have plans today? I have a meeting with Dirk Jonson."

Dirk was Jim's big client. He was the reason I was able to be at home and not back in the corporate world. Had Jim not landed this freelance client, I would be stuck in the nine to five grind, pumping milk every three hours and missing Laurie like crazy.

"I was hoping you could watch Laurie. I have an appointment, too."

After leaving Sara's place the day before, I had phoned Bruce and requested a meeting. He'd invited me over around noon.

Jim grabbed a sport coat out of the closet. "Can you ask your mom? I have to leave in a few minutes."

I didn't have to be at Bruce's until noon so I climbed back into bed. Jim kissed my cheek and disappeared down the hallway. I propped myself on a pillow and dialed Mom.

"What are you up to?" I asked her.

"Oh, darling, I'm almost out the door. Why?"

"I wanted to see if you could babysit. Jim just left for a meeting and I have one this afternoon with Helene's husband. But don't worry about it. I'll take Laurie along."

"Is that safe? Isn't he a suspect?"

"No. You're thinking of Alan, that's Margaret's husband."

"No, I'm not. I mean the widower. Isn't the widower always a suspect?"

"Hmmm. Well, I suppose . . . no. Come on, Mom, don't fuel my paranoia. Even if he was guilty of something, he's not going to try anything at his own house. That would point the finger directly at him, don't you think?"

"I guess you're right," Mom said.

"Where are you off to?" I asked.

"Napa. Wine tasting with Albert." Mom giggled.

"Sounds like fun, but is wine healthy for Galigani?"

"Well, it's not like we'll be chugalugging!"

"You don't even drink, Mom."

"Just a taste, darling. Nothing drastic. We're taking my car."

"Be careful," I said.

At 11 A.M. I bathed Laurie. I'd scrubbed the lint out between her fingers with a Q-tip.

Where did all the lint come from?

It seemed that no sooner had I removed it than it was back. The only thing I could guess was that she constantly had her hands in her mouth. Maybe the fact that her hands were wet made any blanket or piece of cloth fuzz stick between the little webs in her hands.

I stuck a little rubber ducky in the bath with Laurie. She watched it float around. I let her enjoy the soak and sang "Row, Row, Row Your Boat" to her.

I toweled her and dressed her, then I basically force-fed her. I knew it was a bit early—our routine was to nurse around noon—but if I wanted to be on time, I had to feed her now. Plus, it would eliminate any awkwardness in front of Bruce.

She seemed to take well enough to the early feeding, but when I burped her, she spit up all over her clean polka-dot top and my blouse, too, somehow missing the burp cloth entirely.

I laid her in the bassinet and hurried to my bedroom to change my top.

When I returned to the nursery, she was gazing at the teddy bear mobile in her bassinet.

Why did she seem to find something to amuse herself only when I needed to run out the door? Why couldn't she amuse herself with the mobile when I was, say, napping?

"Come on, Peanuty Pie," I said, scooping her up and placing her on the changing table.

She cooed and grinned at me.

"Yes! You'd be really cute if you didn't smell like spit-up." I leaned into her and rubbed my nose against her. She cooed again.

I selected a clean top for her with tiny sunflowers on it. As soon as I slid it over her head, she turned and spit up again.

Darn it!

Maybe feeding Laurie early hadn't been such a good idea. I was now officially late. I mopped her up and started again, this time with a top that buttoned down the front, hoping it would jiggle her less and cause less pressure on her belly.

She seemed content. I packed her into the car seat and took off toward Nob Hill, a good thirty minutes from my house.

Bruce lived in an upscale condo on the third floor. I was winded by the first floor. When I reached his place, I had to lean against the doorframe for support. I was huffing and puffing and refused to ring the bell until I could regain at least a scrap of composure.

When I finally rang the bell, Bruce opened the door wearing blue plaid shorts and a red Hawaiian top. Despite his wardrobe choices, he was still handsome. He was tall and lean, but his shoulders were slumped with grief. I could imagine that Helene and he had made a stunning couple.

"Kate, come on in."

The condo faced north and the view of the bay was breathtaking.

He glanced at Laurie peacefully sleeping in her portable car seat bucket. "She's beautiful."

"Thank you."

"Let me help you," he said, reaching out to take Laurie's bucket from my hand.

A mama bear instinct overtook me and I clutched the handle of the car seat so hard my knuckles turned white. "Oh no, no, it's okay. I got her."

Bruce looked taken aback. "Don't be silly. Those car seats get heavy." He reached out again and this time wrapped his hand around the handle.

What was wrong with me? What did I expect him to do with Laurie?

I tried to release my grasp. But something inside me wouldn't, so when Bruce pulled on the car seat, he took me along with it.

He looked confused and froze. He released the bucket as if it had stung him.

I wanted the ground to open and swallow me up.

I let out a nervous laugh. "Sorry, I wasn't sure you had her."

What an idiot I am! It was Mom's fault for planting the "guilty widower" seed in my head!

Bruce ran his hand up and down his thigh in a self-soothing gesture. He cleared his throat. "Um. I have some salmon on the grill. Downside to these condos is there's no yard. Upside is the roof access."

We made our way awkwardly through the living room. Bruce led and I carted the bucket. The condo was impeccably clean. White Berber carpets, cream leather couches, glass coffee and side tables.

He steered me toward the kitchen. A small interior staircase loomed ahead of me. I hesitated.

"Shall we head to the roof?" he asked.

Even though I hadn't actually seen Helene dead, images

of her lying at the bottom of the stairs flooded my head, followed by an image of Bruce pushing her down the stairs. Immediately followed by an image of Bruce pushing me off the roof.

Bruce glanced curiously at me. "It's a nice day out. The weather is outstanding for November."

I looked into his sad eyes and suddenly felt ridiculous. He wouldn't harm anyone.

"Earthquake weather," I said, climbing the narrow winding staircase.

When I emerged into the bright sunlight, I was startled to see Celia there manning the grill.

She flashed me a bright smile. "Kate! Oh, and you brought your baby!" She dropped the tongs on a small side table and rushed over to coo at Laurie.

What was she doing here?

I recalled the touch and hushed conversation they'd shared at the funeral. Could they be having an affair?

I watched Bruce watch Celia. His eyes flashed bright for a moment, then the sadness returned. He picked up the discarded tongs and poked at the salmon.

"My friend caught this fish in Canada. Shipped it back just a few days ago. This is the freshest salmon we can hope to have in California for a while, what with the season closure and all."

Celia picked up a beer, took a sip, then put her hand to her stomach. "Gosh, I've been feeling sick all day." She hesitantly glanced at Bruce.

Morning sickness?

Bruce looked up from the grill. "Oh. Uh . . . if you're not feeling well . . . Do you want to go home? Oh . . . I'm your ride." He glanced at Laurie and me, then back to Celia. Celia had a sour look on her face.

"Do you want me to call you a cab?"

Celia hesitated. She clutched her stomach. "I hate to miss out on the salmon . . . but maybe I'll feel better if I lie down for a while."

"Sure. You can lie down in the guest room," Bruce said.

Celia moved toward the stairs. She turned to me. "Will you promise to come check on me in twenty minutes? I don't want to miss the party."

Party? How strange.

A widower and a PI meeting was hardly a party. Something was definitely going on.

She descended the stairs. Bruce pulled the salmon off the grill and placed a few pieces alongside some vegetable shish kebabs on a pumpkin-colored platter.

He garnished the fish with some lemon slices and placed the platter in the middle of a picnic table that looked like it should have been center stage in a photo shoot for Pottery Barn.

He indicated for me to help myself.

I served myself a piece of fish and shish kebab. The smell of salmon was unbelievably delicious.

Bruce stared longing at the platter. "Haven't had much of an appetite lately."

I wanted to dig in, but now it looked like I would be dining alone. Was that wise? How did I know the fish was safe?

I chided myself. I couldn't stand the paranoia any longer. Or the hunger for that matter. Anyway, hadn't I already decided Bruce wouldn't harm me in his own house?

I broke the fish apart with my fork and sampled it. It was moist, hot, and delicious.

Bruce looked at Laurie in her car seat bucket and sighed. "Before this is over, I hope I have a couple of those."

"Before what is over?" I asked.

"This life."

"You and Helene didn't have any children, is that right?"

Bruce nodded. "Helene couldn't have kids."

I made no attempt to hide my surprise. "Really? I thought Margaret said you didn't want kids. She said Helene was fighting the biological clock."

Now it was Bruce's turn to be surprised. His face showed first dismay then something between defeat and sadness. "I suppose it shouldn't surprise me. Helene was always one surprise after another. I could probably tell you this. I don't see what difference it makes now that she's gone."

Bruce leaned in toward me and lowered his voice. "About a year after we were married, Helene was brutally raped. It was bad, really bad." He shook his head back and forth. "We didn't realize at first that it would prevent us from having kids . . . but . . . sometimes things are just out of your control. I understand why Helene never said anything to Margaret. But me not wanting kids? No. No way. I'd always joked with my parents that I'd have enough to man a basketball team . . ."

He looked up and squinted at the sun. We sat in silence for a moment.

"I'm sorry," I said.

He closed his eyes. "Thank you." He opened his eyes and looked at Laurie again. "In fact, we were hoping to adopt. That's why Celia's here. She was helping Helene and I coordinate an adoption with a priest in Costa Rica."

"Oh?"

"She knows a priest, Father Pedro at San Rafael Catholic Church, who wanted to help this teenage girl who got . . . well anyway, the baby is due next month. Helene was traveling pretty regularly out there and everything was progressing smoothly, but now . . ." He grimaced. "Now it's hard to imagine being a daddy with no mommy."

Sadness overcame me and my eyes began to well with tears. Before I could speak, my cell phone rang. We both glanced at my ultrafashionable diaper purse—an old Jansport travel backpack that was doubling as a diaper bag, purse, and catchall.

Bruce rose. "Go ahead and get that if you need to. You want a margarita or a beer or something? I think I need a drink."

I dug into the backpack for the offending noise and shook my head. Bruce disappeared down the steps as I examined the incoming call. I didn't recognize the number but pressed the accept button anyway.

"Hello?"

"Kate? This is Hank . . . um . . . your mom's friend?"

Hank? This was Mom's other boyfriend. What was he doing calling me?

"Yeah. Hi, Hank."

"Sorry to bother you, Kate. It's just that I was concerned about your mom. I haven't heard from her in a couple days and, well, we're leaving tonight on our Mexican cruise. I wanted to be sure she had all the information . . . and . . . well, at our age you can't be too careful, right? Just wanted to know that she was okay."

What could I say? She's wine tasting with another fellow?

"Oh, Hank, that is so sweet. Yes, Mom is fine. Just busy. But she's totally fine. I'm sure she'll be there tonight. She's really looking forward to the trip. Shall I have her call you?"

"I don't want to be a bother . . ."

"I'm sure it's not a bother . . . let me take down your number."

What did I know? Maybe Mom was giving him the brush-off. Still, I didn't have to be the one to break the bad news, right?

I rummaged frantically through my diaper purse, but couldn't come up with a pen in time. I double-checked the number he gave me against the one my phone had picked up. We said good-bye and hung up. I contemplated dialing Mom right then, but decided against it. Bruce would be back any minute.

I studied Laurie, still snoozing in her bucket. I reached over and felt her tummy extend and deflate. Good.

I finished the salmon and grilled corn on my plate and waited.

What was taking Bruce so long?

Maybe he was checking on Celia.

Bored, I decided to dial Mom.

She picked up on the third ring. "Kate? Is everything all right?"

I smiled to myself. Now that Mom had a cell phone, she seemed proud to be "on call" 24/7. "Everything's fine, except your boyfriend called me looking for you."

"My who?"

"Hank called me, Mom."

"Oh dear! Well, yes, yes, thank you for the message, Kate."

I imagined her trying to act coy with Galigani at her side. A wicked impulse struck me. "You owe me, Mom. I *lied* for you! Kept your fish on the line, so to speak."

"Yes, dear. Well, thank you very much for that. I appreciate it. Oh! Look at this—we're at Cakebread Cellars!"

"It's okay, you can try and act busy, but I need you to work on Galigani for me. If he's well enough to gallivant through Napa with you, then he's well enough to supervise me or whatever. Besides, I really don't need any supervision."

"I have to go, honey. Kiss little Laurie for me. Thanks for calling."

"Will you do it?"

"Mmm-hmm," Mom answered in a singsong fashion and disconnected.

I pulled out my notebook and rummaged deeper into my backpack. I had to have something to write with. I'd never make it as a PI without a pen!

I finally found a pencil with a very dull tip in one of the pack's side pockets. Still enough to jot some ideas down:

1. Why would Helene lie to Margaret about Bruce not wanting kids?
2. What did Helene's death mean to Bruce? Another chance at marriage and having kids? What about the impending adoption?

Finally, I heard Bruce's footsteps on the staircase. He was carrying a mixed drink in one hand and a beer in the other. He resumed his seat across from me and set both drinks in front of himself.

"Bruce, are you planning any construction projects?"

He sighed. "Yeah. Helene and I wanted to put an extension on the condo. Because of the baby."

"Did you decide to cancel the project?"

He shook his head. "Well, I'm not sure yet what I'm going to do."

"Do you know if Helene canceled the project?"

"No. She wouldn't have canceled the project. Why would she cancel? No."

So maybe Sara was right and Helene hadn't canceled the construction, but why would Evelyn lie?

Bruce took a sip of the mixed drink. "I'd love to have children. But hell, I'm not around much. How am I going to raise a kid all by myself?"

I watched as his face contorted. Anger flashed across his eyes and was replaced by a distant look. He gripped the mixed drink, then made a satisfied sound as he drained the glass. "I work all the time. I have very demanding clients. Even this." He waved his hand around. "My being out this week. Sure the firm will send out a letter to my clients, but it's very hard to be away."

He pushed the empty glass away from himself and grabbed the beer.

"I know you spoke with the ME. Can you share anything with me that might help me figure out what happened that night?"

He fingered the beer and sat in silence. "He didn't tell me much. Just asked if Helene used drugs. I told him she didn't. He kind of kept questioning me along those lines. Asked about drinking and smoking and stuff. Helene drank that night, sure." He took a swig of beer. "We all did. But I don't think she drank enough to have alcohol poisoning or anything. And she was using these nicotine patches to try and get off the cancer sticks. We both wanted the house to be smoke free for when the baby came. But that's it. That's pretty much all I could tell him."

"Bruce, early in the evening, do you remember being at the bar with Helene, Margaret, and her husband? Margaret told me you all were at the bar and then Sara and her husband came over. Apparently you men were discussing investments—"

"Oh! Yeah, sure. Howard was grilling me on the market. It's not a surprise we're all very concerned about it tanking."

"Do you think maybe Helene and Margaret got their drinks mixed up?" I asked.

Bruce looked curiously blank. "I don't know. Where are you going with this?"

It didn't feel right to share Margaret's fears with him. How could I tell him his wife may have accidentally been murdered?

No. I didn't know that for sure anyway. I shouldn't get him upset about something I couldn't yet prove.

Instead I said, "Can you think of anyone that would want to hurt Helene?"

"I really don't know, Kate. As far as I know, she was pretty well liked. I mean in the mommy group and everything . . . even though, you know, she wasn't one of them yet."

"What about her relationship with Evelyn?"

Bruce looked blank.

"Evelyn was in the mommy group. There was an incident with her kid biting Sara's baby . . ."

Bruce finished the beer. "I didn't keep track of the ins and outs of the group. You should ask Margaret."

I nodded.

He hung his head. "You know, Kate, my grandma died a few weeks ago. She had terminal cancer. And she was old and all, and we expected it . . . but Helene . . ."

He covered his face with his hands.

I sat in silence while he collected himself. "I'm going to do all I can to try and figure out what happened to Helene."

He stood. "Thank you, Kate. Margaret said you're great. I'm sure SF's finest can use all the help they can get, and if Margaret says that's you, then that's enough for me."

Margaret had said I was great?

Nothing like a little peer pressure.

I packed my notebook into my backpack. Bruce wrapped his hands around Laurie's bucket handle. "Do you want me to carry her down?"

"Please."

We walked down the staircase. Bruce settled Laurie at my feet and headed straight to the bar. He poured himself another whiskey.

"Were you going to drive Celia home?" I asked.

Bruce glanced at his watch. "Oh, geez. I forgot about Celia. She's been out a long time. I hope she's okay."

"I can probably take her home. Do you want me to check on her?"

"Thanks, Kate. That'd be great." He drained his glass and refilled it. "First door on the right."

I watched him settle himself into the couch and study his drink.

Poor guy.

I knocked on the guest bedroom door.

No answer.

I cracked the door and peeked in. Celia was lying on top of the covers, her shoes still on. Her hands folded across her stomach.

"Celia," I whispered from the doorway.

She lay perfectly still. I cleared my throat and whispered a little louder. "Celia!"

When she didn't move, I entered the room and laid my hand gently on hers. She was cold. I shook her. "Celia!"

She was pale and deathly still.

Uh-oh!

I grabbed her wrist and shook her furiously. “Wake up!”

When she didn’t move, I raced toward the door. I rammed my shoulder into the doorway and winced. Pain shot down my arm. I grabbed my shoulder.

“Bruce! Bruce, call 9-1-1!”

Bruce jumped to his feet. “What’s the matter? Did you hurt yourself?”

“I’m okay.” I rubbed my shoulder. “It’s Celia.”

• CHAPTER FOURTEEN •

Sucker

Bruce and I sat on the couch, each holding a tumbler of whiskey. We heard sirens making their way down the street. I was shaking uncontrollably and Bruce kept telling me to drink the whiskey. I couldn't make myself do it.

As the sirens screamed closer, Laurie stirred in her bucket. She opened one eye and peered up at me.

Go back to sleep, I prayed.

The second eye opened and both stared at me.

I froze, hoping my statue stance might bore her back to sleep.

Now her mouth opened to match both eyes.

I cringed.

Laurie screamed fiendishly loud as though she were being poked with hot needles.

Bruce looked at her curiously. I picked her up and nestled her into my neck as the sirens came to a halt under

Bruce's window. He stood and crossed the room, ready to buzz the EMTs up.

Laurie's cries replaced the noise of the sirens. It felt as if there were an ambulance in the room with us. I cooed, rocked, bounced, and did everything I could think of. Her screaming wouldn't stop. I knew what she wanted.

How could I nurse her here and right now?

The EMTs, two guys in black uniforms, entered the condo and went down the hall with Bruce. Momentarily alone, I dug out a blanket from my backpack and searched for a private space to nurse Laurie.

The condo was all open space and windows.

Laurie continued to howl. I selected a chair and strategically placed it with its back to the hallway and facing a corner of the living room instead of a window. I wrapped the blanket around myself and snuggled Laurie under it, trying my best to nurse her with a modicum of modesty. She was immediately silenced.

I could hear voices down the hall. Every inch of me, except the part physically attached to the baby, wanted to be a fly on the wall of the guest bedroom. From the commotion, it sounded like they were giving CPR.

She couldn't be dead.

That was impossible. No one her age just lies down feeling sick to her stomach and dies. Do they?

God. Please let Celia be all right.

Helene had probably been poisoned. Could Celia have been poisoned? By whom?

Uh-oh!

Anxiety crept through my chest.

Bruce and I were the only ones here. Could he have given her something?

Maybe while I was on the phone? He was downstairs all that time.

No! She was sick before that.

What about the salmon? I was the only one that ate it, though.

Unless Celia had tasted some before I came.

If I was poisoned, too—could I poison little Laurie through my breast milk?

Suddenly it was hard to breathe. Did my stomach hurt? It did!

Was it just me? Was it hypochondria?

Focus on your stomach, Kate! Does it really hurt?

I felt nauseous.

Jesus, Bruce wouldn't poison Celia and me in his own home, would he? Why hadn't he eaten any salmon, for crying out loud! Why had I eaten it?

I pulled my breast from Laurie. She attempted to latch on again. I pulled the nursing bra into place. Laurie whimpered, then cried out.

Well, she wouldn't die from crying, but I couldn't risk poisoning her.

I jumped up and hurried down the hallway. Thankfully the motion soothed Laurie and she quieted down.

Bruce greeted me with dark eyes. "It doesn't look good."

"Is she . . . ?"

One EMT was crouched over Celia, while the other rose and barked something into a walkie-talkie secured on his suspender.

Bile was building in my throat. I felt my blood rush to my toes.

The EMT watched me. "Ma'am?"

I handed Laurie to him and rushed to the bathroom. I got sick in the toilet.

The EMT stood in the doorway of the bathroom. "Can I get you anything?"

From my position on the floor, I watched as another pair of boots sped into the bedroom.

"She said she was feeling sick. She just went to lie down," I said, holding my head in my hands.

The EMT nestled Laurie in one arm and ran a washcloth under the faucet. He handed me the cold cloth. "We have to get her to emergency, she's in critical condition."

"The owner, the guy, Bruce . . . his wife was poisoned last week. Could Celia have been poisoned?"

"It's difficult to say at this point, ma'am."

Laurie looked amazingly content in his arms.

"I ate some salmon here. I was the only one who ate it. I didn't see Celia eat anything and Bruce didn't either. Could I have been poisoned?"

I was half expecting him to laugh. I wanted him to tell me I was being irrational. Instead a grave look crossed his face and he pulled a flashlight from his breast pocket. He shone the light into my eyes.

My throat was dry and breathing was suddenly difficult.

The EMT wrapped his fingers around my wrist and remained silent as he took my pulse.

Voices drifted in from the hallway. I heard sharp commands being tossed back and forth, but was unable to make anything out. A stretcher carrying Celia floated past the open bathroom door.

My tongue felt like it was thickening and stuck to the roof of my mouth.

"Oh, God, if I've been poisoned, what about my daughter? I just nursed her."

The EMT nodded calmly and looked at Laurie snuggled into his arm. "I think we need to take you both into emergency. We'll get your stomach pumped and put the baby in observation. Is there anyone I can call for you?"

The room seemed to do a 360 around me. I pressed my hands against the floor for stability as I spurted out Jim's cell phone number.

The medic told me to remain seated, then took Laurie out to the hallway. I heard frantic whispers and then the other EMT poked his head in. "Don't worry, ma'am, we're going back down to get the stretcher and take care of you in a jiffy." He disappeared.

His hurried speech was followed by an eerie silence. I waited for what seemed like a long time, even though I knew it could be only a few minutes at the most.

My little Laurie, my love! Please, God, don't let her be poisoned.

Panic rose in my chest and my body was wracked with sobs.

Bruce poked his head into the bathroom. "Kate, are you all right?"

I couldn't make eye contact with him. It took all my effort to shake my head.

"Were you close to Celia?" Bruce's confusion showed through his tone.

I shook my head again and sobbed.

Bruce tapped nervously at the doorway frame. "Right. Right. It still is very upsetting."

I met his gaze. "The salmon, Bruce."

Bruce took a step back as though I'd punched him. "What?

You can't think . . . you think the salmon was . . . bad? It was as fresh as—"

"Not *bad*! Poison! Helene was poisoned. Celia's in critical condition. I ate the salmon and now I'm sick."

"You can't think . . . Kate! I prepared the salmon myself."

"I'm sure you did!" I spat.

"Kate, I swear there was nothing wrong with the salmon. I didn't kill Helene or Celia. You can't seriously think that."

Just then one of the EMTs pressed his way past Bruce. "Excuse us, sir."

The other EMT laid the stretcher across the floor straddling the bathroom and the hallway. "Okay, ma'am, easy does it. Just lie down here."

"Where's my baby?" I sobbed.

"Don't worry, ma'am, we've secured her in the ambulance. Your husband is on his way to the hospital."

I crawled onto the stretcher and felt myself being suspended in midair. I glanced at Bruce. He looked as pale as Celia had. Only he was standing on his own and *alive*.

The EMTs paused at the front door, adjusting their grips on the stretcher. Bruce looked down at me. "Kate, I swear it. I swear the food was fine."

I simply moaned.

One of the EMTs answered for me. "Sir, we have to get her to the hospital."

The urgency in his voice caused Bruce to step back and succeeded in sending me into another panic. Tears welled in my throat and my mind was on Laurie.

Please, God, no matter what happens to me, please let Laurie be okay.

A vision of Jim raising Laurie alone sent another shock wave through me. My stomach clenched violently.

Although the EMTs descended the three flights of steps smoothly, I still managed to feel guilty about my weight. My fat butt was causing them to move cautiously down the steps, probably delaying emergency treatment that could save Laurie's and my life.

When they pushed the stretcher into the ambulance, I saw Laurie. She was nestled in a see-through plastic crib, much like the one she'd been in at the hospital only a few short weeks ago when she was born. The EMTs had wrapped her in the blanket I had used to shield myself when I nursed her and she seemed content.

I wanted desperately to hold her, but I was strapped down into mobile mode. The ambulance lurched forward. One of the EMTs remained in the back with us. He hovered over Laurie and smiled. "Her color looks good. Her heart rate is steady. I think she's going to be fine."

His comments settled my nerves a bit, but I still felt tears spilling out of my eyes. The ride to the hospital was short, and somehow the fact that the driver hadn't put the sirens on did much to calm me.

We couldn't be in such bad shape if they didn't use the sirens, could we?

"Where's Celia?" I asked.

"The other team went on ahead of us," he said.

When we arrived at the hospital, Laurie was attended to first. A pediatrician conferred with one of the EMTs as they hovered over her crib. Jim suddenly appeared.

"Jim!" I practically screamed from the stretcher.

"Honey!" He rushed over to me and embraced me. "What happened? How are you feeling?"

"Terrible. My stomach is killing me. I got sick, but they're still going to have my stomach pumped! Celia's in critical condition. Helene was poisoned—"

"Shhh. Hold on, honey. I'm having a hard time following. Who is Celia?"

A nurse appeared at my side. "Mrs. Connolly, I'm going to take you in now."

Jim looked panicked. "Wait, I—"

"Stay with Laurie, please!"

Jim nodded and looked solemn. Tears streamed down my cheeks.

• CHAPTER FIFTEEN •

Emergency

I was wheeled into another room. A team of doctors and nurses hovered over me. There were at least six people in the room with me.

A man dressed in scrubs stepped forward, "Mrs. Connolly, I'm Dr. Wong. As you know, we're going to perform a gastric irrigation. You will experience minor discomfort. But the procedure is brief, after which you'll be given activated charcoal to absorb any poison that might remain."

Good God! Charcoal! They are going to give me charcoal!

Like briquettes?

I must have nodded because Dr. Wong said, "Good."

"Wait, wait. My baby! Will she have to have charcoal? Irrigation?"

Dr. Wong blinked at me. "Dr. Monroe is attending to

her now. Unless she starts to show severe symptoms, they'll wait for our findings before they proceed with a treatment plan."

Severe symptoms. What have I done!

A woman leaned over and touched my shoulder. "Kate, I'm Nancy. I'll be assisting Dr. Wong. Try to relax and turn over onto your left side. We'll be inserting this tube through your mouth, into the esophagus, and down to your stomach."

Think happy thoughts. Beach thoughts. Don't focus on the tube. I'm on the beach. The water is lapping against the sand. The air is refreshing. No. Not cold! Hot, it's hot. I am on the beach in Hawaii. Don't think about the tube.

The nurse sprayed a numbing agent into my mouth and down my throat. Even though it smelled like spearmint, it tasted like tin. She inserted the tube into my mouth and I experienced the most horrendous feeling as she shoved it down my throat. Like when a long noodle gets stuck in your throat and you don't know if you need to swallow or try and hack it out.

My gag reflex kicked into high gear and I felt like I was somewhere between puking and suffocating.

This was worse than labor!

Nancy leaned in close. "You are doing great. Dr. Wong is starting the irrigation now. This will only take about ten minutes."

Ten minutes! Oh God! I don't have enough beach thoughts for ten minutes.

Think healthy thoughts. Healthy me. Healthy Laurie. Everyone healthy, fine, pink, happy. There. At least one minute must have gone by. Right? Only nine left.

Dr. Wong semigrunted.

What did that mean?

He watched the fluid leaving my stomach. I glanced down, causing myself to go cross-eyed and only glimpsed some rose-colored liquid. The tube was connected to a bag but I couldn't make anything else out.

What was he grunting about?

"Good, Kate. Everything is good," Nancy soothed.

Dr. Wong nodded.

Okay, relax. Maybe only eight minutes left.

How many seconds is that? Think 8 times 60 is . . . wait, okay 8 times 5 is 40. 40 plus 8 is 48. Good God, what had happened to my math skills? Take 48, add the 0, so 480 seconds. If I count to 480 slowly, the procedure will be done. And actually, it took me so long to do the math that probably one minute has already gone by. Oh . . . what is 7 times 60?

Nancy rubbed my arm. I tried to get back into my beach reverie, but Dr. Wong was up and moving around distracting me.

I had to swallow but with a tube in my throat, how was I supposed to do that?

Quick! Think about something else!

How many more seconds?

I watched Dr. Wong open a package and fiddle with the bag that was connected to the tube in my mouth.

Nancy squeezed my elbow. "We're just completing the rinse and are preparing for the charcoal. More than halfway through now, honey. You're doing fine."

Dr. Wong handed the bag to another physician, who was focused on a monitor. He took the bag and promptly left the room.

I imagined them examining the contents for the poison in order to figure out how to treat Laurie.

Was she going to have to have this awful tube inserted?

The thought of Laurie threw me into overdrive and tears streamed down my face.

"Calm down, honey. We're almost through here. You're going to be fine." Nancy patted my arm.

Trying to suppress the sobs was making my breathing speed up. But breathing fast with a tube down your throat is really difficult so I willed myself to stop panicking.

Laurie was with a doctor and Jim. Surely they were taking good care of her.

Dr. Wong prepared a syringe.

"We're going to take a small sample of blood to send to the lab," Nancy said as she wrapped a rubber tie around my arm.

I wanted to nod my understanding, but didn't want to move the tube.

Screw it.

They were going to take my blood whether I nodded or not.

I hardly felt the pinprick of the needle over the tube, which seemed to be growing inside my throat. Weren't ten minutes up yet?

After they drew the blood, Dr. Wong examined the package attached to the tube and nodded to Nancy.

She leaned over and said, "Okay, Kate, the procedure is complete. I'm going to remove the tube now. You'll feel a little discomfort as I do this."

"A little," of course, turned out to be an understatement. It felt like she was ripping out my throat. What followed was a severe case of dry heaves.

Nancy rubbed my shoulder. "Yes, yes. This is normal. Take your time."

I recovered a bit and lay down on my back. It had been the worst experience of my life, bar none.

Please, God, don't let Laurie have to have her stomach pumped!

Dr. Wong leaned into me. "Kate, the contents of your stomach and your blood will be analyzed in the lab. We'll be monitoring you for symptoms. I need you to try and rest as much as possible."

I nodded.

I guessed that they would compare my results to Celia's and Helene's in order to figure out a treatment for Laurie. With the procedure over, I had nowhere to turn my thoughts except to Laurie.

An image of her, with all sorts of tubes attached to her tiny body, popped into my head. This image charged me with so much emotion that my heart felt like it was collapsing onto itself and suffocating me.

I prayed and wept.

•CHAPTER SIXTEEN•

Faux Pas

I awoke with a start. Jim was sitting on the end of the bed, holding my feet in his lap. Suddenly the events of the previous hours flooded my mind. I was in the recovery room at the hospital, everything looking foreign and sparse. I bolted upright.

"Laurie! Where is she? How is—" A sob choked off the rest of my words.

Jim rubbed my feet. "Laurie is fine. She's being spoiled rotten over in the pediatric unit. The nurses keep passing her around and cooing at her. She's loving it."

I swallowed hard. My throat was extremely sore and dry from the procedure and crying made it feel worse, but I couldn't help myself. Tears streamed down my cheeks as relief overwhelmed me. "She's okay? What did they do? Did they pump her stomach?"

"No. They didn't have to do anything to her. She was perfectly fine," Jim soothed.

"I . . . I . . . didn't poison her through my milk?" I sobbed.

Jim squeezed my feet. "The doctor doesn't think you were poisoned."

I stared at him.

Not poisoned?

This *was* good. This was *very* good. Laurie hadn't had to be treated. I had not been poisoned!

Why didn't I feel elated?

Because I'd had my stomach pumped for NOTHING!

"What about my symptoms?" I asked.

"What symptoms, honey?"

"I threw up. My tongue was getting thick. It was hard to breathe. I was sick."

"Honey, those weren't symptoms of poisoning. The doctor says most likely you were experiencing a panic attack."

I shook my head. "No. No. I was sick. I threw up in the toilet at Bruce's condo. What if I flushed the evidence?"

"They're going to run the test anyway, but they probably won't have results for a week or so. The doc said you didn't have the same stuff going as Celia. He's pretty sure your results are going to be negative."

"But if they don't know for sure, what about Laurie?"

"She never showed any signs of distress. No shallow breathing, drowsiness, slowed heart rate, and whatever all else. The doctor rattled off so many symptoms that I lost track. Point being, she didn't have any of them."

Thank God for all the doctors and nurses, going to

medical school, studying so hard, and sacrificing so much to be able to help us!

"How is Celia?" I asked.

"She's in stable condition. She was almost unconscious by the time they got her here. So they think her results are going to show something. But anyway, they were able to pump her stomach in time and expect a full recovery." Jim's expression was grave. "You saved her life."

We sat in silence for a moment.

"My throat is killing me," I said.

Jim handed me a cup of water with a straw from the bedside table. I sipped the water and felt it burn going down. Swallowing made the pain worse.

We sat in silence for a moment then tears sprang to my eyes again. "When can I see Laurie? Is she really okay?"

Jim got up from the end of the bed and moved toward me. He wrapped his arms around me. "She's really okay. They didn't need to pump her tummy or even give her any medication. They watched all her vital signs for over six hours."

I started to wipe my tears but gave up and buried my face in Jim's chest and bawled.

Jim stroked my hair and rocked me back and forth. "Everything is fine, honey. I think you're a little stressed out. But you're fine. Laurie's fine. Everybody's fine."

I looked up from Jim's chest into his eyes and nodded.

"I love you, honey. Just close your eyes and rest for a while. They said you'll probably be released as soon as Dr. Wong gives you a final evaluation. I'm going to check on Laurie and see when they will release her." He rose from the hospital bed.

"Wait! I want to go with you. I have to see Petunia." I

swung my legs out of the bed, feeling a chill through the thin hospital gown.

"No, honey. You need to stay put and wait for the doctor." His brow creased with concern. "Are you hungry? Should I order a pizza or something. I mean, your stomach's empty, right?"

I groaned. The thought of eating made my throat constrict. I couldn't imagine swallowing anything solid for a hundred years.

"Soup, probably."

Jim nodded and pulled open the room door. "Course, yeah, right. Soup is good food." He offered me a smile. "I'll be back as soon as I can."

He shut the door behind him.

I sat back on the bed, ignoring the chill I felt. I had needlessly put Laurie and myself in harm's way. The guilt I felt was debilitating. Freezing in the hospital gown would be punishment for my crimes.

And yet . . .

Had I really put Laurie and me in danger? Or was it only a perceived danger?

After all, I hadn't been poisoned. I had only freaked out a bit. Had a "panic attack."

Big deal. Didn't all new moms have panic attacks at one point or another?

I mean, what was the difference in panicking to see if Laurie was still breathing in her sleep and thinking I'd been poisoned by a murderer?

I buried my head in my hands. Good Lord, maybe I really was losing my mind.

My thoughts turned to Celia. She would recover.

I had saved her life.

See. I did have value. Even if I was going crazy. Celia was alive today because of me.

Had Bruce killed Helene?

What did this mean about Alan? Was Margaret really in any danger? Had she been imagining Alan's suspicious behavior?

A nurse peeked in. "Mrs. Connolly, Dr. Wong will be another fifteen to twenty minutes."

"Okay, thank you. Can I get dressed?"

"Not yet. He'll need to examine you again before discharge. Do you need anything? More water?"

"No. Can you tell me what room Celia . . . oh, I don't remember her last name . . ."

"Martinez?" the nurse asked.

Martinez? Was that it?

"The woman who was brought in just before you?" the nurse asked.

I nodded.

"She's in Room 1712. Right around the corner." She left the room.

I spotted a pair of slipper socks on the bedside table and ripped open the plastic package. After putting them on, I left the room to locate Celia. I knocked at her door.

"Come in," she called.

She was sitting in bed propped up with a bunch of pillows. She was pale but looked astonishingly well rested. She seemed startled to see me.

"Kate! What are you doing here?"

I approached the bed. "I came to see how you were recovering."

"Why are you in a hospital gown?"

She offered me the only chair in the small room. I sat and recounted the events that had transpired after she had lost consciousness the best I could. When I finished, my throat was sore and raw. I imagined hers would still be also. I pushed the bedside cart/table, which had a pitcher of water and a cup with a straw on it, toward Celia. Next to the water was a business card from SFPD. I couldn't make out the name. Celia watched me and nodded.

"Thank you," she said, reaching for the cup.

"How are you feeling?" I asked.

"As good as can be expected." She took a sip of water. "Oooh. It hurts to swallow!"

"I know."

She put the cup down. "I'm happy to be alive, though."

"Have you talked to the police?" I asked.

"They were here earlier." She indicated the card that was on the table.

I took the opportunity to take a closer look. Officer McNearny. Homicide.

Celia's lips twisted to the right, her beautiful face becoming a hard mask. "I can't believe Bruce tried to kill me. I would have never thought him capable of it. If you hadn't called 9-1-1, Kate . . ." She faltered. "I can't even go there."

But actually I hadn't called 9-1-1. Bruce had . . .

I recalled the hushed conversation between Bruce and Celia. I had thought something romantic could or had developed between them, but then he mentioned the pending adoption. His trying to kill her made no sense, unless he thought she knew something.

"Did you suspect anything?" I asked.

Celia pushed the buttons on the bed, first lowering herself and then overcorrecting to a sitting position. She kicked off the covers in frustration.

"I hate this stupid bed!" She rose, shuffled to the door,

and looked into the hallway. She turned back to me, and her shoulders slumped. "Sorry. I don't know when they're supposed to release me and I'm getting anxious to go."

I stood. "I'll go. Dr. Wong is supposed to be checking on me soon anyway."

"No. No, don't go. You asked if I suspected anything." She crossed back to the bed and jumped on top of it, opting not to get under the covers. Her delicate legs and feet dangled over the side.

I waited for her to continue.

"I didn't outright suspect him or really even think about it until he tried to kill me. I don't know why he would kill Helene and then try to kill me. Maybe he thought I knew something or saw something. At least that's what the homicide cop suggested." She looked expectantly at me. "Do you know why? Were they having marital problems?"

I shrugged. "Well, you certainly knew them better than me. All I know is Margaret told me Helene wanted kids but Bruce didn't. But weren't you helping them to adopt?"

Celia's mouth clamped shut and she gripped at the covers. "Oh. Who told you about that?"

"Bruce did."

Her grip relaxed and she released the bed cover. "Helene really wanted kids, I'd heard about this situation in Costa Rica. My second cousin . . . she's only fifteen . . . Anyway, I was trying to help Helene and my cousin. But now that she's gone . . ." She pressed her lips together so tightly they turned white. "That's why I was there talking to Bruce. My cousin is ready to deliver and now she doesn't know what she's going to do."

"Bruce wants to back out?"

She nodded and sat up straighter. "It doesn't matter anyway. The guy's a murderer. Now, I wouldn't let him even look at my little cousin."

The nurse poked her head in the door. "Oh, there you are, Mrs. Connolly. Dr Wong will be able to see you in a few minutes."

"What about me?" Celia asked.

"I'll be back with your dinner." The nurse left.

Celia made a face. "Sounds like I'm staying for a while. I hate hospitals. That's why I offer an alternative to women giving birth."

I rose from the chair. "Celia, I was thinking. How do you suppose he did it?"

Celia looked as though she was considering the question for the first time.

"It wasn't in the salmon," I added.

"Probably in my drink or something."

"Did you taste anything?"

Celia glanced upward as if trying to recall. "Hmm. Now that you mention it. My beer did taste rather . . . metallic. But sometimes beer does, so I didn't think anything of it."

I returned to my room to find McNearny sitting on the chair next to the bed.

Uh-oh!

I glanced down at my hospital gown. Not the kind of look a gal wants while having company. I desperately searched the room for a robe.

None.

"Can I help you?" I demanded.

McNearny stared at me. "How are you feeling?"

I shrugged.

He cleared his throat and stood. "Well, glad to see you're up and about."

Was he?

I had to be cautious; it would be just like him to try and get me off my guard.

He motioned for me to take a seat on the bed. I sat and pulled the sheet up to my neck, more or less defensively. He sat back down on the chair. We waited each other out in silence.

After a minute he said, "Maybe you can help. What happened today?"

I briefly recounted the details of my lunch at Bruce's. He shook his head back and forth in complete and utter disapproval as I spoke.

"What were you doing there in the first place?"

"I wanted to find out what Helene and Sara had been fighting about that night on the cruise."

"And what was it? Is it relevant?"

"Apparently they fought about a construction project and whether or not it was being canceled."

He scowled. "Who cares about that?"

My hands clenched involuntarily. "Well, I also wanted to know if he'd seen anything that night. Like Helene drinking Margaret's drink—"

"I told you to limit your actions to the doctor!" McNearny growled.

"Well . . . I . . ."

He stood. "Do not step on this investigation. I'm not interested in idle gossip about who is canceling projects. I'm canceling you. You got that? Believe it or not, SFPD was here before you broke onto the scene. We have the training and experience necessary to handle this. It's not amateur hour. Amateurs end up in the hospital!"

I remained quiet, duly reprimanded.

He leaned in a bit. "Either that or they end up in jail for interference!"

• CHAPTER SEVENTEEN •

Second Wind

To Do:

1. Talk with Galigani—what are the real dangers of this business?
2. Stock up on soup and tea.
3. Dust and clean house—yuck!
4. ~~Catch up on laundry.~~ Ask Jim to do laundry.
5. Laurie swim classes?
6. Be a better mom—stay out of trouble—do NOT endanger Laurie.

The following morning, I puttered around the kitchen making coffee, still not sure if I would be able to drink any. My throat continued to hurt and only tea seemed to go down. It was 9:00 A.M., and Jim and Laurie were still sleeping.

The nurses had pumped Laurie full of formula and it seemed to knock her out overnight. We had been up to breastfeed only once, around 3:00 A.M.

Hmmm. Something to keep in mind.

When we got home last night, after the hospital escapade, Jim had made me promise not to investigate without guidance. He'd said if Galigani wasn't willing to sponsor me as an intern and supervise me, then I'd have to stop investigating.

Actually, the arrangement was fine with me. I hated being scolded by McNearny. What if he arrested me?

No.

I would be a stay-at-home mom! Full-time mother! Completely dedicated and 100 percent devoted to my little flower!

The temperature had dropped overnight and it looked like we were in for a bit of a cold spell. At least by San Francisco standards, high forties. I planned to snuggle under a fleece blanket, drink tea, be with Laurie, and watch TV all day.

After all, isn't that what new moms were supposed to do?

No running around and thinking I had consumed something deadly.

I flicked on the TV and at the first commercial break got antsy. I peeked at my cell phone and noticed the voice mail indicator on. I'd missed three calls yesterday.

Hmmm.

No!

I'm a stay-at-home. One hundred percent mom. If I listened to my voice mails, I might get sucked in again. I padded to the middle of room, where Laurie was lightly sleeping in the bassinet. She fidgeted and swung her arms. I touched her cheek, and despite the fuzzy sleeper, she seemed cold.

When would I be allowed to use a blanket in her bassinet? She had broken out of the swaddle a few weeks prior, and keeping her warm in this weather was going to become a concern.

My eyes flicked back to my cell phone. There wasn't any harm in checking messages, was there? All I would be doing was listening. Maybe there was an important message, even something urgent.

I grabbed my cell phone as the doorbell rang. I made my way to the front door and looked through the peek hole. There was a pregnant belly poking its way through a bouquet of flowers. My best friend, Paula, was standing behind the bouquet.

I flung the door open and a gust of wind hit me in the face. I grabbed Paula around the neck, crushing the flowers between us. "Oh, my God, what are you doing here?"

Paula, a born designer, was wearing a white cashmere overcoat and was wrapped in pink accessories. Pink gloves, scarf, and hat. They matched her cheeks.

She stepped inside and handed me the flowers. "These are for you."

"For what?"

"I called yesterday and Jim told me you had been in the hospital. I wanted to come see you right away."

A delicate Parisian shopping bag hung from her wrist. She unlatched it and handed it to me. "Something for the little one. Where is she?"

I directed her to the living room. Paula immediately spotted the bassinet and rushed to unbundle herself. She thrust all her pink accessories at me, even her Dolce & Gabbana purse—also in pink.

I hung everything in the hall closet. "I wasn't expecting you home so soon."

"I came home to have the baby!" she said, reflexively rubbing her belly.

"But you're not due, for what, another couple of months, right?"

"Yeah, yeah, but I wanted to be home before I got too far along to travel."

"What about David and Danny?" I asked.

Paula and her husband, David, had relocated to Paris several months ago with their two-year-old, Danny. David worked for a top consulting firm and they'd requested he take an assignment in France, holding the promise of a promotion over his head. "At home getting settled in," Paula said. In moments she had scoped Laurie up. "Kate! She's so darling."

Laurie remarkably remained asleep in her arms.

"Who do you look like?" Paula asked Laurie. "You have your dad's forehead. What about your eyes?" She jiggled Laurie. "Hey, wake up there, kid. I'm talking to you."

I nudged Paula shoulder. "Don't you dare!"

Paula laughed and continued her conversation with a snoozing Laurie. "I'm having a girl, too. You guys will be best friends, just like your mommy and me. I can't wait."

I gestured for her to have a seat.

"Where's Jim?" Paula asked.

"Still sleeping."

Paula raised an eyebrow. "You are the luckiest person I know. What new mother can actually sit down and have a conversation with a girlfriend while her newborn and husband sleep?"

I waved a hand at her. "I'm sure the peace and quiet will be short lived. Coffee?"

She sat on an easy chair in front of the couch and nestled Laurie into the crook of her arm. "I'm dying for a cup of coffee, but I'm doing the caffeine-free thing until the baby is born."

"I have decaf tea."

Giving me a thumbs-up, she kicked off her pink ballet slipper flats and propped her swollen feet on my coffee table as I headed to the kitchen. When I returned with two steaming mugs of tea, she said, "Kate, you look great. Did you wear one of those girdle things after giving birth?"

I stopped in my tracks. "What girdle things?"

"You know, like the kind I wore after having Danny. You wear it for the first six weeks after giving birth and it pulls your tummy right in."

"What! I'm as big as a house! You never told me this! And Laurie's already seven weeks! Is it too late?"

Paula laughed. "You are not as big as a house. Where do you get that stuff? I just told you, you look great."

I pulled up my shirt to show her my stomach. "Look at this!" I said, pinching a fold between my fingers.

"Oh, you're just a little swollen. That's what the girdle thingy helps with. It compresses your muscles or something and helps with the swelling."

"Am I too late?"

Paula shrugged and took a tea mug from my hand. "I don't know, I don't think so, I think they recommend the first six weeks, but I'll send you the web link. You can read all about it."

There was a product out there that helped you get back to your prebaby shape and I'd missed it? What the hell kind of investigator was I?

I resumed my perch on the couch, covering my legs with the blanket. "Are you warm enough?"

She nodded and indicated her belly. "You know, running hotter than usual. Tell me what happened."

"You mean yesterday?" I asked.

She sipped her tea and nodded.

"What did Jim tell you?" I asked.

She laughed. "Just the basics. Don't worry—we still have plenty of things for you to explain."

I gave her a brief account of the happenings since Helene's death and ended by saying, "I freaked out yesterday and had a panic attack."

"I always knew you'd end up nuts."

I pushed her shoulder. "Shut up."

"Either that or drive the rest of us crazy." Paula sipped her tea and winked at me. "Better you than me, sister."

"Thanks."

"Yeah. Well, hey, I would have done the same thing. Christ, Kate, you practically found a dead woman."

"I didn't know your own mind could cause you to get physically sick like that. I mean, Paula, I was really sick. I threw up and had awful stomach cramps, I was dizzy, I was—"

"Kate!" Paula pulled her feet off the coffee table, leaned toward me, and grabbed my hand. "It's not an everyday thing. Of course you made yourself sick. Who wouldn't? Remember when we were twelve and you got your first period? I'm the one who ended up in bed with phantom menstrual cramps."

I laughed at the memory. I had been confused about what was going on with my body, and Paula, who always knew infinitely more about women stuff because of her older sisters, had to be put to bed with Midol and a heating pad. As it turned out, Paula didn't get her first menstrual cycle until almost a year later. I somehow weathered my first period without the medicine and attention, but simply went home and found Mom's sanitary pads in the bathroom closet.

"That was different. We didn't know what was going on then."

"Well, you didn't know what was going on yesterday. Hell, the guy could have poisoned you."

"No. It really doesn't make any sense. Intellectually, I knew that. Even if he is guilty of murdering his wife, he's not going to poison an investigator at his place. That would be insane."

"Well, he poisoned the midwife at his place basically in front of you. That sounds pretty crazy or *stupid* to me," Paula said.

"I don't know. What bothers me is that Margaret sort of set me up to believe it was Alan all along, and now I'm not sure if she really thinks that or if I was duped."

Paula sipped her tea. "What's your theory?"

I sighed. "I don't have one."

Paula rubbed her belly thoughtfully and made a little *hmmm* sound. "If Margaret or Alan weren't there yesterday, then there's no way they could have poisoned Celia, right?"

"Well, I don't really know anything about what she might have been given. How long had she been there before I arrived? I mean, could she have been given something before getting to Bruce's place? How long does it take for a poison to work or whatever before someone starts to feel the effects?"

Paula shrugged. "What kind of poison was it?"

"We won't know until the medical examiner releases the toxicology report."

"When's that?"

I pressed my hands against my tea mug to warm them. "At least a week, I think." After a moment, I said, "How was Paris?"

Paula folded her hands under her pregnant belly. "Very French. It was wonderful, and at the same time that I was sad to leave, I'm ecstatic to be home."

My phone rang.

"Probably my mom calling from Mexico." I grabbed the receiver.

"Kate, it's Bruce. I'm so glad you're all right."

I almost dropped the phone.

Paula brought her feet off the table and sat up. "Who is it?"

"Bruce," I mouthed, sitting next to her and holding the phone out a bit.

She leaned forward to eavesdrop.

"What is the purpose of your call, please?" I asked.

"Oh . . . um . . . can we meet?"

Before I could scream "No!" Paula grabbed my knee. I shook my head at her. She nodded emphatically. I put the phone on mute.

"Are you crazy? I'm not meeting him!" I said.

"Tell him to meet you at the café down the street. I'll go with you."

I shook my head. "I promised Jim I wouldn't investigate—"

Paula waved me off. "Don't tell him."

"I can't lie to him."

"I didn't say lie. I said don't tell him."

"Do you do that with David?" I asked.

"*Pfft.* All the time."

"I can't," I said. "What if—"

"Stop it! You're meant for this line of work. Nothing will happen. It's a public place and I'll be right there."

"How are you supposed to protect me?" I asked, indicating her belly.

"Ah, together we'll be okay."

"Yeah, the postpartum detective and her prenatal sidekick."

• CHAPTER EIGHTEEN • •

Redirected

To Do:

1. ✓ ~~Stock up on soup & tea.~~
2. Catch up on e-mails.
3. ~~Clean the house.~~ Find maid/nanny.
4. Laurie swim classes?—Yes—sign up.
5. Order girdle thing.

I watched from across the street as Paula entered the café. Only the tables in the window were visible. She disappeared; presumably she was at the counter ordering.

I pulled out my cell phone and retrieved the messages I had ignored earlier: one from Mom, one from Paula, and one from Margaret. Mom had called as she was getting ready to board her flight to Mexico:

"Darling! When I was in Napa today at Cakebread Cellars, I talked Albert into being your mentor and letting you use his license. My flight is boarding now but I'll be home in a few days. Call you then. Love you! Kisses to Laurie and Jim."

I closed my eyes.

What did I feel? Relief? Betrayal?

I was extremely relieved Mom had gotten on her flight and missed Jim's call about Laurie and me. But at the same time I felt like I was betraying her. If she knew about the hospital, she'd tell Albert Galigani to forget sponsoring me.

But if I had his sponsorship, Jim would let me continue on the case . . .

Paula's message:

"Girl! I am home! Paris was très magnifique *but I'm happy to be back. What are you doing tomorrow?"*

Margaret's message:

"Kate! Bruce just called me on his way to the police station. He said you and Celia were rushed to the hospital . . . Oh my God. I hope you are all right. Please call me."

As I was about to dial Margaret, Paula came back into view and sat in one of the window tables. She placed a paper cup on the sill, then pulled out her cell phone and connected a pair of headphones to it. She put the headphones on and tapped her foot to no music, our sign that she thought Bruce was there.

I crossed the street and entered the café. Bruce was sitting in a table in the corner, close enough to Paula for her to eavesdrop comfortably.

He stood as he saw me and smiled nervously. "Kate, thank you so much for meeting me." His eyes lowered to his hands and he seemed to be searching for words.

I positioned the chair opposite him in such a way that I could face him and see Paula at the next table. I sat. "It's okay, Bruce. Sit down."

He crumpled into his chair looking much slimmer than he had a few short days before.

What, the guy doesn't eat for a day and he withers away to nothing?

Life's so unfair.

He had beard stubble and looked exhausted, although his hair was impeccable along with his sweater and jeans. In fact, the jeans looked ironed.

Do people really iron their jeans?

"Can I get you a latte or a cap or something?" Bruce asked.

I shook my head. He fiddled with his cup and nodded.

On the walk over, Paula and I had decided ordering coffee here was probably safe. But while waiting on the corner, I'd imagined Bruce slipping a mickey into my coffee. How ridiculous could I get? Yet, it was easier on my neurotic mind just to skip the drink entirely instead of obsessively watching for any sleight of hand.

"So you were at the police station yesterday? Want to bring me up to date?" I asked.

"How did you know?" he asked.

Before I could answer he said, "Oh, Margaret, right?"

I nodded. "She left me a message."

He closed his eyes. "Jesus, Kate. These have been the worst days of my life. First Helene, that awful night on the boat . . . Then yesterday. Celia getting sick, you and your baby being rushed to the hospital . . . She's okay, right? Your baby?"

I nodded.

Bruce swallowed. "And then when you were being taken by the EMTs, you thought . . . you thought it was me. Hell, the cops sure do. They came by my place and escorted me—that's what they called it—escorted me downtown for questioning. I thought finding out Helene was dead was the worst low of my life. And I think it was. But being questioned for her murder. It just . . ."

He put his face in his hands and took several deep breaths.

I glanced at Paula; the expression on her face was skeptical.

Bruce looked up at me. "The only thing left to happen is the stock market can crash." He laughed maniacally and several patrons turned to look at us. Bruce ran his fingers through his hair. "Sorry. Christ, I'm losing it."

I sat in silence, watching him and waiting for him to continue.

After a moment he said, "You wouldn't believe the calls I've been getting. Clients I've had for years, good clients, great clients, calling me to give condolences and then at the same time asking me about their portfolio. Like I give a rat's ass, right now, what the hell their IRA's doing."

As if on cue, his BlackBerry buzzed on the table.

"Screw off," Bruce said, hitting a button on the phone to silence it.

"Have you hired an attorney?" I asked.

Bruce nodded. "Sure. I didn't know any criminal defense guys, but fortunately a strategic partner I have, an estates lawyer, recommended a buddy of his. Guy by the name of Gary Barramendi. Good guy. Works fast. The mere mention of the guy's name had everybody over there shaking in their boots, so maybe I got lucky."

I made a mental note to commit the attorney's name to memory. I'd ask Galigani about him.

"What did you tell the police?"

"Nothing. Gary put the muzzle on me superquick. He said that a charge is waiting in the wings. As soon as the evidence piles up against me. Witnesses or whatever. See, that's why I need you, Kate. I was with you the entire time up on the deck. You know I didn't poison Celia."

There had been a while he'd been gone. I had been on the phone with Mom.

I bit my lips.

And then, what about before I arrived? Surely he could have given her something before I got there.

"I don't think you poisoned her while I was there. She was already feeling ill when I got there."

Bruce looked crestfallen. "You think I did it."

I shrugged my shoulders noncommittally.

A few strangers wandered into the café and proceeded to order at the counter. The whipping sounds of milk being steamed and the smell of espresso made my mouth water.

Bruce frowned. "But why would I try to hurt Celia when I knew you were coming over? That would be insane! I know you're a PI, for Christ's sake!"

"It does set you up with a pretty nice alibi."

Bruce scratched his head. "This is going from bad to worse. You think I asked you over for lunch so I could poison Celia and then point to you as the witness who says I didn't do it?"

"I don't know how likely that possibility is, Bruce." I pressed my lips together and fixed my eyes on him.

He covered his mouth. "This is rich." He fiddled with his empty coffee cup and muttered, "I need a real frigging drink." He closed his eyes and stewed.

I glanced at Paula, she nodded encouragingly at me.

I still couldn't think of why he would want to hurt Celia, so I asked, "Why did they say you poisoned her anyhow?"

His eyes flicked open. "What?"

"What motive did the cops try and pin on you?"

Bruce smiled sadly. "They didn't give me a motive, per se. The questions they asked all centered around how Celia must have known something. Must have had something on me and I would have wanted her out of the way. And they didn't disguise the fact that they thought I was stupid for trying to kill her in front of you. Sort of like a jackass drawing a neon arrow above his own head."

"What can you tell me about Margaret?"

Bruce shrugged. "What do you want to know?"

"Was her husband cheating on her?"

He glanced at his nails, suddenly looking spent. "See, that's something Helene would have known. And if she did, she never said anything about it to me. What does Margaret say about it?"

"She thinks her husband is trying to kill her, that he mistakenly killed Helene that night instead."

The color drained from Bruce's face. He looked as if I'd landed a punch square in the solar plexus. "What!"

"I believed her at first, but now it makes no sense. Alan didn't poison Celia yesterday."

Bruce turned red and raised his voice. "We don't even know if she was poisoned yet."

Paula sat up at attention.

Bruce covered his face with his hands. "I can't take much more of this. I need those toxicology results to come out, so I can prove that I had nothing to do with any of this."

"How would you prove that?" I asked.

He shrugged. "I don't know. Hopefully, Gary can think of a way. Will you talk to him?"

I sat back in my chair, a bit stunned. "About what?"

"Tell him what you know. I think he can help us."

"Us?"

"Well, okay, me. Gary can help me, but I think you need to help Gary."

I saw Paula craning to get my attention. Once she had it, she nodded firmly.

"All right, I'll meet with Gary. Give him my number, and he and I can set up a meeting."

Bruce nodded distractedly as he picked up his Black-Berry and pressed several buttons. His fingers flashed across the phone. When he'd finished, he looked up at me. "Okay. Done. I asked him to share my file with you."

Share his file?

I couldn't believe my luck! I was going to get my *unlicensed* hands on some real information!

We said good-bye and I watched him leave. As soon as he was out of sight, Paula slipped into his empty chair.

"Girl, your life has gotten so exciting without me!"

•CHAPTER NINETEEN•

Rolling Over

To Do:

1. Meet with Gary Barramendi.
2. ✓ ~~Catch up on mail.~~
3. ~~Clean the house.~~ Find maid/nanny—how can we afford?
4. ✓ ~~Order girdle thing.~~
5. Shop for shoes.
6. Thanksgiving!!! Prep, prep, prep!

Jim had woken up early and gone for a run. I felt slightly guilty for not working out, but figured the soup diet I'd been on the last two days might count for a purge and be good enough.

I put Laurie on her playmat for tummy time. I tucked her arms under her so that she was propped up by them. "All right, missy, this is Sergeant Mommy, hold that head up ninety degrees."

Laurie cooed and kicked her legs up and back as though she wanted to shuttle across the floor. Her head bobbed around a bit, but she was safe enough for me to duck into the kitchen and get coffee.

I grabbed the phone and threw some bread into the toaster, trying to make breakfast and catch up on phone calls at the same time. I listened to the phone ring as I buttered my toast. Margaret didn't pick up. I left her a condensed status message and asked her to phone me back.

Then I called Galigani. "Mom said you were willing to sponsor me. Can we meet for lunch?"

"I'd love to meet you, darling. Where and when?"

"Can we meet today? I have a meeting with Gary Barramendi tomorrow and I need—"

"You're meeting with Gary the Grizzly! He eats cupcakes like you for breakfast."

"Thanks."

Galigani guffawed. "There's a great Thai place near my house, want to try it?"

"See you around noon?"

I picked up my toast and coffee and made my way to the living room, where Laurie was on her playmat. She was on her back with a stunned expression on her face. I rushed to her, dropping my breakfast off on the coffee table.

"Laurie! Did you roll over?"

She stared up and grinned.

I tickled her tummy and she kicked her feet up at me. "I can't believe you rolled over for the first time while I was in the other room."

How could I have missed this milestone!

I put her back onto her tummy. "Do it again!"

Laurie cried. She put her head down between her arms and flapped her legs and wailed.

I picked her up. "Don't cry, Petunia. I know it's hard." I rubbed her back. "That tummy time is awful, just awful."

Laurie curled up against me gratefully.

"Next time will you wait until I'm in the room to have a turning point?"

I stood outside Galigani's house and rang the bell. When he opened the door, he smiled. "Ready to go? Or do you want to come in?"

"I'm ready. Let's go," I said.

Galigani grabbed a jacket from a clothes tree and slid it on. He smoothed down his mustache as though putting on the jacket had caused it to go astray. "It's walking distance."

The few short blocks to the Thai restaurant winded us both. Galigani, who'd had heart surgery a few weeks back, and I, with my postpartum legs and butt, made a sorry team. We studied each other at the entrance of the restaurant.

"Good thing nobody was chasing us," I said.

Galigani howled. "The walk is good for me, though; got to get myself in shape."

I nodded. "Yeah. Me, too. At least now we can have lunch and feel like we earned it."

He opened the restaurant door for me and laughed. "Right. One Thai iced tea with the half and half they put in it and any calories we just burned go out the door."

I shrugged. "We still have to walk back. I need to fuel up."

He smiled. "I love your attitude, kid."

A hostess with silky black hair done up in a bun seated us in a window booth. She wore a traditional dress in red and gold. She placed menus on our table with a dazzling smile and winked at Galigani. He pushed the menu aside, and she laughed.

"The usual?" she asked.

"You better believe it," Galigani answered.

She nodded. "I'll give your friend a minute."

I perused the menu and settled on peanut satay. Galigani nodded his approval.

Our iced teas arrived at the table. When the waitress left, Galigani said, "Bring me up to speed."

"Okay." I reached for my diaper purse and attempted to pull out my notebook. Even though Laurie was home with Jim, I was still lugging the bag around. This morning, it seemed to make more sense than to swap to a traditional purse, but as I rummaged past diapers and wipes, the extra outfit, the nursing shawl, the sling, and the burp cloth, I wondered how the heck I'd come to that decision.

"There must be twenty pounds of gear in here," I mumbled.

No wonder the few blocks' walk had been so taxing.

I finally located my notebook and pulled it out.

- *Helene Chambers, deceased on November 5th. Bay dinner cruise. Cause of death, still undetermined, but apparent overdose. Parents deceased, no siblings, no children. Survived by Bruce Chambers (husband).*

- *Spoke with Evelyn. She states she witnessed an argument on the cruise between the deceased and*

Sara. States that the deceased was canceling a construction project. Sara denies this claim and Bruce (widower) said he knows nothing about the cancellation.

- *Evelyn was ousted from mommy group because her kid bites. She is considering home birth with Celia (same midwife Margaret Lipe used).*
- *Attended Helene's service—Homicide Inspectors McNearny and Jones were in attendance.*
- *Margaret Lipe—told me she suspected her own husband (Dr. Alan Lipe) of having an affair and said she thought he had mistakenly killed Helene instead of her. Neighbor, Miss No-Nonsense, Sara has confirmed Alan's affair. So far haven't been able to identify other woman.*
- *Celia Martin was hospitalized on November 15th after being at Bruce's house. Doctors suspect overdose. She told me she consumed metallic-tasting beer. Awaiting lab results.*
- *Bruce Chambers—questioned by police for murder (Helene) and attempted murder (Celia). Attorney Gary Barramendi. Motive? Was planning adoption of Costa Rican infant, coordinated by Celia Martin.*

After reading my notebook, Galigani took a long sip of iced tea and sat in silence for a moment. Finally, he stroked his mustache and asked, "When are they going to release the tox results?"

"I don't know. Another week?"

"The ME doesn't normally do a tox screen."

"How do you know?"

"Kid, I've been doing this a long time. Believe me, the ME and I are buds, we golf together, we smoke cigars together, we drink brandy together. The ME's job is to shut a case as quickly as possible. Tox screens take time and cost taxpayers' money. They normally don't do 'em unless they're pressed."

The waitress arrived with our lunches. The smell of garlic wafted over to me from Galigani's plate.

"Wow! Your shrimp looks delicious," I said. "I should have ordered that."

Galigani scooped a portion of his serving on my plate. "We'll split it."

I pushed half of my peanut satay onto his plate. "I'm not sure I understand what you're saying about the ME," I said.

Galigani wrapped noodles around his fork. "Someone pushed him for the tox screen. But why? I can ask him. And I can get a copy of the records. You want me to do that?"

"Could you? That would be great. Gary Barramendi is going to share Bruce's file with—"

Galigani dropped his fork. "Barramendi is sharing info with you?"

I shrugged. "I guess so. Bruce asked him to anyway."

Galigani guffawed. "Kid, if you get in with Barramendi, your career is set!"

"What do you mean?"

Galigani looked at me as if I was from outer space. "He's the highest-profile criminal defense attorney on the West Coast. He's always featured on CNN, MSNBC, and FOX News. Didn't you know that?"

I shook my head.

Galigani laughed. "Good God, Kate. Talk about beginner's luck. I don't know how you do it!"

"Now you're making me nervous! Do what?"

"I tried for years to work with Barramendi's office. Of course, former cop and defense guys don't normally make nice. So it's no surprise that we never connected. But this guy, if he likes you, can give you regular PI cases, make you a media darling, completely fast-track your career. Just don't mention my name."

Now it was my turn to drop my fork. "Why can't I mention your name? I'm working under your license, right?"

"Sure. I'll fill out the paperwork and you can work for me under my license. But don't make a big deal out of it to Barramendi. Like I said, I'm a former cop."

"Something else has been bothering me," I said.

Galigani waited for me to continue.

"McNearny and Jones were at Helene's funeral."

"Sure," Galigani said. "Especially if your client called the ME and told them she suspected something. That would have raised a flag for them and then homicide would want to go to the services to take a look around."

"But she called after the funeral."

Galigani played with his mustache. "They could have been there because of the fight . . . Uniforms took statements from everyone on the boat, right?"

I nodded.

"Let's see if I can poke around and get some info, they know something we don't," Galigani said.

When I arrived home, Jim handed off a howling Laurie and a UPS package to me.

I tried to juggle Laurie while reading the label on the package. It was my girdle! A few weeks ago, I couldn't imagine getting so excited about a girdle—but here I was practically giddy.

Laurie continued to fuss.

"What's wrong with her?" I asked Jim.

He shrugged. "I wish I knew. She's fed, has a clean diaper, and hasn't stopped crying for at least fifteen minutes."

I cuddled Laurie to me and rubbed her back, trying to soothe her. The rubbing coaxed an enormous burp out of her, which suddenly silenced her.

Jim looked shocked. "Oh."

I raised an eyebrow at him. "You remembered to feed her, but forgot about the burping thing?"

Jim matched my expression. "Apparently."

I laughed.

"Well, I'm glad it's nothing serious," he said. "I was starting to get worried. How was lunch?"

"We had Thai. It was great." I passed the UPS package to Jim. "Can you open this for me?"

Jim ripped open the package and pulled the girdle out. "What is this?"

I launched into a dissertation about the benefits of "binding" one's tummy after childbirth.

Jim seemed stunned by my passion on the subject. From our office/nursery we heard his cell phone ring. He passed the girdle to me and went to answer the phone.

I shuffled to our bedroom and laid Laurie down in her bassinet. She immediately protested, but not so persistently as to deter me from trying on the girdle.

I read the instructions and opened the package, but before I could try it on, Jim came into the room.

"That was Dirk Jonson. He wants to meet tomorrow over lunch, said he loved my concepts."

Dirk was the reason I could even try my hand at this PI business. Now I had a meeting with the top dog of criminal defense at the same time Dirk had called a meeting with Jim. My husband, yes, but also my primary babysitter, and with Mom in Mexico, what could I do?

Lugging Laurie around would look completely unprofessional, wouldn't it?

"Oh. I'm supposed to—"

"Sorry, honey, I need to go polish up some stuff for them." He headed out of the room. "What's for dinner?"

Uh. Dinner.

"I'll think of something," I called after him.

I dialed Paula and told her about my meeting with Gary Barramendi.

Paula practically screamed in my ear. "A media darling! Kate, you have to go!"

"But I have to watch Laurie."

"Are you crazy? I'll watch her. Swing her by here. I'll be home all day with my little beast. No problem."

"But you're pregnant."

"So?" Paula demanded.

"I don't want to put a seven-week-old burden on a pregnant lady!"

"Shut up. I can handle your little cherub with my hands tied behind my back."

"Wait . . . um . . . Does Danny bite?"

"No! Don't worry, I would never let Danny bite Laurie. Why do you ask?"

"One of the moms got kicked out of Roo & You because her kid bit a baby."

"Really? Isn't that kinda harsh? Don't all kids do things

at one point or another that you can't control? We try our best, but sometimes, girl, the kids are not your own."

"Hmmm. Maybe there was more to it. She's pretty pushy. Anyway, I'll see you tomorrow and thank you!"

"Okay, no prob," Paula said.

"Hey, Paula, one more thing . . ."

"What?"

"Galigani told me not to mention his name when I was with 'The Grizzly,' so what do I do if he asks about my license?"

"Hmm. Tell him you applied for a license and are waiting on the paperwork to be processed."

"Lie?"

"That's not a lie. It's a *petite* misrepresentation of the facts."

"I haven't applied for a license. It's a bald-faced lie."

"The guy is criminal defense—you think he cares about one tiny misstatement?"

I sighed. "You're impossible."

Paula laughed. "See you tomorrow. Make sure to look sharp. That'll distract him and secure your rightful destiny as a media darling."

• CHAPTER TWENTY •

The Grizzly

To Do:

1. Meet with Gary Barramendi.
2. Shop for shoes.
3. Practice some recipes for Thanksgiving.
4. Groceries.
5. Laurie—need the memento book—already missed milestone!

I'd had a fitful night. Tossing and turning while Laurie was sound asleep and then finally drifting off just as she would wake for a feeding. While I nursed her, I contemplated my restlessness.

I was definitely nervous about meeting with Mr. Barramendi, but was that all? No, the weight of the case was getting to me. And now to make matters worse, I'd have to lie to Barramendi about Galigani or avoid the topic altogether.

I had never been good at lying. Something people find hard to believe as soon as they discover I have an acting degree. But acting is different. You take on the role of a character. You're not actually lying about yourself.

And then again. Wait.

Yes. Tomorrow I would play the part of a character. I would meet with Barramendi as my "future self." A self-assured, successful PI. A licensed PI.

In the morning I woke with a start to the alarm. Laurie was still asleep and Jim was getting dressed for his meeting. He stood in front of our closet examining dress shirts.

"Good morning," I said, propping myself up in bed.

"Hi, honey. I made coffee," Jim said.

"Thank you."

Jim selected a blue striped dress shirt and put it on.

He looked great. My mind immediately snapped to what I was going to wear. Did anything fit?

As soon as Jim said good-bye, I jumped to the task of getting ready.

First I nursed and burped Laurie then laid her back in the bassinet. She was still awake but seemed content to study a white bunny rattle that I handed her.

I stopped suddenly; today Laurie was two months old!

I picked her up out of the bassinet. "Oh! My darling!" I squeezed her to me. "Two months already. So short a time and yet it feels like you've been part of my life forever."

Laurie cooed and attempted to put the bunny rattle into her mouth.

"You like the bunny? Mommy's going to get you something for your . . . what? Second month birthday? Okay, that works." I kissed Laurie's head and put her down.

Need to add shopping for Laurie to the to-do list!

Next I showered, then pulled out my new girdle and wrapped it around myself. It was simple enough to use. It wrapped around my tummy and hips and fastened on the side with a long Velcro fitting.

I positioned it in place and frantically started going through items in my closet. I found a favorite burgundy silk blouse and tried it on. To my astonishment, it fit nicely. I then selected some trousers. The first three pairs I tried on were way too tight, but the fourth pair worked.

Way to go, girdle!

Shoes?

Ah. Another problem!

My postpartum feet didn't fit any of my pre-Laurie shoes. I finally found some loafers that would barely pass.

I glanced at the clock. I needed to get Laurie loaded into the car and out of the house in the next few minutes if I was going to be on time, and I still needed to pack her diaper bag.

Why hadn't I packed the stupid diaper bag last night?

I hurried to do my hair and makeup.

At least Laurie was now sound asleep; that would be a help in getting out the door. I ran to the freezer and found a few bags of frozen milk. Just over 4 ounces. Enough for one feeding.

Darn. I needed to build up a bigger supply if I was going to have to keep leaving Laurie with a sitter. Another thing to add to my list!

I hustled Laurie into the car. She barely roused. Why didn't she sleep like this for me? Why only when I left her with someone?

I drove to Paula's and pulled into her driveway like a madwoman.

I unclipped the car seat from the base and grabbed the diaper bag, lugging the entire load up Paula's front steps.

Paula opened the door ensconced in a violet terry robe.

"Good morning!" I said, pushing my way past her and into the entrance to unburden my arms.

Paula let out a low whistle. "Look at you, girl! You are looking hot!"

"Thanks. It takes effort now, you know."

Paula laughed. "Oh yeah! Hey, what's up with your shoes?"

I glanced down at my loafers and shrugged. "They're what fit."

Paula tsked. "Oh no. Follow me."

Paula retreated down the hallway. I looked at Laurie sound asleep in her car seat. I quickly put my hand on her and felt reassured by the rise and fall of her belly.

I walked down the hallway to Paula's bedroom, stopping first to peek in on Danny. Paula had hand painted the room in baby blue with a mural of Thomas the Tank Engine on one wall. Sure looked a lot more inviting than Laurie's nursery that doubled as Jim's and my office.

I worried about having the computer in Laurie's nursery. Was it giving off any weird energy waves that I should be concerned about?

Add that to my to-do list: look up safety of computers in nursery!

Currently, she was spending the night in our room in

her portable bassinet, but soon she would outgrow that and have to sleep down the hall. My heart dropped. She would be down the hall! So far away from me.

A big kid in her crib in her own room.

I peered over at Danny asleep in his crib. I marveled at how long he appeared; it seemed like only yesterday he had been an infant like Laurie.

I touched his soft hair. "Hey, buddy, you're gonna be a big brother soon."

He was fidgeting a bit and his mouth started to move as though he wanted to nurse or have a pacifier. Still asleep, his hand shot to his mouth and he started sucking his thumb.

"You're still a baby, too! I love you, little buddy." I pulled his blanket up around him and headed toward Paula's bedroom.

I found her digging in her closet.

"Size?" she asked.

"Pre-Laurie was seven."

"So eight?" Paula asked from inside the closet.

"I guess. I'm still trying to come to terms with it."

Paula laughed and rummaged deeper into the closet.

"I have some frozen breast milk for Laurie in the diaper bag. She could be hungry when she wakes up. I also brought some formula, just in case I'm not back in time for the feeding after that. Oh, shoot . . ."

"What?" Paula asked from inside the closet.

"I didn't think about a purse. All my gear, my wallet, cell phone, notebook, and stuff is in the diaper bag."

Paula emerged from the closet with the classiest pair of Ferragamo burgundy pumps I'd ever seen. They matched my blouse exactly. I gasped.

Paula grimaced. "Just my luck. I was a size eight pre-Danny, now I'm a nine, so you can have them."

I grabbed her around the neck and kissed her cheek, then slipped into the shoes. They felt simply divine. "Ooh, I feel so *in*!"

She laughed as she kicked the loafers I'd been wearing across the room. "Well, those are definitely *out*."

"I'm matchy-matchy now!" I exclaimed. "You are a lifesaver!"

Paula let out a self-satisfied sigh. "I know. And you don't even know the half of it. I have the matching bag for you."

She reached inside the closet and pulled out the purse. A lovely handbag that was large enough for my notebook, but sleek enough to belong to a media darling.

I sighed. "Paula! It's beautiful."

"You know my thing about bags and shoes."

I studied my reflection in the mirror, posing with the shoes and holding the handbag to me. "I look like I can fake it, huh?"

Paula smiled widely. "Of course, girlfriend! Fake it 'til you make it."

When I arrived at Gary Barramendi's office, I was greeted by a receptionist, who had on a Dior suit and more expensive shoes than I did. Her honey-colored hair was pinned at the sides and down in the back, framing her round young face. She looked to be in her early twenties. She assured me she would let Gary know I had arrived and showed me to a waiting room.

The waiting room boasted huge windows with a glorious view of Alcatraz. There was a station with coffee, tea, and water in the corner of the room, and in the center were several high-back chairs near a table covered with magazines.

On the wall opposite the windows a full-length mirror reflected views of Alcatraz throughout the room. But instead of focusing me on the view, it focused me on the image of me.

I had forgotten to put breast pads inside my bra.

Oh God! What if I leaked!

I pulled the door of the waiting room open and peeked out into the hallway. No trace of the receptionist or anyone else, but a ladies' room sign was prominent. I made a mad dash into the ladies' room and quickly pulled some tissues from a box on the marbled counter.

I folded a few sheets of tissue neatly and stuffed them into my bra. The result gave me square breasts.

I pulled the tissues out and tried a single sheet on each side. The padding was not as noticeable. I prayed only one sheet would be enough.

I returned to the waiting room and fiddled with the magazines. The glossy rags depicted yachting, golfing, and travel that I could only dream about. I wondered about Gary's clientele. Were they all that high-end?

I was totally out of my league. Each magazine I flipped through made me feel worse and worse, until I was a nervous wreck.

What was I doing here?

Women who had sat in this waiting room before me certainly didn't have tissues stuffed in their bras. Or worse, girdles to hold in their postpartum bellies. And they definitely, definitely didn't sit here in borrowed designer shoes with the accompanying handbag!

In the midst of my insecurity, the receptionist returned and ushered me into Gary's office.

The office was enormous, with an astonishing view of the Bay Bridge. I felt as if I could lean out his window and touch traffic.

Gary Barramendi stood when I entered and offered me a warm handshake.

I was suddenly disarmed. He was young. Not what I had been expecting at all. He was very tall. Perhaps six-six. And extremely thin, bordering on gawky. He had dark bushy hair. His features appeared to be pushed together from all different angles and the left side of his face was almost completely different from the right side, yet everything was fused in the middle by his large nose.

Despite his unconventional face and stature, his smile was warm and his handshake firm and friendly, putting me at ease instantly.

"Hey. Gary Barramendi. Nice to meet you. I understand you know Bruce Chambers."

"Yes." I shook his hand with my best businesslike handshake and said, "Kate Connolly, pleasure to meet you."

Gary motioned to the sofa that hugged the left wall of the office. "Have a seat."

I was starting to feel confident. Gary wasn't a grizzly! This was going to be a good meeting.

I was channeling my future self. Confident, smart, proactive.

I was feeling great!

I placed my beautiful burgundy Ferragamo handbag on the couch and took a seat next to it. Suddenly a horrifying loud ripping sound reverberated around the room.

I froze.

The Velcro closing on my girdle had given way. The

entire thing came undone under my shirt. The buttons on my silk blouse threatened to pop and the material between each button gapped hideously open.

I moaned and swayed, feeling a bit faint.

Please, please, earth, swallow me whole.

•CHAPTER TWENTY-ONE•

Two's Better Than One?

Gary cleared his throat. "Kate. There's a restroom here to the right." He motioned across the room.

His voice sounded as though it was coming at me through a tunnel. I sat frozen, my mouth agape. I looked up at him with my mouth still open, feeling like a walleye fish.

He smiled. "The restroom's right there," he repeated.

"I just had a baby. I bought this stupid girdle thing online. I wanted to look professional . . ."

"A baby? That's so sweet. Got any pictures?"

"Uh."

I didn't have any pictures! Not one.

What kind of mother was I?

I'd left my baby to come on this wild-goose chase in an outfit that didn't fit. Not only was I a bad mother, but an idiot, too!

Suddenly, tears streamed down my face.

Gary grabbed a box of tissues from his desk and sat next to me. "How old is your baby?"

I swallowed hard and sort of gulped my tears, trying to bring myself back to the present. "Two months."

Gary nodded sympathetically and handed me the tissue box. "My sister just had a baby. Beautiful little girl. She's four months. Me? I'm not married, so no kids yet. But man, they are something, huh?"

I nodded, slightly dumbfounded at the kindness of this stranger.

Gary stood and straightened his slacks. "Listen, I'm going to pull Bruce's file. Take whatever time you need. Should I have Mandy make us some coffee?"

I stood and straightened my slacks, too, as if on cue. Suddenly my head was clear. I was here for business and I needed to get on with it.

"Yes. Coffee would be nice. I'll just be a moment."

I headed to the restroom as Gary left the office.

Once in the safety of the bathroom, I evaluated myself in the mirror. It was worse than I had imagined. The blouse that I had been so pleased with and felt so pretty in now looked like a sausage casing gone bad. It was stretched to the limit. I had raccoon eyes from my streaky mascara and my hair was totally flat.

I unbuttoned my blouse and re-Velcroed the girdle. I then checked the tissue I had stuffed into my bra. It was soaked, but thankfully hadn't leaked.

I shoved clean dry tissue into my bra, then redid the buttons on the blouse. Miraculously, it looked fine again.

I sat on the toilet and tested the Velcro. It held. I stood, then sat again and rocked back and forth. The Velcro slipped a bit. I jumped as though I'd just been bitten and redid the girdle a little looser. This time the blouse didn't look as great as before, but the Velcro didn't slip either. I decided that was the better option.

I washed my face and cleaned off the mascara, then teased my hair a bit for some volume. Overall, physically the effect was fine. Not fabulous, but passable.

What about feeling like an idiot, though?

Nothing I could do about that but suck it up.

Stop pretending I was somebody I wasn't. Thin, confident, experienced. And start telling the truth.

When I emerged from the restroom, Gary was seated comfortably on the couch looking completely untraumatized. In fact, he looked so relaxed holding a cup of coffee in one hand and flipping through a file that rested on his lap with the other, that I wondered if I had imagined the entire incident.

He looked up when I entered and smiled. "We won't get the preliminary report the uniforms took on the evening of November fifth or any of the medical examiner's findings from the toxicology screen unless they formally charge Bruce. The only thing in here are my notes from the police interview the other day." He closed the file and rose, indicated a coffee tray on a side table. "Help yourself. I'm going to ask Mandy to photocopy this for you."

He left the room and I poured myself a cup of coffee. I sat on the couch and tested the girdle. Everything held. I tried not to focus on the girdle and sipped the coffee instead.

Gary returned, smiling. "Here we go. This is the full transcription from the interview."

He handed me the file and I opened it.

It looked like somebody had written the pages in German. I fought to keep my eyes from glazing over from the legalese.

Might as well start with something I knew.

I recounted for him my first meeting with Helene and Margaret and then began on the dinner cruise.

"You were on the cruise?" Gary asked.

I nodded. "Yeah. It was my first night meeting most of the mommy group."

Gary looked confused.

I waved away his concern. "Long story. Anyway, what I do know is that there were reports of Helene and Sara fighting just before Helene's demise."

Gary didn't try to hide his surprise. His eyebrows rose, although due to the asymmetry of his face, his right eyebrow shot up quite high while his left one moved only slightly. I had to smile in spite of myself.

"Where did you get this information?" he asked.

"Another former member of the Roo & You group. She was asked to leave the group because her kid bit a baby."

Gary rose, crossed to his desk, and picked up a legal pad. "Really? I used to be a biter."

I laughed. "Is that where you got your nickname?"

Gary looked taken aback.

Oops. Perhaps I shouldn't have mentioned that.

"You know about my nickname?"

I swallowed. Well, my foot was in it now. May as well proceed.

"Sure. Gary the Grizzly."

He laughed and looked pleased with himself. "My reputation precedes me, huh?"

I smiled.

He scribbled something on the legal pad. "Okay, what else do you know?"

I explained that, according to several sources, Dr. Alan Lipe was having an affair. That he and his wife, Margaret, had fought that evening and Margaret suspected he may have poisoned Helene by mistake.

Gary took notes. When I finished, he looked up. "What else you got?"

"What else do *you* got?" I countered.

Gary smiled. "Ah. Tough cookie, huh? You want a little quid pro quo?"

I nodded.

"I'm giving you a copy of my client's interrogation."

"He asked you to," I answered.

Gary chewed on the cap of his pen and squinted at me. "Are we on the same team here?"

"What do you mean?"

"Has Bruce hired you, or what?"

I glanced around the room. "Not exactly."

"Who are you working for?" Gary asked.

Time to come clean.

"I was hired by Margaret Lipe."

Gary nodded. "You think Bruce is guilty."

"I don't know what to think," I said. "It was just Bruce, Celia, and I at his place, and I know I didn't poison Celia."

"What does Margaret Lipe think?" Gary asked.

I hesitated. Frankly I didn't know what Margaret thought about the attempt on Celia's life, because she hadn't called me back.

How much should I disclose to Gary?

Did I have any obligation of confidentiality to Margaret?

"Well, Margaret suspected Alan, and I understand that for Helene's murder—but what about Celia? If it was just the three of us at Bruce's house, how can it be anyone other than Bruce?" I asked.

"Maybe Celia was with the doctor right before she showed up at Bruce's. Maybe she's the other woman and the doc told her he was going to get rid of his wife and then botched it. But now Celia knows about the accident and he's scared she'll say something to the police, so he slips her something on her way to Bruce's."

"If that's the case, wouldn't Celia tell the police that her lover killed Helene and then maybe tried to poison her?"

Gary shrugged. "Maybe she hasn't put it all together. Or maybe she's protecting him. You'd be surprised about the things people don't tell the police. Well, probably you wouldn't, if you've been doing PI work long."

I tried to look as experienced as I could by composing my features into a serious reflective look and nodded.

He must have bought into my acting because he said, "Let's start there, with the midwife. She knows something. Stake her out, see where she goes. Maybe we'll get lucky." He chomped on the pen cap thoughtfully. "You think we can come to an arrangement?" he asked.

I studied his eyes. "What kind of an arrangement?"

"I have a PI I use to look into things. Because you know my time . . ."

"Right. Your time is pretty valuable."

Gary smiled.

"Your reputation precedes you." I laughed.

"Now, see! Sweet-talk like that will get you everywhere. I mean nowhere," he corrected, shaking a finger at me, but with his disarming grin lighting up his face. "What I'm thinking is I can hire a PI, but they'd have to run around and do the same work you just did. So, I'd be behind the curve—"

"Isn't what you're proposing a conflict of interest?" I asked.

"Whose interest?"

"My client's. Sort of breach of confidentiality."

Gary frowned. "You're not bound to confidentiality. Unless, of course, you bound yourself in your own contract. Which I hope you didn't. Because it wouldn't stand up in a court of law and you'd just be misleading your client. You should let me review that for you. Anyway, as you know under the Business and Professions Code, Article 6, Disciplinary Proceedings, Sections 7561–7567, you are free to report illegal activity as you see fit or risk suspension of your license, fees, jail time, you name it—whatever the Review Board decides."

All right, so I didn't have to worry about confidentiality, but how could I tell him I had no worries about a license suspension either?

"Why don't you tell me exactly what you're proposing?" I asked.

"Simple, you work for me. I'll double your hourly rate. Or are you working on a project basis?"

"Hourly."

"Great. Hourly. I'll double your rate. You can continue to work independently, so keep your contract with Margaret, I don't care about that. But let me know everything you find out. I mean everything. I'd like a daily report. Doable?"

• CHAPTER TWENTY-TWO •

Unstable

To Do:

1. Stake out Celia.
2. Build up milk supply.
3. Buy Laurie swing contraption thing (like baby Amanda) for two-month milestone.
4. Research safety re: computers in nursery.
5. Look up Business and Professions Code, Article 6.

"He wants you to work for him?" Paula asked.

"I don't know if I can do that, though, ethically, you know?" I was seated at her dining room table nursing Laurie.

Paula had swaddled Laurie in a special swaddling blanket with Velcro closures on the sides and around her belly. When I complained and told her Laurie had outgrown the swaddle, she'd pooh-poohed me and told me that babies slept much better swaddled. I could hardly argue as apparently Laurie had been sacked out since I'd left.

I rubbed Laurie's cheek and secretly thought the swaddle looked like a straitjacket. "I'll break you out of it as soon as we leave, Sugarplum," I whispered in her ear. "I'm an expert in breaking out of Velcro."

Paula was working furiously on a scrapbook of Danny's first year, and Danny was running back and forth between the dining room and his bedroom bringing us Lego pieces, one at a time.

Each time Danny returned from his room, he'd hand me a piece saying, "'Go piece."

I'd say, "Yes! Lego piece," then oohed and aahed as he attached the piece to the tower he was building.

Paula gave me a dismissive wave. "Come on, Kate. You know I'm the last person you should be discussing ethics with. Take the money! Of course you should work for him."

"But that would be double billing or something like that."

Paula laughed. "Well, duh. That's the beauty of it."

I sighed and helped Danny connect a piece to the tower. He yelped with happiness and then charged back to his room.

Paula scrunched her face. "I promised myself I would finish this darn book before the baby came. I can't have Danny's first year looming over me when I have the other one's first year to capture. But I swear I hate this scrapbooking."

"You do? But you're so good at it."

"Why would you think I'm good at it? I never do it."

I looked around the table. She had neatly arranged the photos in one stack, stickers in another stack, and colored paper in a third stack. "Well, look at all the organization and care you've put into it."

"It's all a façade," Paula said.

I laughed. Danny zoomed back into the room and handed me a Lego piece. "Danny's good at building—why don't you let him put it all together?"

Paula sighed. "The end result would probably be the same."

At home, I fussed with dinner. On the drive from Paula's I thought I'd had a wonderful time-saving idea. Crock pot cooking! Just throw all the ingredients into a pot and voilà—dinner!

When I got home, I realized that would mean I actually had to have the ingredients on hand, not to mention the six- or seven-hour lead time for cooking.

While inventorying the fridge, I grabbed a piece of cheese and popped it into my mouth. Then, I looked in the cupboard for some crackers.

Hmmm, did we have any wine?

I found a bottle and opened it, pouring myself a glass.

I had recently read an article online that allowed breast-feeding moms one to two glasses of alcohol a day. What a hoot! I thought I wasn't supposed to have any alcohol. Well, everything in moderation. Certainly the occasional glass of wine wasn't going to hurt Laurie. And definitely the last few days had been trying. I needed something to take the edge off.

I continued my search for crackers.

Maybe I could make a little appetizer plate for Jim and me—cheese, crackers, nuts, and fruit . . .

My daydream was cut short with the discovery that we didn't have any crackers, nuts, or fruit.

Man! I had to get to the store.

I took a sip of wine, sliced another piece of cheese, and ate it anyway. Didn't wine count for fruit?

I cracked open the file from Gary. It was a transcript of Inspectors Jones and McNearny questioning Bruce. Only they hadn't been able to ask him much. Gary had coached Bruce and he'd only made a small statement about being grieved over his wife and shocked about the incident at his house. He repeated the same statement to most of the questions until Gary put a sudden stop to the questioning by quoting a statute and ending the interview.

Short and simple, they needed to officially charge him if they were going to get any answers. And without evidence, they couldn't charge him.

I grabbed the phone and dialed Margaret. I got no answer but left her a second message. Where was she? She was supposed to be at her mother's but there was no answer there either.

What kind of investigator can't get in touch with her client?

I heard the front door creak open and knew my time for dinner prep had run out.

I'm a failure as a housewife.

Jim clunked down the hallway and peered into the kitchen. He inhaled deeply. "Hi, honey."

"What's wrong?"

He let out his breath and dropped his briefcase on the floor. "My client put a hold on the project."

"What does that mean?"

"Did you watch the news today?"

I shook my head.

"The market's crashed. People are kind of freaking out. So, Dirk wasn't able to secure funding for the project."

My mind flashed on Bruce Chambers. His clients would be scared, too.

"What does it mean for us?" I asked.

Jim shrugged. "Well, we don't have much in the market, so in that regard we're fine. But if they don't get funding for my project, that means I'm out of work again."

During my maternity leave from my corporate job, Jim had been let go from his. He'd been able to land a freelance client and the income had been large enough, or so we thought, to last us awhile so I had left my corporate gig.

I felt my heart constrict. "They gave you a retainer, though."

Jim closed his eyes. "That's not a guarantee. My contract states that if the project moves forward, I apply it to the cost of the project. If they back out in the first sixty days, I have to return fifty percent."

I grabbed the stovetop for support.

He wrapped his arms around my shoulders and pulled me into him. "Don't worry, honey. Things will be okay. If this falls through, I'll find something else."

I wanted to say that I would go back to my secure corporate income, but I choked on the words.

There was no way. I couldn't go back now. I had tasted the freedom and excitement of entrepreneurship. Even with doubts surrounding a steady income stream, nothing could bring me to sacrifice myself to the doldrums of my office job again.

Could it?

Laurie squeaked from the nursery. She had been asleep for about an hour in the crib and that was the maximum she had ever slept at the dinnertime hour, what Jim and I were beginning to call the "witching hour."

"I'll get the squirrel," Jim said. As he left the kitchen, he asked the inevitable, "What's for dinner?"

"Nothing," I called after him.

Jim laughed. "Okay, open a can of soup. We're on austerity anyway."

I groaned. "But I'm nursing and I'm really hungry."

Jim returned to the kitchen with Laurie bundled in his arms. "Okay, screw it. Let's order a pizza."

I squinted at him and bit my lip. "I may have good news."

Jim raised an eyebrow. "Good. Something to celebrate. What is it?"

"I got a pseudo–job offer today. I think it will keep up our income stream anyway."

Jim held Laurie out to look into her face. "Mommy got a job offer," he said.

Laurie was holding her head so well these days we no longer cradled it. Yet as Jim was holding her up and she was looking at him happily and gurgling, her head started to wobble and she suddenly pitched herself headfirst into Jim's chest.

"Whoa," Jim said. "She's excited."

We laughed.

"What kind of offer?" he asked.

I filled him in on the details.

His face displayed an array of emotions as I recounted Gary's offer. I left out the girdle-popping incident—no need to sound like a complete moron in front of my number one fan.

When I'd finished talking, he was silent for a moment.

Finally I asked, "So do you approve? Can I take him up on it?"

He shuffled Laurie from one shoulder to the other. "Kate, I don't ever want to keep you from doing something you want to do." He wrapped his free arm around me. "I just want you to be safe. Promise me you'll be careful."

I kissed him. "I promise."

• CHAPTER TWENTY-THREE •

Watchful

To Do:

1. ✓ ~~Look up Business and Professions Code, Article 6.~~
2. Throw out stupid girdle and exercise—there is no substitute.
3. Find Margaret—why isn't she calling me back?
4. Get Laurie outfit for Thanksgiving.
5. Groceries!!!

In the morning I looked out my front window and saw our neighbor Kenny washing his van. It was an old white van with tinted windows.

A van?

His van would be perfect for a stakeout!

I rapped on the window. He looked up and waved when he saw me. I picked Laurie up, wrapped her in a blanket, then ran down the stairs.

"Hi, Kenny, can I use your van? I want to check something out."

"Sure. Is your car in the shop?"

"No. I need to go on a stakeout," I said proudly.

Kenny bobbed his head up and down. "Cool."

I observed Celia's midwife center from inside Kenny's van. There was no activity.

Wow. I was on a stakeout.

I'd done a stakeout on my first case, but Jim had been with me, so it felt more like I was hanging out with my husband—which I was—instead of a stakeout. And following Alan last week didn't count because that was really only following—so now it was official—my first stakeout.

And I actually felt prepared. I had stopped by Mom's to water her plants and borrowed her binoculars, then I'd bought lunch.

Practically a legitimate PI.

And with two paying clients no less!

Where was Margaret?

I unwrapped the bagel I'd purchased from the shop up the street. Cream cheese dripped over the side but the tomatoes and spinach were still crisp. If I waited any longer to eat it, the veggies would start to wilt.

Oh, well, better eat it now. If Celia kept me waiting too long, I could always get something else from the shop.

Wait. What if I missed her leaving?

I used my binoculars to check out the shop.

Binoculars! A real PI tool.

Oh, I was growing, growing, growing!

Never mind the fact that I had borrowed them from Mom.

The shop was within view, but if I went inside and, say, I was at the counter ordering, then I wouldn't be able to see the entrance of Celia's midwife center. I couldn't risk missing her.

Darn.

I bit into the bagel anyway. It was absolutely divine. Either that or I was extremely hungry—which I was. After a few bites the bagel was gone.

Now I was out of food but still hungry.

I sipped on my latte. It was too bitter to drink fast.

Good. That would give me something to do and maybe curb my appetite a bit if I drank it slowly.

I tapped my foot and waited.

What was the deal with stakeouts? Why had I been so excited? This was boring. How long would I have to wait for some action?

What was I hoping for anyway?

Wait.

A car just turned the corner.

Yippee! Action.

Maybe someone was coming to see Celia. I strained to identify the car. It didn't look like Alan's Lexus.

It was a Toyota. It drove right past me.

Darn!

I fidgeted around the van. Kenny had some pretty good gear in here. I picked up a trombone. Man, it was heavy. My cell phone rang and I dropped the instrument as though I'd been caught in the act of stealing it.

I fished my cell phone out of my purse. "Yes."

"Kate! How's the stakeout?"

It was Kenny.

"Boring. How do you play this thing? It's really heavy."

"Are you messing with my stuff?" Kenny laughed. "Why is it boring?"

"I ate all my food and nothing is happening."

"What'd you bring with you?"

"A bagel."

"That is boring."

I laughed. "So, what's up? Do you need your van back?"

"You've only been gone thirty minutes."

"Is that it?"

"Do you want some company?" Kenny asked.

"Not yours."

Kenny laughed. "I can bring you some chips or something."

Hmmm.

Catering à la seventeen-year-old.

"Chips sound good," I said.

"I can't bring beer or anything. I'm not drinking age," Kenny said.

"I'm on a stakeout! This is serious business. I'm not here to drink beer."

"You have to have something to drink with chips."

"I'm drinking coffee," I said.

"Coffee doesn't go with chips."

"Okay, bring some soda then. Something with caffeine," I said.

"Okay," Kenny said cheerfully.

"All right, see you soon."

"Uh, Kate?"

"What."

"Uh, are you going to come pick me up or what? Because you have my van."

Christ.

"I can't leave the site, Kenny."

"Bummer."

Three hours had passed since I'd first parked the van and now I had a more serious problem than hunger and boredom. I needed a hospitality break.

Should I risk going down the street to the shop and use the restroom?

I thought about Laurie. Surely she'd be hungry by now and my breasts were starting to burn. Before leaving home, I'd examined my breast pump. It had a car attachment for power that plugged into a standard car charger. But who wanted to pump in the car?

After all, it wasn't like there was any kind of privacy in a car. What did other moms do? Use a nursing wrap?

I recalled a news item about one mom getting pulled over because she was breastfeeding while driving. Now *that* was taking multitasking to a whole new level.

I'd tried distracting myself from my bodily needs by killing the time on the phone. I called Jim to check on Laurie; he reported that Laurie was watching him from across the room and making coo-coo eyes at him.

I dialed Paula and caught up with a few friends I hadn't spoken to in a while. I called my brother long-distance; he had moved cross-country for work and this would be the first Thanksgiving we wouldn't be together. I chatted with Kiku. my future sister-in-law. She filled me in on some planning details for her wedding with Jim's brother, George. Considering George was on probation due to his antics during my first case, things were going relatively well for them and their new baby. I even called Kenny back a few times.

As soon as I decided that I simply had to go down the street to that shop, the door to the midwife center swung open.

Oh yes!

Action.

I grabbed the binoculars and put them to my eyes, only I was so excited that I did it backward and the effect was that Celia looked miles away. I quickly switched them around and Celia zoomed right up to me, giving me the impression that she could reach out and touch me. I pulled away from the binoculars to verify Celia's distance.

She was half a block away and hadn't bothered to notice the van at all.

She was dressed in a track suit with running shoes. I watched as she reached her car, a yellow VW bug, and got in.

I jumped into the driver's seat of the van and started the engine.

Please, Celia, bring me a clue.

It could blow the case wide open if she drove straight to Alan's clinic and engaged him in a juicy kiss.

Either that or maybe she'd be going to see a client. Then I could at least get a trail on her activities, find out more about her from someone outside Roo & You.

I followed her car to a local gym. She parked and went inside.

There was no way I could wait here for her to finish a workout. Nothing for me to do, but go home to Laurie and Jim empty handed, or empty headed—whatever the case may be.

As I started home, I found myself driving right back to the midwife center.

Why was I here?

I parked in front and walked up to the entrance. With Celia gone, perhaps I could get a look inside. I peeked through the glass window.

The floor was a blue-green marble, and on the reception console matching tile had been laid in a wave pattern across the front. On top of the reception console was a stack of pamphlets and a vase of red roses.

Who had given her the roses?

The center looked freshly remodeled. Where did Celia get the money to have her own center? How much did midwives charge anyway? Was she billing back to the insurance companies? I couldn't imagine she was bringing in enough money to own the building, but if she rented the center, the lease payment had to be considerable.

If she was having an affair with Alan, maybe he was helping her with the payments. Doctors made pretty good dough. He had a private practice and he lived in a nice neighborhood, big house.

By far the nicest home I'd been in lately was Bruce's, though, with the rooftop access and incredible view. Suddenly a thought hit me. Everything that was true for Alan could be true for Bruce.

Bruce had great income as an investment banker. And there were those odd moments I'd witnessed between Bruce and Celia, at the service and then again at his house.

Maybe Bruce had killed Helene to get her out of the way so he could be with Celia, but then somehow things went wrong with Celia.

Could I run a search on his credit card? Find out where

he was spending time and money? Had he bought those roses on the counter?

I made a mental note to ask Galigani about background and credit checks. Now that I was officially under his wing, he could give me database access to some specialized data providers for licensed private investigators.

From down the street, I heard a car engine. Out of reflex, I turned to look and nearly passed out. It was a yellow VW bug, Celia's car.

Shoot!

What was she doing back so fast?

She parked in front of the center and hopped out of the car.

Had she forgotten something? Did she know I had been outside watching her? Had she returned to catch me red-handed?

As she walked up to the building, she said, "Hello, Kate."

What do I say? What do I say? What do I say?

I smiled. "Hi!"

She nodded at me expectantly.

"Uh . . . hi!" I said again, adding a wave this time and smiling bigger.

"Have you been here long?" she asked.

How could I be here long, you just left!

"Uh . . . no."

She reached into her gym bag and pulled out keys. "What are you doing here?"

"I was in the neighborhood. I was curious about your birthing center."

Celia scratched her chin. "Really, next time do you think you'll go natural?"

I laughed. "Margaret practically has me convinced," I lied.

She unlocked the door and pushed it open. "Why don't you come in and check it out?"

I followed her inside.

"I thought maybe you were here because you had some news . . . ?"

"News?"

She shrugged. "I guess I was hoping you were going to tell me that the results from the hospital were ready."

"The hospital wouldn't release your results to me."

She eyed me. "Really, I thought because you're an investigator, you might get the results from the medical examiner." She sat down on a waiting room chair and looked crushed. "I was hoping that the results would be in and they would show conclusively that Bruce poisoned me with the same thing he used to poison Helene. I keep waiting for someone to tell me he's in jail."

Her shoulders slumped and she looked ready to cry.

What was I thinking? This woman had been poisoned. Surely if she was dating Bruce and suspected him, she would have made the affair known.

It had to be Alan.

I crouched down next to her. "Celia, about that day, what can you tell about the morning? Did you see anybody else, maybe earlier in the day? Before going to Bruce's house?"

She sniffled and snapped to attention. "Just my normal client list." She stood and crossed to the reception area. She looked at the appointment book on the counter, running her finger down a daily column. "The fifteenth? Hmmm, pretty dead really. Just Evelyn came in for her appointment. She's getting close now and coming in weekly."

Right. Evelyn had told me about the appointment.

"Did you go anywhere before Bruce's?" I asked.

"Let's see." She paced around and looked thoughtful as though she was trying to re-create events in her mind. "I had the appointment with Evelyn in the morning at ten A.M. then left here and went to Bruce's. He'd called me the night before and asked me to meet with him. He said he wanted to talk about the adoption."

I leaned against the arm of the waiting chair. "Did you stop anywhere along the way? To get coffee? Or pick up dry cleaning?"

Or see your boyfriend, Alan?

She shook her head. "No. I don't typically buy coffee—it's so expensive! Four-fifty for a cup? No way." She glanced down at her track suit. "And dry cleaning? I don't know if anything in my closet is dry clean only."

Maybe she could afford the rent because she wasn't spending money on coffee or dry cleaning bills.

"This is a nice place you have here. How long have you been here?"

"The center is brand-new. Sara's husband, you know Sara, right?"

I nodded.

"He remodeled it for me. He's a contractor—gave me a great price. The place used to be a record store. I got a deal on the rent because the area is low foot traffic, which is fine with me, because people don't usually select a midwife by spontaneously walking in. Let me show you around."

I followed her to a back room. There was a beautiful birthing pool in the center of the room. Around the sides of the room were large exercise balls, a shelf with towels, and several laundry baskets. Celia dimmed the lights and pressed Play on the stereo. There were small lights around the baseboards and the room seemed to glow.

"This room is where most of my moms deliver. There's an exam room next door. Did you want to see that?"

I shook my head. "No. This is wonderful."

And it was. It was truly beautiful and relaxing. I still couldn't see myself giving birth outside of a hospital, but now I understood the draw.

"Did Margaret give birth here?"

"No, she was my first client in the Bay Area after I moved up from L.A. She had Marcus at her home."

I imagined Celia assisting Margaret giving birth. Margaret—swollen belly, sweating, tired, probably swearing at Alan, juxtaposed next to Celia—olive skin, calm, beautiful.

How could a father witnessing the birth of his baby choose to be with the midwife instead of the mother of his own child?

At that moment in my mind, Alan was worse than pond scum.

"I've always wanted my own center," Celia continued. "So, I got this lease and fixed up the place. I need to find some staff now. Do you know anyone?"

I shook my head.

Celia led me back up to the front.

I pointed to the roses on the reception console. "Boyfriend?"

She smiled. "No. The roses are from me. The one thing I allowed myself to splurge on when I got out of the hospital."

• CHAPTER TWENTY-FOUR •

Research

To Do:

1. Why would anyone poison Celia?
2. Where is Margaret?
3. Must get house in order for Thanksgiving!
4. Shop, cook, clean.
5. Drink water.
6. Exercise—or will have nothing to wear for Thanksgiving!

On my way home, I'd stopped in at the library to pick up my reserved copy of *The Complete Idiot's Guide to Private Investigation*. While there I checked out a few picture books for Laurie and a cookbook for Jim.

By the time I arrived home, I was famished and exhausted. Laurie needed attention, but fortunately Jim had taken a stab at dinner. Spaghetti and meatballs—nothing fancy, just frozen ones—with some canned sauce. But beggars can't be choosers.

I ate three bowls before I felt satisfied and then shortly afterward felt overstuffed and regretted the extra helpings.

Hopefully the cookbook would help us be a little more creative with our meals. There was even a section on homemade baby food!

Over dinner, Jim told me I'd missed a call from my mom.

"She's back?" I asked.

"Yeah. She's coming over in the morning. I suggest you don't tell her about your foray in the hospital. Not unless you have a death wish."

I had been anxious to get to bed to catch up on lost sleep, but once my head hit the pillow, I tossed and turned. The night of the cruise was still fresh in my mind, not to mention my venture to the emergency room. I felt like talking to Jim, but he was emitting soft snoring sounds. I peeked at Laurie, snoozing peacefully in the bassinet next to our bed.

I turned on the bedside table lamp and cracked open *The Complete Idiot's Guide to Private Investigation*. I read the section on research then climbed out of bed and padded down the hallway. In the office, I logged on to the computer and fumbled my way through a bit of background information on Bruce. I was able to review his personal website as a financial advisor and pull a credit report for him.

He had great credit, but that didn't tell me much. I e-mailed Galigani and requested he help me with subscribing to one of the databases licensed PIs had access to.

For lack of anything better to do, I googled "Celia Martin midwife"—a gazillion things came up but nothing of value. I clicked through several articles on midwives and the benefits of home births. I read a disturbing account of a pregnant woman in Miami who had disappeared on her way to a natural child birthing center. Her husband was deployed in the military. The woman was on her own to have the baby and had selected a midwife to assist. Only she'd never made it to the center. One of her neighbors had reported seeing her leave the house in labor and had offered to drive her. She'd declined, telling him it was the early stages of labor and she was not having regular contractions.

The authorities suspected she'd gone into active labor while driving and had an accident. Although when the car was finally recovered, months later, there was no evidence of the mother or baby.

The midwife wasn't named, but Celia had told me she was from L.A., so while it had nothing to do with the case I was working on, the story nevertheless upset me.

Must be the hormones!

Tears ran down my face as I thought of the demise of this military wife and soon to be mother, not to mention the loss of the innocent life inside her.

I refined the search to "Celia Martin midwife Los Angeles," but no direct links came up.

I went to bed dejected.

* * *

The following morning I was sitting on the couch reading the PI book when Mom rang my doorbell. I opened the door to find her dressed in a poncho and mariachi hat. On her feet were bright red Converse high-tops and in one hand she held a plastic bag.

"I thought you got in last night." I motioned for her to come into the house.

She looked confused. "I did."

"Then why are you still dressed like that?"

Mom laughed. "The poncho and hat are for Jim and this is for you and Laurie." She handed me the plastic bag.

I peeked inside. A matching pair of red Converse and a set of maracas.

"The shoes are for you and the maracas for Laurie. Where is she?"

"Why did you get me Converse?"

"Because they're comfortable. Look at this!" She ran in place. "My bunions were killing me on the cruise. I could barely walk, but then I found these in a two-for sale."

"Two-for?"

"Two for one! I thought of you!"

I kissed her. "Thanks, Mom."

Mom looked offended. "Why do you say it like that?"

"Like what? All I said was thanks!"

"You're not going to wear them, are you?"

"Well, I don't normally wear Converse. They're for teenagers. Boy teenagers."

Maybe I'd give them to Kenny.

"That's not true," Mom said.

"I'll try them on." I sat on the couch and kicked off my house slippers. "Thank you for getting Galigani to sponsor me," I said, lacing up the left shoe.

Mom nodded and took off the hat and poncho, then proceeded to place the items on my dining room table. "Coffee?" she asked.

"In the kitchen." I laced up the shoe.

Hmmm. It was comfortable.

"Where are Jim and Laurie?" Mom called as she disappeared to the kitchen.

"Jim went for a run. Laurie's in the nursery."

Mom reappeared in the living room and placed her cup on the coffee table. She grabbed the maracas and headed to the nursery singing a goofy made-up song and shaking the maracas like crazy.

"Mom, you're going to wake her."

I heard Laurie let out a loud scream that escalated to a pitch that could break crystal. I ran into the nursery with my Converse on my feet.

Hey, I ran fast in these shoes.

Mom had Laurie in her arms. "I don't know why she doesn't like the maracas. She's going to be just like her mommy—difficult to shop for."

We decided to bathe the Laurie as I filled Mom in on the last few days. I told her about Celia being hospitalized but left out the part about me and Laurie.

As I put warm water in the baby tub, Mom undressed Laurie. She placed her in the tub and poured a few cupfuls of water over her. Laurie cooed from pure enjoyment. I pulled out the Magic Moments cradle cap cream.

Mom frowned. "What's that?"

"It's special cream so she doesn't get cradle cap."

Mom examined Laurie's head. "She doesn't have cradle cap."

"I know. I've been using this stuff. Smell." I stuck the bottle under Mom's nose.

Mom crinkled her nose. “You don’t need special cream, just use soap and water. That’s what I did with you and your brother.”

“That’s because they didn’t have Magic Moments when I was a baby,” I taunted her.

“How much did you pay for that?”

“Too much probably, and it wasn’t a two-for sale,” I said.

Mom laughed at me. “You were had!”

The phone rang, interrupting us. I left Mom to bathe Laurie and answered the call.

“Kate? This is Mandy from Gary Barramendi’s office.”

I snapped to attention. “Yes! Hi. Um, uh . . . I mean, hello!”

“Gary would like the daily report. I’ll transfer you now.”

Daily report?

Oh no! I had forgotten. What was I supposed to tell him?

I cleared my throat, hoping to sound professional and not like I’d just been bathing my infant and arguing with my mother.

“Good morning, Mrs. Connolly. Any news?” Gary asked.

“Good morning.” Good, my voice sounded fine—intelligent even! “Yes. I interviewed Celia yesterday.”

There! I did have something to report!

“Interview? I thought you were going to stake her out.”

Shoot!

“Uh . . .”

“Anything relevant?” he probed.

What could I tell him about? The stakeout and interview had been a complete dud?

Before I could think of an answer, Gary said, "That's my other line, I have to take it. I'll look forward to reading the transcript."

"Transcript?" I squawked.

"You do tape your interviews, don't you?"

I was supposed to tape them?

"Uh . . . no . . . I mean . . . yes. Of course. Just not this one. I had a problem with my . . . device."

"It happens. Okay, type up a summary and fax it to Mandy."

I hung up as the front door squeaked open.

Jim appeared, dripping from his run. "Look at what the cat dragged in," he said.

Paula trailed him. "Looks more like you've been dragged. What happened to you?" she teased.

Jim laughed, greeted Mom, then kissed me. "I'm jumping in the shower."

Mom stopped him. "Wait! Look at what I brought back for you!"

She handed a towel-wrapped Laurie to me and proceeded to put on the poncho. She threw the mariachi hat onto the floor and sang the tune to the "Mexican Hat Dance."

Paula laughed hysterically watching Mom dance around in the red Converse and poncho.

Jim looked concerned. "Is that safe?"

Mom frowned. "What's unsafe about it?"

Paula pointed to my feet, still clad in the Converse, and giggled. Jim simply shook his head.

"I love the 'Mexican Hat Dance,'" Paula said.

"The '*Jarabe Tapatío*'!" Mom exclaimed with the worst Spanish accent imaginable. "How was Paris?"

As they caught up with each other, Jim showered and I got Laurie dressed. When I'd finished, I joined them in the living room and brought Paula up to speed on my interview with Celia.

"Was Celia on that cruise?" Paula asked.

"No," I said.

"If she's not a suspect for killing Helene, why didn't you just ask her if she's seeing Alan?" Paula asked. "If I was dating a married man who was suspected of murder, I'd want to know."

Mom rubbed her chin thoughtfully. "People don't generally tell the truth about affairs, though. Do they? Especially to someone she knows is friendly with the wife. No. If she's in love with him, then she'll protect him."

"Not if he poisoned her," Paula said.

"We don't know that, and even still," Mom said, "maybe they're working together. Maybe she allowed the podiatrist to give her a little something to knock her out but not kill her. If he's a doctor, he would know about dosages and the like."

I sat to attention.

Paula shook her head. "That's crazy."

"Is it?" I asked.

I hadn't considered that option. Could Celia and Alan be working together? Or Celia and Bruce, for that matter?

"You should just ask her about Alan," Paula insisted.

I shook my head. "She knows I'm working for Margaret. She knows I would report it to her."

We sat in silence for a moment.

Suddenly Paula said, "I could ask her. I'll go to her midwife center and pretend I'm looking for a midwife. She won't suspect me of being connected to you."

Mom jumped up. "And I can see the podiatrist! He can look at my bunions!"

Paula leapt up. She and Mom sprang into a spontaneous rendition of the "*Jarabe Tapatío*." I turned Laurie on my lap so she was sitting up and facing them. She let out a little giggle and pedaled her feet as though she wanted to dance, too.

I watched them dance with more verve than a sixty-year-old woman with bunions and seven-months-pregnant woman should have.

When they'd finished, I said, "Even though I think you two should really get out a bit more, I can't let you do this."

"What?" Mom exclaimed. "Why not? We're the perfect undercover team! No one will suspect a thing!"

"You have no training or experience," I said.

This comment launched them into hysterics. Paula could barely breathe as she grabbed my copy of *The Complete Idiot's Guide* and waved it around, making Mom double over and gasp for air.

Jim appeared, freshly showered and looking relaxed. "If there's going to be more singing and dancing here, I'll have to leave immediately," he said.

"Don't worry!" Paula patted his shoulder. "Mom and I are on a mission. We'll be out of here shortly!"

I pressed the bridge of my nose. "Are you sure about this, guys?"

Mom and Paula nodded emphatically. Jim simply looked from one to the other then back at me.

"You both have good pretexts. I learned that this morning," I said, pointing to the book Paula still had in her hand.

"I don't know what that is," Mom said, "but don't worry, darling, we'll do it for free."

"Don't you have to get back to Danny?" I asked Paula.

"My in-laws took Danny to the lake cabin last night and David's at work. So, I have nothing better to do."

"If you're bored, you can always stay here and do laundry," I said.

Paula and Mom both shook their heads.

"All right," I said reluctantly. "Honey, can you run down to Radio Shack for us? I need you to buy some stuff for a tap."

"A what?" Jim asked.

"Gary wants all my interviews to be recorded and this book I'm reading has a chapter on how to do it."

"I can record mine on my phone! It's got a cool voice recording feature," Paula said.

"No. You can't do that. What are you going to do?" I imitated Paula voice: "Celia, tell me if you're having an affair with Alan. Clunk." I pantomimed putting down the phone on the table. "Pretty conspicuous."

"I wouldn't do it like that," Paula said.

"I thought you couldn't record anybody without their permission. It's illegal," Jim said.

"Technically yes, that's true. But I'm not going to submit it as evidence or anything. If we get any information relevant to the case, then Gary would have to depose them."

"Depose, ooh. You're using fancy words now," Paula said.

"Can you tell I've been studying? Anyway, I just want

to feel like I was there or you two will end up having to repeat the entire conversation for me and it's very likely we could miss something."

"Yeah. I'm ready to be wired!" Mom said.

Jim patted her arm. "Don't worry, Mom, you already are."

•CHAPTER TWENTY-FIVE•

Preparation

We sent Jim with a list of items to our neighborhood Radio Shack. Then Mom proceeded to dial Dr. Alan Lipe's office looking for an appointment. I warned her that he was booked up for a month and I'd only gotten my appointment because of a cancellation. She ignored me and dialed.

Paula, wanting to appear convincing, was at my computer researching midwives and the benefits of home births. With my primary PI tools in use, the computer and the phone, I reclined on the couch with Laurie in one arm and the *Idiot's Guide* in the other. As soon as I began to read, my doorbell rang.

I put Laurie in her bouncy chair and answered the door. It was Galigani.

"Hey, what are you doing here?" I asked, motioning him inside.

"I got your e-mail. I figured I could help you set up some accounts and . . ." He spotted Mom and Paula. "I didn't know you were having a party—"

Mom hung up and practically bounded over in her Converse. "Albert!"

He gave her a warm hug and kiss on the cheek.

"How was your cruise, Vera?" he asked Mom.

As far as I knew, Mom had told him that she was going with friends and I cringed to see how she would answer, but fortunately for Mom, Paula saved her by joining us and introducing herself.

Laurie began to cry from the bouncy chair.

"She's hungry." I picked her and headed to the bedroom to nurse her. Paula and Mom stayed in the living room with Galigani and filled him in.

By the time I'd finished with Laurie and laid her down for a nap, Jim had returned with the purchases. In addition to getting all the items on the list, he bought Laurie a stuffed purple puppy that had an imbedded digital recorder. He placed it next to Laurie in the crib to record her cute little coos.

Galigani assisted me with setting up the devices we were going to use for Paula and Mom. The microphones were just slightly bigger then a memory card and the receiver/recorder part was about the size and shape of a cell phone. I tested all the parts, and for fun recorded myself giving a grave warning to Paula.

My voice came out of the device. *"Paula, can you hear me? Do NOT get caught. This is serious business and I'm depending on you to get the secrets of the universe and report back to me."*

Paula listened to the recording, blowing air into each

cheek alternately and frowning. When the recorder clicked off, Paula's face relaxed and she smiled. "This is gonna be fun."

We secured the equipment to the inside of Paula's maternity blouse and instructed her to go to the garden and tape a conversation with Jim. Satisfied with our testing, we sent Paula and Mom out into the field. Paula was going to drop in on Celia and Mom had scored an appointment with her general doctor. She was planning on getting a real referral to Alan's practice in the hopes that she might actually get her bunion problem taken care of.

After Mom and Paula left, Galigani helped me learn the ropes on background checks and grilled me a bit over my meeting with Gary. I shared with him the transcript of the interview from Gary and Bruce's meeting with Inspectors McNearny and Jones.

Galigani perused the report. "Does Mac know you're still working on this case?"

McNearny and Galigani had been partners years ago. From comments Galigani made occasionally, I was never sure how close or not they actually were.

I recapped my meetings with McNearny.

Galigani scratched his head. "He said it was okay for you to follow Alan?"

I nodded.

Galigani sighed. "Then it's a waste of time for your mom and Paula to pursue him."

"Why?"

"If Mac didn't mind you investigating him, then he's not the guy. They have information we don't have. Remember they talked to all the people on the boat that night. No. They're looking into someone else."

* * *

Around 3 P.M., directly after I had nursed Laurie and put her down for a nap, Paula returned from Celia's.

We made tea and camped out in my kitchen nook.

We put the recorder on the table between us and pressed Play. Paula's voice came on:

Paula: Okay I'm in the car outside of Celia's center. Testing 123.

The recorder clicked.

Paula: All right. I just played my test and it worked. I hope I don't botch things.

Sounds of Paula getting out of the car. The car door slams.

Paula: I'm walking toward the entrance. I'm going to shut up now so she doesn't think I'm some weirdo who talks to herself.

Sounds of a door opening.

Paula: Hello?

Celia: Oh hi. Can I help you?

Sounds of shuffling.

"We can fast-forward a bit. This part's all small talk," Paula said.

I nodded. Paula pressed the forward button on the recorder and held it down for several seconds. When she released it, the recording continued.

Celia: Are you interested in a home birth?

Paula: Yeah. I had my son at the hospital and I'd like to try—

Celia: Did you have a bad experience?

Paula: No. Not really. Just, you know, I don't really like hospitals.

Celia: Most healthy people don't. That's one of the

benefits of the home births. There's less stress and fear in a home.

Paula: Do you . . . I mean would you do it at my house?

Celia: Whatever you're comfortable with. This can be your home away from home. A lot of people prefer the center, and remember, not everyone who wants a home birth has a home. This center is for everyone. Would you like to see the birthing room?

Paula: Uh . . . no.

I raised an eyebrow at Paula. She paused the tape.

"Why didn't you go look at the room?" I asked.

"For what? I'm not actually going to have my baby there, you know. Not even for you."

I laughed. "Still. You could have checked it out. It's actually kind of nice."

Paula giggled. "I knew that would kill you. You can't stand the thought that I had an opportunity to poke around and didn't."

"Well, you have to be sort of convincing. I mean, you're there on the pretext of wanting to hire a midwife and then you don't even look at the facility."

Paula waved her hand. "Ah, no big deal. She gave me this and I oohed and aahed at all the right places."

She pulled a glossy brochure from her purse. It contained several pictures of the birthing room, complete with a birth tub and balls.

"Did you ask her about her boyfriend?" I asked.

Paula nodded and pressed the Play button on the recorder.

Paula: How long have you been doing this?

Celia: Almost three years.

Paula: Are you certified?

Celia: Of course.

I sipped my tea. "You asked her for certification?"

Paula nodded. "Yeah. I was trying to get a groove on her. She gave me enough rubbish on the benefits of home births and births in a 'home away from home' to make me think she was legit."

She fidgeted with the recorder and the playback resumed.

Paula: So are you a nurse?

Celia: I was. Yes. In Miami. An ob-gyn nurse. Then I decided to go into business for myself and really focus on what I love. You know if you just give your dreams a chance, it can change your life. You're dreaming of having your baby without all the trappings of the hospital. I can help you.

When are you due? Who's your doctor now?

Paula: Uh. In March. Dr. Reynolds.

Celia: Do you have her number?

Paula: What?

Celia: I can call your doctor and begin the process to find out if you're a good candidate for home birth—

Paula: Oh no. I mean, I have to think about it. You know, talk to my husband. You know how men are. Are you married?

Celia: No.

Paula: You have a boyfriend?

Celia: Not at the moment.

Silence.

I raised an eyebrow. Paula held up her hand, indicating for me to wait.

Celia: I was seeing someone, but well . . . things got complicated.

Paula: I'm sorry. Affairs of the heart can be complicated. Was it recent?

Celia: Yes. Very.

Paula: My toughest breakup was this married guy I was seeing. It wasn't one of those, was it?

Celia: Actually . . .

Paula: Oh, sweetheart. I'm so sorry. I couldn't take it. I couldn't stand being second. Well, he would tell me I was first, but he wouldn't leave her—

Celia: Yes. That's it. We broke it off because he won't leave her.

Paula: Don't worry—there's plenty of Tom, Dick, and Alans out there.

I laughed.

Paula stopped the tape. "That's pretty much it."

"Wait! What was her reaction when you mentioned Alan?"

"Nothing. She just kind of looked sad and shrugged. The rest of the tape is her persuading me to leave my OB and become her client. You know, having a home birth gives you maximum control over your birth experience, blah blah. You can listen to it later; hearing the sales pitch once was enough for me."

"Tell me how you really feel about it."

Paula laughed. "Well, I got her to say she was with a married guy. But not who. I didn't know how to get that part without downright asking her—are you seeing a podiatrist name Alan?"

"It's okay. You did great. Good stuff to go on." I raised my eyebrow at her. "I never knew you had a thing for married men. I promise I won't tell your husband. Unless . . . I wonder how much my silence is worth to you . . ."

Paula jogged my elbow. "Don't be a twit. That lie was

only to elicit her feelings of camaraderie. If this tape surfaces on the Internet, I know where to find you."

I laughed, then hugged her. "You're the best. Thank you for suffering for me."

She rolled her eyes. "Okay, okay, you don't have to slobber all over me. Just keep in mind that you owe me one."

That evening I tried my hand at chicken cacciatore, pulling the recipe straight from the library cookbook with the only modification being that I liberally splashed wine into the pot.

While tasting the sauce, Mom called me and reported that her doctor had given her a referral to Dr. Lipe and she had scored an appointment for the morning. We agreed she would come straight to my house after the visit.

I dialed Margaret and left another message.

While waiting for the chicken to finish cooking, I typed up the tape from Paula and e-mailed it to Gary's office then called it a day.

Dejected, I sat down to dinner.

"Honey! This is outstanding," Jim raved.

"Glad you like it." I was holding Laurie and staring into her beautiful little face.

How could she be so complete and so tiny at the same time?

"What's wrong, honey?" Jim asked.

I picked at the chicken and sighed. "I'm bummed that I'm not making more progress on the case. I wanted to solve it before Thanksgiving and just have a peaceful holiday with you guys."

Jim squeezed me hand. "Don't worry, honey, if you fail

at the PI biz, you can still make me chicken cacciatore anytime."

I cleared the plates and kicked Jim on my way to the kitchen.

• CHAPTER TWENTY-SIX •

Talking

To Do:

1. Why would anyone poison Celia?
2. Where is Margaret?
3. Must get house in order for Thanksgiving! (in progress).
4. Shop, cook, clean (in progress).
5. ✓ ~~Drink water.~~
6. ~~Exercise—or will have nothing to wear for Thanksgiving!~~
7. Pick up exercise regimen after the holiday.

The following afternoon, I was busy trimming a keepsake lock from Laurie when Mom showed up on my doorstep with a little swagger in her step.

I ushered her into the house and showed her the lock of hair I'd placed in the delicate pink ballerina box Paula had brought Laurie from Paris.

"Oh! It's darling!" She rubbed Laurie's cheeks and cooed at her. Laurie watched Mom's face and stuck her little puppy tongue out.

I'd read that this is an infant's way of communicating. They're trying to imitate the way a mouth moves during speech. They even take turns, watching you first, as though they are having a conversation with you.

Mom laughed and proceeded to stick her tongue out at Laurie. Laurie rolled her tongue and gurgled. Mom did the same. Pretty soon I had a couple of drooling fools on my hands.

"Did you find anything out from Alan?" I asked.

"Maybe," Mom said with a smug look on her face. "Listen to the tape. It's in my purse. Oh, and bring me my Cheaters. I want to cut some of Laurie's hair for me, too."

I grabbed the recorder and handed Mom her glasses. She immediately went into action and clipped the only remaining long hair Laurie had.

Laurie was beginning to lose the hair on the back of her head and I feared she'd go completely bald before I could save some baby hair. But now after the radical haircut Mom had given her, I wondered if it had been a wise decision.

I pressed the Play button on the device.

Mom: Good morning. I have an appointment with Dr. Lipe. Is that you, Joan?

Joan: Vera! How are you? I didn't make the connection that it was you!

I pressed Stop on the recorder and raised my hands to Mom. "You know her?"

Mom laughed. "Isn't that a coincidence? I met her a few weeks ago at a dinner party. I told you about her. She's the lady who wanted to take home some leftover crackers, remember?"

"I can't believe you know her." I pressed Play again on the recorder.

Joan: Let me take you right in.

Sounds of a door opening and shuffling.

"This next part is my visit with the doctor. He gave me a good solution for my bunions."

I pressed Stop on the recording. "Let me guess. You need an orthotic."

"Yes!" Mom said excitedly.

"Okay, you can spare me the details of the visit," I said, fast-forwarding the device a bit. "Did you get any more information?"

"Oh yes. Let me see." Mom took the recorder and pressed a few buttons back and forth. "Here we go."

Mom: Okay, Joan. Looks like I need to come back. Do you have anything for next week?

Joan: Let me check.

Sounds of pages turning.

Joan: Next week the doctor is out due to the holiday. How about the first week in December?

Mom: Yes, that will work. The doctor is so handsome, isn't he?

Joan (giggling): Oh! You think so?

Mom: I'm sure a lot of woman do. Is he married?

Joan: Well, yes. Currently, but you know there's such a high rate of divorce these days.

Mom: Oh. That's too bad. You think he's heading for a divorce?

Silence.

Joan (whispering): He was seeing the wife's best friend.

Mom: Tsk, tsk, tsk.

Joan (whispering): But she (long pause) died!

Mom (sharp intake of breathe): Oh!

Joan: It was in the papers. So tragic. A bay dinner cruise.

Mom: Oh dear!

Joan: He hasn't been the same since.

Mom stopped the tape and thumped me on the back. "What do you think about your ol' mom now?" She laughed and whooped. "You don't mind the gossip so much when it yields you a juicy bit, do you?"

I held my head, feeling like if I didn't, my brain would explode and then there would be one more thing to clean up around here.

The phone rang.

"Want me to get that?" Mom asked. "You look a little pale."

It was Helene? Alan had been sleeping with Helene?

No wonder. Margaret said he'd been getting home on time after the night on the boat. Of course, because his mistress was dead.

My answering machine kicked on. Galigani's voice filled the air.

"Kid! I got something for you. The doc was sleeping with the vic. Call me."

Mom grabbed the phone before Galigani could hang

up. "Hello, Albert. Just one second, Kate's right here . . . Oh tonight? . . . Sure, I'd love to have dinner with you."

My chest felt tight and my head throbbed. Lives were going on all around, Mom had a date, Celia had her business, Paula would have her baby soon, but Helene was dead and gone.

Why? Why would Alan have killed his mistress? Had she threatened to tell Margaret? Could he have done it? Maybe he'd killed her by accident as Margaret had feared.

Mom passed me the phone. I semigrunted.

Galigani laughed. "What's the matter, kid? We're making progress."

"How did you find out it was Helene?" I asked.

"This is confidential. Okay? You *cannot* disclose to Barramendi, understand?"

There was a lump forming in my throat the size of a walnut.

I was so in over my head.

I swallowed past the lump. "Yeah," my voice cracked.

"I'm holding the police report from the night on the cruise. Officer Lee questioned you. Do you remember?"

"Yes. I remember."

"Well, there were a few officers there and Officer Rebecca Burke took a statement from one witness who'd overheard a discussion between Helene and Alan."

I recalled the woman officer on board. I had seen her talking to a silver-haired woman who had been gesticulating madly.

"According to the statement," Galigani said, "the witness overheard a discussion between the deceased and Alan. He was planning to leave his wife. There was some talk of moving to North Carolina together. Then they were interrupted by another woman. The doc left the scene and the two women had an argument. The deceased was canceling a home extension or construction project. The other woman got very agitated. That's when our witness decided to clear out of there and in the process ended up spilling her drink on the woman."

Sara.

So if Alan and Helene were planning on running away together, it made sense that Helene would cancel the home remodeling plans. And it would also make sense that Bruce didn't know she'd done it. But what about the adoption? Hadn't Helene wanted kids? Had she really been planning to leave Bruce and stop the adoption proceedings?

Maybe she only seemed to be agreeing with Alan about moving to North Carolina. Maybe she was scared of him.

"What do you think?" I asked Galigani. "You think the doc did it?"

"It's not the doc."

"Why do you say that?"

"There is another very important thing in the prelim report," Galigani said.

I rubbed my temples. "What's that?"

"The doc's the one who pushed the ME to run a tox screen. There's no way he'd do that if he killed her. I told you McNearny knew something we didn't."

"How did you get him to share this report with you?"

"I didn't. Mac doesn't share. He's by the book and he's tough."

"Who then? Did you woo the lady officer?"

Mom, who was hovering near me rocking Laurie back and forth, scowled at the mention of another lady and I had to laugh at her double standard.

"Jones," Galigani said. "He was taking a couple days off, spending a little time with his kid. I dropped in on him and we had a couple beers. Don't mention any of this to anybody or we'll have no one left to play in the sandbox with. *Capisce*?"

"I *capisce* all right," I said.

Did Bruce know about the affair?

That would fit. He'd found out about the affair and killed Helene, then he must have feared Celia knew something and took a whack at her.

"So you think Bruce did it?" I asked Galigani.

"No. Killing the wife maybe, but the midwife at his place makes no sense. I think it might have been Margaret."

"Margaret?" I asked.

Mom nodded her agreement.

Margaret? If she was guilty, then I was a ruse designed to throw suspicion off her. Why else would someone guilty hire a PI?

Had I been used as a pawn?

No! Couldn't be.

"As far as I know, Margaret wasn't with Celia that day of the poisoning. Only Bruce, Evelyn, and I saw her that day. And why would Margaret poison Celia anyway? She had been her midwife."

"What about at Bruce's house?" Mom asked.

"What?" Galigani and I asked at the same time. I put Galigani on speaker phone and Mom got close to the microphone.

"Maybe Margaret was over at Bruce's before Celia got there. Maybe she mixed a little cocktail intended for Bruce."

"Why, though?" I asked.

Mom shrugged. "I can only do so much work for free."

Galigani snorted through the phone line. "I'm working on getting the tox results right now. Maybe they'll shed a little light on some of this stuff, but let's not hold our breath."

After Mom left, I tried phoning Margaret and ended up leaving another voice mail. She had effectively disappeared. I wondered if "going to her mother's" was a euphemism for "skipping town."

Both Mom and Galigani had suggested Margaret was the murderer, but if my client was guilty—what did it make me?

Was I just being prideful?

Had Margaret played me? Perhaps she had found out about Helene's betrayal. Or had she legitimately believed she was in danger from Alan?

And what about Evelyn? She'd been on the cruise and had seen Celia the day of the poisoning. But what possible motive could she have for killing Helene, or Celia for that matter?

Was getting kicked out of a mommy group motive enough to kill someone?

Hardly.

No matter how peeved it had made her, I couldn't see it being cause for murder. Unless there was something else to the story?

Why had she been on the cruise anyway? She must have known that the night would be fraught with friction. It seemed silly to insist on going when she knew she would be seated with a bunch of women who didn't like her.

And then there was the fact that her husband was leaving the country for a work assignment. Wouldn't she rather have had a private date night?

Still, as strange as it seemed to me, it didn't gel as a motive for murder. Perhaps she thought getting kicked out of the group was a slight on her kid? Could she be that overprotective as to kill in retaliation for the snub?

And then what would be her motive to hurt Celia?

No. It didn't make sense.

No matter how many times I wrapped my head around it, I came up with Bruce. He had motive because of the affair, and opportunity—he was on the boat and at his house.

I dialed Gary and reported to him about Helene and Alan's affair.

"It's not looking good for Bruce," I said.

There was silence on the phone. Finally Gary said, "Well, we just have to look harder. I think there's something suspicious about Margaret. Check into that."

Another one who wanted to peg it on Margaret!

"I can, of course," I said.

If she'll call me back!

"It's just that the truth may be that Bruce is responsible," I said.

"The truth is overrated," Gary replied as he hung up on me.

For the umpteenth time I reviewed the transcript Gary had given me. Neither Inspector Jones nor Inspector McNearny had questioned Bruce on Helene's affair, yet surely they would have known about it from the preliminary interviews. Why hadn't they asked him?

I reread the report. It was clear that Gary had silenced them before they'd gotten to any substantive questions. They needed evidence. Pure and simple.

And so did I.

• CHAPTER TWENTY-SEVEN •

Risk

To Do:

1. Find proof to nail Bruce.
2. Where is Margaret?
3. Laundry—didn't I just do it?
4. Order turkey.
5. Read to Laurie.
6. Sing to Laurie—Am I falling behind on any more milestones?

Paula and I sat inside my car and waited for Bruce to leave. I'd convinced her to watch his house with me for a while, hoping for an opportunity to search his place.

After about an hour of waiting and making small chit-chat, Paula said, "Maybe we should call him and tell him the condo is on fire and that he needs to leave right away."

I laughed. "It's not a bad idea. What kind of believable reason to get him out immediately could we use?"

"A fire's not believable?" she asked.

"No. I think he'd notice pretty fast that the place wasn't on fire. No firefighters, fire trucks, et cetera."

"I could set the place on fire," Paula offered.

"No."

"Okay, how about I set you on fire for dragging me along, then when the firefighters come and Bruce peeks out of his condo to see what the commotion is about, I sneak into his place and search it," Paula said.

"I hate to break it to you, but a pregnant woman can't really 'sneak' around."

"Well, I hate to break it *to you*, but pregnant women have a lot of pressure on their bladders and sitting inside a car on a stakeout doesn't exactly elicit brilliance." She laughed. "Seriously, can't you call Margaret and ask her to invite him over or something? She *is* your client."

"I'm not sure where she is or where she stands in all this. What if we just go upstairs and talk to him? You can distract him while I search the place."

"What am I supposed to talk to him about? And what are you hoping to find anyway? You think a murderer just keeps stuff lying around?"

I opened the door to the car and jumped out. I walked around to Paula's and pulled open her door. "Come on, you can use his bathroom. I know you're dying to go."

Paula indicated my new Converse. "You're actually willing to be seen in public in those?" Paula asked.

"They're my getaway shoes. Just in case."

We climbed up the stairs to the third-floor condo and rang the bell. After a moment, Bruce came to the door.

"Kate!" He scratched his head and smiled. "Was I expecting you?"

"I was in the neighborhood and I had a few questions for you. Can we come in for a minute?"

He stepped aside. "Sure. Of course. Nice shoes."

Paula snorted.

I smiled. "This is my friend Paula."

She stuck out her hand. "Nice to meet you and all that, can I use your potty?"

Bruce laughed and pointed down the hall. "Help yourself."

Paula disappeared down the hallway, while Bruce and I seated ourselves in his living room. Concern showed on his face. "What's up, Kate? Did Gary send you?"

"No. I was just going through my notes last night and realized there was some stuff I hadn't asked you about."

"Okay, shoot."

I was desperate to find out what Bruce knew of Helene's affair, but didn't want to alienate him before I had a chance to snoop.

"Can you tell me a little more about the adoption?" I asked.

"Well, I don't think it's going through now. Celia won't return my calls, which is understandable. I don't know how to reach Father Pedro's. I feel so badly about everything that I think I should still give the girl the money, you know? Help her out. I mean, what's two hundred and fifty thousand dollars to me?"

"What? Wait a minute. What do you mean, two hundred and fifty thousand dollars?"

"That was the agreement. Helene and I were going to donate money to Father Pedro's orphanage."

"You were *buying* the baby?"

"Well, no. I don't consider it *buying*, more like we needed to give Father Pedro something. You know, get to the top of the line. I've got the money, that's no problem."

"Bruce, that day Celia and I were here. Did anyone else come over?"

He looked thoughtful. "No."

I couldn't contain myself any longer. I had to find out if he'd known about Helene's affair.

I squinted at him. "What can you tell me about the affair?"

"What affair?"

"Between Helene and Alan. When did you find out about it?"

The color drained from Bruce's face. He looked as if I'd landed a punch square in the solar plexus. "Helene was having an affair?"

I nodded slowly.

Bruce swallowed and took an involuntary step back. "How do you know this?"

"Witnesses on the cruise."

Oops!

I wasn't supposed to say anything about having that information!

Yikes, please don't tell Gary. Please don't tell Gary.

Why didn't I just tell him I'd heard it from Alan?

Now, I couldn't very well tell him my mother had snagged the information from Alan's receptionist. That would sound completely stupid—like I was dependent on my mommy for my survival as a PI. Never mind the fact that it was one of her boyfriends who was letting me use his license.

Bruce slouched and allowed his head to fall heavily into his hands. "I didn't know anything about it. Are you sure?"

"I'm sorry. Yes. It's true."

Was he legitimately stunned or had he rehearsed this reaction?

At that moment, Paula emerged from the bathroom and walked down the hallway toward us.

I gestured to the bathroom "May I?"

"Of course," Bruce said.

Paula reached us and said, "I hear you have a great view."

I excused myself and headed down the hall as Paula said, "I love views of the bay. Can we take a peek?"

Bruce, still slightly pale, said, "Um . . . Yeah, sure."

Paula called after me, "We'll be on the roof, Kate."

"No problem," I said over my shoulder.

I stopped at the bathroom door and listened as they climbed the metal staircase. I could hear them chatting overhead. Mostly Paula, Bruce seemingly going through the motions or pretending he was.

I made a mad dash into the master bedroom. There were gorgeous gold curtains and a matching coverlet on the bed. The furniture was handsome and heavy. An antique set of dressers adorned either side of the bed. On top of each dresser were gold candlesticks and several dishes that held knickknacks.

I circled the room quickly. The closet looked in order, nothing out of the ordinary. It would help if I knew what I was looking for, but I was clueless. I entered the master bath and pulled open the medicine chest: cold creams, makeup, makeup remover, and nicotine patches. Looked like Helene had taken Margaret's advice and bought some. I peeked in the package—half empty. Apparently they hadn't worked for her either, because that night on the cruise she still wanted a cigarette.

Sadness filled my gut and I felt a hopelessness overcome me.

What was I looking for?

If I was Bruce, where would I hide a poison? Certainly not in the bathroom. That would be obvious. I returned to the bedroom. If he still had anything incriminating, which he probably didn't—unless he was planning on poisoning someone else . . .

Paula was alone with him upstairs.

Fear raced through me and I took a deep breath, trying to calm myself. I knew she was fine. It was more likely that I'd be caught snooping than anything happening to Paula.

If I were Bruce, I would hide poison . . . where?

I went to one of the dressers and pulled opened the top drawer. My hands were shaking. The drawer held ties and silk handkerchiefs. The balance of the dresser held clothes, and the closest thing I got to poison was a few mothballs.

On top of the dresser the little gold dish held a pair of cuff links and some loose change.

I had to get out of the room. They could return at any second and I would be caught with my hand in the cookie jar.

For my final snooping, because it is beyond my nature to stop myself from snooping before I actually have to, I yanked open Helene's top drawer. It was filled with designer scarves, slips, and bras. I opened the next drawer: panties, hose, and some lingerie. The remaining drawers held sweaters, tops, and finally jeans.

I was out of drawers and out of luck.

On top of her dresser the gold dish held rings, a bracelet, and three pairs of earrings. I fingered the jewelry and the dish slipped a bit, revealing an envelope tucked underneath. It wasn't hidden exactly, more like held in place for safekeeping under the dish. I pulled the envelope out and looked inside.

It was a plane ticket, printed from her home computer. SFO to Costa Rica. It was an open ticket; no date was set. And the *Special Note* on the bottom stated she'd be flying with an infant.

Sadness overtook me. This was Helene's ticket for when the adoption occurred. Of course, no date was set. They were waiting for the baby to be born. And now what? How would this little baby grow up? Without Helene, Bruce wouldn't take the baby. And probably he wasn't a fit father anyway. Celia was most likely right about that.

What about the affair? Could Helene have been ready to back out from the adoption? Bruce wanted kids of his own; he had told me that from the first.

Helene had canceled the addition to the condo. Had Bruce known and just played dumb when I asked him?

It seemed like Helene was planning on leaving him and moving with Alan to North Carolina.

Perhaps Bruce had found out about the affair and Helene's plans, then he killed Helene out of anger and decided to stop the adoption proceedings.

Then poisoned Celia. Why? Maybe he thought she would force the adoption? Now he said he wanted to donate the money to the orphanage.

Buy his way out of looking guilty.

And what did it all matter anyway? Bruce had hired the slickest attorney in town, one who thought the truth was overrated, and now I was working for him!

So much for my hopes as a media darling.

I felt nauseous. I had to leave. Get Paula out of here, as far away from that murderer as possible.

Adrenaline surged within me, causing my hands to shake even further.

I jammed the printout back into the envelope and secured it in place under the dish. I left the bedroom and returned to the living room just as Paula and Bruce were descending the staircase.

"That view is spectacular!" Paula said enthusiastically.

I headed straight for the front door and tugged it open. "Come on, let's go."

Bruce stopped short and looked at me. "Is everything all right, Kate?"

"Uh . . . yeah. My husband called. I gotta run." I reached out and put my hand on Paula's waist. Doing what I could to mask the shaking, I ushered her out the door.

She gave me a knowing look and kept moving.

I crossed the threshold of the doorway and jerked it closed behind me. Paula and I darted down the three flights of steps and pushed through the main condo doors on the first level, squinting into the low November sunlight.

Neither of us spoke until we were inside my car.

"What did you find?" Paula asked, slamming the car door shut.

I started the engine. "Nothing really. It just hit me all of a sudden. It's him. I know he did it. I just have to prove it."

I pulled into traffic and nearly collided with a yellow VW bug.

"Hey!" Paula screeched, clutching the dashboard.

My hands were still shaking. "Sorry," I said.

"Want me to drive?" Paula asked.

"No. I'm fine." I took a deep breath. "I'll focus and get you home safe. Promise."

I dropped Paula off and phoned Jim. I didn't want to be on the phone while driving. I was obviously too keyed up to be safe.

Jim said the only thing worth mentioning was that Laurie had briefly woken up and given him a "scary-eyed" look. Other than that, she was still back asleep in her blue bouncy chair.

I caught him up on my snooping and told him I was going to stop by Galigani's to brainstorm.

I pulled up to Galigani's and rang the bell.

Galigani answered the door. "Hey, kid. Glad you stopped by. I got some more info for ya."

Mom appeared in the doorway behind him and peeked at me over his shoulder.

"Kate, you're completely white. What kind of trouble did you find now?" Mom asked.

They ushered me into the house. We ended up in Galigani's kitchen, where he was making Mom some homemade osso bucco for dinner.

As the smell of garlic and onions frying in olive oil permeated the kitchen, I absently wondering if Mom's other beau, Hank, could cook.

I recounted for them my search of Bruce's place and my suspicions about his not wanting to go through with the adoption.

"I freaked myself out so bad being there and I didn't want to put Paula in any danger. So we ran out as fast as we could," I finished.

"Well," Galigani said. "It's never a bad idea to flee the scene if you're getting any kind of signal about danger."

Mom nodded and rubbed my back. "Do you want something warm to drink? Tea?"

"Tea?" Galigani chuckled. "How about a brandy?"

I declined. "What information do you have for me?"

Galigani stirred the onions, a delicious sizzling and popping sound filling the room. "I heard from Jones, the tox report is in. Helene was killed with a lethal dose of fentanyl. Celia was exposed to fentanyl but did not absorb a lethal dose and your results—"

I cleared my throat as loudly as I could and launched myself up from the table. Galigani, who was standing by the stovetop, immediately stopped talking and stared at me.

I hadn't told Mom about Laurie's and my hospital stay.

Mom squinted at us. "What about Kate's results?"

"Kate's results . . . in that report . . ." Galigani turned his back to Mom, stirred the onions, and winked at me. "The one you were preparing for Gary . . . I'd say . . . Oh, Vera!" He pulled the pan away from the flame. "I need some wine to add to this . . . would you mind? In the dining room above the china cabinet, there's a nice selection of red. Why don't you pick one?"

Mom rolled her eyes. "Stop pretending, the both of you!" She harrumphed, stomping into the dining room. "I know when I'm not wanted."

As soon as the swinging door closed behind Mom, Galigani whispered, "Negative. Nothing in your system and Laurie was clear, too."

Although I had suspected this, I found myself clapping my hand to my chest in relief and collapsing back into the chair with a sigh.

Galigani nodded and placed the pan back over the flame. "Curious, though, that Celia's dosage wasn't lethal, isn't it?"

"What do you think it means?" I asked.

"Either a botched attempt or a warning? Not sure."

I arrived home in a panic. I'd been gone five hours and it felt like a lifetime. I ran upstairs and found Jim on the computer and the house eerily silent.

"Where's Laurie?" I asked.

"Hi, honey," Jim said, absently kissing me.

"Where's my little rose petal?" I demanded, trying to keep hysteria out of my voice.

"Oh, in her bouncy chair."

"Still? She was there when I called you hours ago." I ran to the living room, where we had been housing the bouncy chair. It was set to vibrate and Laurie looked like she was in a deep peaceful sleep.

"How long has she been sleeping?" I asked.

Jim shrugged. "Dunno. Since you left?"

"What! I've been gone five hours. Haven't you fed her?"

Jim looked dumbstruck. "That long? Hmmm." He glanced around the room looking for an answer.

"Well? Did you feed her?"

"No," he admitted.

"Jim, she won't sleep at all tonight." I rushed to Laurie's bouncy chair and pulled her out of it. She startled for a moment, then resumed sleeping.

Jim stared at me. "Really? Are you sure you're supposed to wake her? If she was hungry, wouldn't she wake up on her own?"

I shrugged. Nothing seemed to work. If I let her sleep through the day, she would be awake all night.

But then wouldn't she be awake all night anyway?

I tried to nurse her but she stayed snoozing. I couldn't stand it any longer. I pulled out the dreaded breast pump and finally felt some relief. Six ounces later I was exhausted.

As soon as I cleaned the pump, capped the bottles, and placed them in the fridge, Laurie woke up screaming and howling.

Great. Just great!

Now I was empty and would have to use the milk I had just pumped. There was no winning.

Before going to bed, I researched fentanyl online. It came in transdermal patches and candy form and was primarily prescribed to terminally ill cancer patients.

Hadn't Bruce told me his grandmother had passed away a few weeks ago from cancer?

•CHAPTER TWENTY-EIGHT•

Reward

To Do:

1. ~~Find proof to nail Bruce.~~ It's hopeless—if the police can't do it, what makes me think I can?
2. Where is Margaret?—Who cares? If she doesn't want to call me back, then forget it. Maybe she's in Mexico getting away with murder.
3. ✓ ~~Laundry—didn't I just do it?~~
4. Order turkey—Oh, yeah, holiday, festive, joy, joy, joy.
5. ✓ ~~Read to Laurie.~~
6. ✓ ~~Sing to Laurie—Am I falling behind on any more milestones?~~
7. Buy new pajamas.

I sulked around the store and found what I was looking for in the back. I rummaged through the pajamas in the bin and picked up a teal pair with pink flamingos. I held them up for Laurie to view.

She was nestled in her stroller looking contented.

"What do you think of this set, lemon blossom?"

Laurie's eyes shifted to the hanging purple puppy strapped to the side of her stroller. I pinched the puppy's ear and recorded myself asking in a booming voice, "Do you like the pajamas?"

Laurie pedaled her feet but kept a serious expression on her face.

"Hmmm, you don't like them?" I returned the teal pair and moved a few other sets out of the way. At the bottom of the stack I found a fuzzy pair with fuchsia lips all over. "Well, I'm not even going to ask you. I like these."

I pulled the puppy off the stroller and recorded myself saying, "I'm buying them."

I placed the puppy near Laurie's ear and replayed it for her. She smiled and cooed at my voice then tried to eat the puppy.

I poked around looking for my size as my cell phone rang. I rummaged past the baby paraphernalia in the diaper bag and pulled out my phone. The caller ID read Paula's number.

"Hi," I mumbled.

"What's wrong?" she asked, alarm in her voice.

"Nothing. Just shopping."

"For what?" she asked suspicious.

"PJs."

"For you or for Laurie?"

I sighed. "Me."

"No! Not pajamas! How many pairs have you bought?"

"None yet."

"Where are you?" she asked.

"At Bed Head and More."

"Drop the PJs and step away from the counter right now!"

"I found a pair I really like. Well, two, but Laurie didn't seem so fond of one of them."

"Don't buy them. You'll wear them for weeks and never get out of that mood."

"I'm not in a mood," I said.

Paula knew me too well. If I was seriously down in the dumps, shopping for new pajamas seemed to help. Nothing would comfort me more than a cozy pair of new pajamas.

"Do you think they have footed pajamas for adults?" I asked.

"What?"

"You know, like the kind for kids with the feet. Do they make them for adults?"

"Yeah, that sounds really sexy, Kate. You've gone off the deep end. Come over immediately."

"No. I'm going to buy these, go straight home, and snuggle up in them. They're fleece and fuzzy and superwarm. I'll sleep all week in them, lounge on the couch with Laurie in my lap, and eat bonbons if I want to. I'm going to—"

"Shut up, you nut. You're a mom now, you can't indulge your every whim. Like Laurie is going to let you sleep at all, much less for a week. And Jim? And what about Thanksgiving, you have too—"

"I'm hanging up now. I'm going to buy them. Both pairs and there's nothing you can do about it."

I snapped my phone shut and found my size in both

pairs. I turned the stroller toward the counter, and Laurie's puppy fell to the floor. I picked it up, wiped the drool off it onto my jeans, and shoved it into the diaper purse. When I wheeled Laurie up to the counter, the store phone rang.

The girl working smiled at me as she held up her index finger. "Just a second." She picked up the phone. "Thank you for calling Bed Head and More, may I help you?"

I perused the fashion jewelry while waiting. I picked up a pair of silver earrings and held them to my ear, evaluating them in the mirror behind the counter.

"Uh . . . yes. She's right here," said the girl. "Do you want to talk to her?"

She seemed to be referring to me, but that couldn't be right. I glanced over my shoulder. There was no one else in the store.

She must be referring to another employee in the back or something.

"Oh. Okay," she said into the phone.

I replaced the silver earrings and picked up a pair made of delicate pink beads.

How old did Laurie have to be to get her ears pierced?

"Oh!" The girl's voice dropped several octaves and her eyes darted up at me then down again.

What was going on?

I put the beaded earrings down and wheeled Laurie up to the counter. Now, it was just plain annoying. The girl was obviously having a personal conversation and I was meant to wait it out.

Well, nope. I had some serious lounging around to catch up on. So, she'd better get her butt in gear and check me out.

I placed my pajamas on the counter and smiled. The girl kept her eyes down and almost ducked her head.

"Uh-huh," she said into the phone. "Okay." She hung up and looked at me. "I'm sorry. We're closed."

"What?" I looked at my watch. "It's one fifteen in the afternoon."

She blinked. "Yeah. Sorry."

We stared at each other in an awkward moment. My cell phone rang.

"You called the store, didn't you?" I said into the phone.

The clerk smiled.

"Yeah. Come over," Paula said.

"No!" I exclaimed as stubbornly as I could.

"I'm trying out a new recipe for pumpkin pie."

"Okay."

I sat in Paula's kitchen, stirring the hot cocoa she'd made me and staring out into her garden. Her once green grass had yellowed and all the pots were empty. Keeping up the garden while she'd been away had been too much of an effort to coordinate, so she'd let it go—which, knowing Paula, had probably killed her.

"Don't be so hard on yourself," she said, cutting me a piece of the still steaming pie. "The police have a hard time closing cases, why shouldn't you?"

Danny ran into the kitchen holding a plush blue ball and screamed, "Ball!"

I put my hands out to collect it from him and he gave me the biggest smile I'd seen in a long time.

"Kiss Auntie," Paula said.

Danny leaned into me and said, "Kiss!"

He pressed his lips, tongue, and teeth against my cheek and made his own clicking sound, bringing a smile to my face.

I wrapped my arms around him and pulled his small body onto my lap. "Thank you, buddy, that was the best kiss ever!"

Laurie watched us from the safety of her bucket seat.

"So are you convinced it was Bruce?" Paula asked, liberally dolloping whipped cream onto the pie.

Danny spotted Laurie and screamed excitedly, "Baby Lo-ly!"

"Of course it was Bruce. Only now Gary the Grizzly is going to try and get me to pin it on Margaret."

Danny scrambled out of my lap and ran to the glass door that separated the kitchen from the garden. He placed his pudgy palms on the glass and banged. "Danny garden!"

Paula pulled him away from the glass door. "No. Danny. Cold. Brrr!" Paula picked up the ball and threw it into the other room.

Danny lost interest in the garden, left fingerprints smudged on the glass, and ran out of the room with as much gusto as he had when he'd run in.

"Do you know if Margaret has access to that drug?" Paula asked, placing the pie in front of me.

"Fentanyl? Well, I suppose she could—being married to a doctor, right?" I tore into the pie. The pumpkin was still warm, the cream chilled, and the crust crisp. "Oh my God!"

Paula smiled. "Is it good? Is this the one I should make?"

I shook my head and shoveled another piece into my mouth. "It's terrible. You need to try a different one tomorrow. I'll come over and taste-test. In the meantime, don't eat this one. I'll take it home."

Paula laughed. "I'll give you the recipe. Why do think she hasn't called you back?"

"Margaret? I don't know."

"Maybe it's time you talked to Alan."

I cringed. "You mean tell him his wife suspected him of murder?"

Paula pulled out a Windex bottle. "Oh, I don't know why I bother!" she said, squirting the glass door. "Look at it this way, Kate. You can go talk to the doctor and possibly solve this thing or go home, clean house, and start getting ready for Thanksgiving."

"No. I don't even have fuzzy pajamas to put on."

I drove straight home to drop Laurie off with Jim. I found him in the living room watching the news of the spiraling Dow Jones and praying the downturn wouldn't affect his client so adversely that his contract would be canceled.

"Hi, honey, can you babysit?"

Jim looked up from the television. "You're going out again?"

I nodded.

"Okay. What do I need to do? Feed her? Is there milk?"

I rubbed his shoulders. "Yes, there's three ounces in a little bottle in the fridge."

"Can I microwave it?"

"No, you have to heat water—you can do that in the microwave—then put the bottle into the cup of hot water to heat. Otherwise the nuker will destroy the beneficial properties in the breast milk, whatever they are."

Jim nodded. "When will you be back?" he asked, his brow furrowing.

"I won't be long. I need to go to Sacramento Street."

* * *

It was almost 5:00 P.M. and I hoped Alan would still be at his office finishing paperwork after his final appointment. I pushed open the door to the medical office and entered the waiting room. Joan sat behind the closed-in glass counter. She was in her uniform lab coat, her gray hair curled around her ears.

When I stepped up to the counter, she blinked at me, trying to place me.

I smiled. "Is Dr. Lipe available?"

She frowned. "He's with a patient right now. How may I help you?"

"Will you kindly let him know Kate Connolly is here?"

She stared at me. Did she see a resemblance to my mom? She didn't know I was Vera's daughter. That was the ace in my back pocket should she not wish to cooperate.

Ha! I know you are gossiping about your boss. You better let me get my way!

She pushed herself away from the desk and rose, not hesitating to give me a look of contempt as she disappeared down the hallway.

A few moments later, she pulled open the connecting door. "He'll see you in his office, third door on the right."

She resumed her perch at the counter and I walked down the hallway.

Hmm, no patient, huh?

At the third door I peeked in and saw Alan at his desk. The office was no more than a desk with a computer on it, two chairs, and a bookcase along the far wall, which was actually so close to the desk it seemed that books would crash onto our heads in an earthquake.

He stood when he saw me. The last time I'd been at his office, he'd had dark circles under his eyes. Now the circles were even darker and his clothes were wrinkled, making him look like a train wreck. "Mrs. Connolly, what can I do you for?"

"Thank you for your time." I offered him my hand. "Do you have a few minutes to answer some questions, Doctor?"

He nodded, indicating for me to sit. "Of course, of course. Uh . . . about your feet?" He stared at my Converse-clad feet.

"No."

He clenched his fist then relaxed it and seated himself.

"It was brought to my attention that after Helene was killed, you asked for a full toxicology scan from the medical examiner," I said.

He seemed surprised. "Yes. That night on the boat, I told the EMTs and the police to please request a full tox screen."

"Can you tell me why?"

He rubbed at his face. "I thought her death was odd. I didn't think the fall down the stairs had killed her. Her neck wasn't broken, her skull hadn't cracked. No trauma from the fall that I would deem severe or deadly. So, I reasoned that the medical examiner would call the cause of death an internal organ failure. Like, say, heart failure. While technically that may have been true, I wanted to know what caused the heart failure. I thought we at least deserved to know."

"Were you close to Helene?"

"Sure. She was Margaret's best friend."

It was confession time, I needed to get everything I could out of Alan and I didn't think confrontation would be best.

I titled my head and softened my voice. "You wanted to know because you were in love with her?"

Alan eyes opened wide. "What?"

"I have it on pretty good authority that you were having an affair with Helene."

His face turned red. "What authority? Who said this? Who have you been talking to?" He jumped out of his chair. "Who's saying I'm having an affair?"

Okay, maybe eliciting a confession wasn't going to be as easy as I'd thought.

I remained seated. I couldn't disclose that I had access through Galigani to things I shouldn't have had access to.

An ugly vein was pulsating on his forehead. "And what about my wife? Did you mention this outrageous gossip to her?"

My hand involuntarily came to my throat, maybe because he looked like he could strangle me. It kicked up a self-protection instinct in me. "No. I haven't been able to reach her."

Suddenly my stomach clenched and I tasted bile in the back of my throat.

My God! Where was Margaret? Had something happened to her?

A bubble of anxiety crept along my spine and I did my best to suppress the shudder it was causing me. Alan, who was still hovering over me, suddenly dropped into his chair as though he'd just realized how physically imposing he was in this confined space.

"Margaret didn't know about Helene. She suspected I was seeing someone, but she didn't know it was . . ." He rubbed at his temple. "Please don't tell her. She left me. There's no point in her knowing now, is there? She took the kids and went to her mother's. You can reach her there."

"She hired me to investigate you. She thought you were trying to kill her."

Alan's hands dropped to his side. "What? That's absurd!"

"I left several messages for her. She hasn't returned my calls."

Alan's eyes narrowed. "I spoke with her yesterday. Let me give you her mother's number."

He proceeded to write the same phone number Margaret had left for me on her last voice mail.

"Do you have her mother's address?"

Alan scowled, but jotted an address down for me nonetheless. "Look, I don't know where this is going, but even though Margaret and I were having problems, I would certainly never physically harm her. I'm a doctor, for Christ's sake."

He glared at me, waiting for me to respond, but I simply closed my mouth and looked at him. He tapped at his desk. "Helene and I fell in love. Things weren't working in her marriage. She wanted kids and we thought . . ." He sank his head into his hands.

"What about adoption? I thought Helene and Bruce were arranging for an adoption."

Alan dropped his hands to the desk. He held on to the edge of the desk as though he were afraid it would run off on him. After a moment, he said, "We thought I could get custody of my kids. Margaret . . . well . . . she's had some stability problems." He moved his head from side to side, evaluating what to say next. "She was addicted to prescription painkillers for a long time. I'm sure any judge would give me custody. Helene was excited about the opportunity to raise my kids."

He wouldn't "harm" Margaret, but he'd take her kids away.

Might as well kill her.

I remembered Margaret asking me to keep quiet on Alan's access to drugs. Now that I knew she had an addiction, this made sense.

I stood.

He stood with me, his face lined with sadness. "I need to know what happened to Helene. Do you have any additional information?"

I was furious. He was a cheat. Had practically destroyed his poor wife and was colluding to steal the kids from her. The entire thing made me feel sick to my stomach and I didn't want to help him in any way.

And Helene?

What kind of person had an affair with her best friend's husband and schemed to take her kids?

I shook my head. "You'll have to speak with the homicide cops. Inspector McNearny is assigned."

He nodded as I stepped to the door.

"Doctor, one last question. Can you tell me where you were on Tuesday the fifteenth?"

His eyes narrowed. "Here. I had appointments all day."

•CHAPTER TWENTY-NINE•

Praying

I dialed Margaret from my car. I left her a bit of a panicked voice mail announcing that if she didn't call me back shortly, I was driving to her parents' house to find her.

I hung up and dialed Jim. "Is everything okay with you and Laurie? I want to follow a lead."

"What lead?" Jim asked.

I explained to him my increasing concern about Margaret. He assured me that he could manage Laurie but made me promise to phone the police at the first sign of any trouble.

Margaret's folks lived in Palo Alto, a short drive out of San Francisco. Night was falling quickly and I noticed the full moon rising. The sky turned orange and pink as the sun set on another day. I ran through my to-do list in my mind. Thanksgiving was fast approaching and I still needed to make a lot of preparations, starting with a detailed honey-do list for Jim.

I arrived at the address Alan had jotted down for me and parked my car at the curb near a large Dumpster. It didn't appear as if anyone was home. There were no cars in the driveway or lights on in the house.

Maybe the cars were parked in the garage and everyone could be at the back of the house for all I knew. I walked up the jasmine-lined walkway. Only moonlight illuminated the path but I could identify the flowers by their sweet scent. It was the same scent as Laurie's shampoo and it made me miss her terribly.

What was I doing here instead of home with her and Jim?

I waved my arms around hoping to trigger an automatic eye on the walkway light. Nothing came on. On the front porch was a tricycle with a baseball in the basket.

In the corner of the porch, I noticed a few shards of glass glinting in the moonlight. The glass from a small window on the front door was missing. It appeared someone had broken the window and made an attempt at cleaning up. Only they'd missed a few pieces.

I rang the bell and waited.

Please, Margaret, open the door.

Where could she be? And why wasn't she retuning my calls? If she was fine, where was she now? She had two small children—where were they? And what about her parents? It was a cold Tuesday night, not like there was much partying going on.

I wrapped my jacket around myself tighter and rang the bell again, leaning on it so a continuous ring sounded.

I contemplated calling McNearny. But what would I say? I think my client is missing?

What about the shards of glass and the broken window?

Had someone broken in?

Could I reach inside the door and unlock it? Then what?

No.

The last time I'd gone into someone's house who wasn't answering the door, I'd found her dead. And that had resulted in a downtown interrogation and countless nightmares.

I released the doorbell and headed down the walkway away from the house. Maybe I could see something from the street. I walked passed the Dumpster and stood next to my car.

What was a Dumpster doing in this high-end neighborhood?

Maybe they were moving.

An uneasy feeling settled into my stomach—all my defenses on alert. Images of Margaret's twisted and ravaged body surrounded by garbage filled my mind.

No! Kate, come on, don't lose it.

She is *not* in the Dumpster!

A crackling sound emanated from some nearby bushes.

A mouse?

A squirrel?

A murderer hiding out?

I swallowed past the fear that was building inside me. Why had I come here alone? I should call McNearny, just dial him now. Who cared if I looked like a fool?

Instead, I pressed my car keychain's automatic horn alarm. The car lights went on and the horn blasted alternately. With all the noise, I couldn't tell if the scurrying crackling sounds from the bushes had ceased. I pressed the alarm button again to stop it.

The bushes were silent.

But what did that prove? If someone was hiding out, wouldn't they be quiet now that I'd just blasted my horn?

Suddenly a light went on in the house.

Someone was inside.

I rushed up the walkway away from the bushes.

Wait.

What if it was an intruder?

I froze.

Maybe I should get into my car and call the police.

Nervous and not sure what to do, I spun around on my heel as the front door swung open and the porch light flooded the stoop. Margaret stood before me, her hair a tangled mess. She wore an oversized white button-down oxford shirt and black and white pants in what can only be described as a cow pattern. Nevertheless, probably because she was tall and thin, the ridiculous pants seemed to work on her.

"Kate! Oh! I didn't realize it was you. I thought maybe it was Alan and I didn't want to get the door. Then I heard the car alarm . . . is everything all right?"

I was standing with both hands clasped over my wildly beating heart, fearing it might pop out of my chest as in a silly cartoon. "Margaret! Thank God you're okay! Why haven't you returned my calls?"

"Come in." She stepped aside and let me enter the enormous family room.

The room was dark with a cathedral-style ceiling, exposed beams, and glossy hardwood floors. Margaret turned on a small side table lamp. The décor was casual with a wide-screen television that hung from the main wall and some bean bag chairs thrown across the floor.

She motioned for me to take a seat in a brown leather wing-back chair that faced the bean bags.

"Have you been calling me?" she asked. "I thought I left you a voice mail on . . . oh, the other day . . . when was it?" She scratched her head. "I don't know. Sorry, I've been kind of out of it. Have you learned anything?" she asked.

I semicollapsed into the chair, hoping my heart would slow down. "Margaret, what happened to the window? I was worried sick about you!"

She glanced at the front door. "Oh. My two-year-old threw his baseball into it."

Well, at least that was one mystery solved.

I leaned forward in my chair. "Can you tell me where you were on the fifteenth?"

She sank into one of the bean bags. "What?"

"Last Tuesday the fifteenth. Do you remember? That was the day Celia and I ended up in the hospital. Can you tell me where you were?' "

"I'm sorry I didn't visit you." She folded her skinny spider legs under her. "So much is going on here. My mom took the boys to dinner at Chuck E. Cheese tonight, just to give me a little breathing room. Since leaving Alan, I've been . . ." She waved her hand around and appeared distracted.

I must have woken her. She seemed out of it. That or . . .

Was she using again?

"Did you go to Bruce's house that day?"

"No." She looked thoughtful as she ran her hands through her hair, trying to smooth over the tangles. "I don't think so. The fifteenth was the day I left Alan. It's the day I came here."

"Can you retrace your steps for me?"

"I think so, why?"

"It's important. Please."

She scratched at the nape of her neck, then smoothed down her hair. "Let's see. I went grocery shopping. The nanny came to watch the boys and help me pack. Then I came here."

"Did you see Celia that day?"

Margaret's expression changed.

My heart dropped.

She sat a little straighter. "I did see Celia, as a matter of fact. I saw her at the little sandwich shop near my house."

Darn!

I had been hoping that Margaret would have been nowhere near Celia. Now she'd had access to both Celia and Helene. Although since she had so readily admitted seeing Celia, she could hardly be guilty, could she?

"Celia was with Howard," Margaret continued. "You know Sara's husband, right? I thought it was strange—them being together, but I remembered she hired him to do the midwife center. So they were probably having a follow-up meeting."

I covered my mouth with my hand.

Could Howard be the married man?

Did Miss No-Nonsense know about or suspect his infidelity? I recalled her outrage about Alan cheating on Margaret and her outspoken opinion that Margaret should leave the "two-timer." I wondered how she would feel now that the shoe might be on the other foot.

"Margaret, that day outside your house I told you I was going to speak with Sara, and well, it might have just been me, but it seemed like you didn't want me to talk to her."

She sighed. "I figured you were going to ask her if she knew about Alan's infidelity and . . ." She shrugged. "I guess I was embarrassed. You know airing dirty laundry in front of the neighbors."

I glanced at my watch. "When are you expecting your mom?"

I dreaded telling her about Alan's affair with Helene and wanted to be sure that I didn't leave her alone and vulnerable to taking anything. I wanted to be sure someone would be with her before I left.

Margaret glanced at a handsome cuckoo clock standing in the corner. "Maybe in about fifteen minutes, why?"

"You were right. Alan was having an affair."

Margaret nodded, her eyes welling with tears. "I knew it. I knew it." She bit her fist and her eyes glazed over.

I waited for her to look at me. When she seemed to have collected herself, I continued, "Margaret, this is going to be difficult to hear but I found out he was seeing Helene."

Her mouth opened and closed. One leg shot straight out as if she wanted to get up then she seemed to rethink it and fell back deeper into the bean bag. "What? No, no! That can't be right! Why would you say such a thing?"

"I heard it straight from Alan. He told me he and Helene were going to move away together. She was canceling plans for her home extension."

"He was going to leave me? They were going to move away together?"

I couldn't bring myself to tell her about their plans to get custody of her children. What did it matter now anyway? She'd been through enough.

Instead, I said softly, "That's what he said."

Margaret wept silently.

I listened to the ticking of the cuckoo clock.

After a moment she wiped her eyes and said, "Helene never . . . why? How could she do that to me, Kate? How could he do that?"

The weight of the betrayal was stifling the room.

"I also was able to confirm that Helene was indeed poisoned," I said.

Margaret sat straight up. "Alan did poison her? But why?"

"I don't think Alan did it. No. I don't think it was Alan," I said.

Margaret searched my eyes. "Who else then? Was it Bruce? Did he know about the affair? I feel so stupid. Was I the only one buffaloed?"

I was silent. A car drove by, filling the room momentarily with light. As the car passed, the room was covered in dark shadows again, lit only by the table lamp beside me.

"Do you think Bruce killed Helene?" she pressed.

I opened my palms to her, inviting her theory.

"Why would he kill her?" Margaret asked. "He was barely home—practically never even noticed her. Was it pride?" She rose off the bean bag and started pacing. "Let me guess: Killing her was a cheaper solution than divorce. She would get half of everything and my husband, too."

She stopped pacing and stood before me. "Why did she do it, Kate? She could have had anyone. She was pretty and desirable and unattached—well, I mean, relatively. I know she was married but they didn't have any kids. She could have just started over with someone else.

Someone who wanted kids. Why did she have to take *my* husband?"

"You think Bruce didn't want kids?" I asked.

Margaret nodded. "Well, I don't know but Helene wanted them so much and he just didn't seem to be interested."

"What about the adoption then?"

Margaret frowned. "What adoption?"

"Celia was helping Helene and Bruce coordinate an adoption from Costa Rica."

Margaret's face went blank. "She was? Helene wanted to adopt? I never knew—she never said anything to me. I guess she was full of surprises . . ." Margaret's lips puckered with bitterness. "She never said a word."

I watched Margaret carefully, not even certain what I was looking for.

She seemed very emotional and was continually wiping her eyes and nose with the back of her hand.

Could she have known about the affair all along?

How could she not know her best friend was sleeping with her husband? What if she had killed Helene out of retaliation and all this pacing around was just an act?

She was standing directly in front of me—practically on top of me. I realized my shoulders were hiked up to my ears.

Was I expecting her to pounce on me?

I forced my shoulders down and stood, reclaiming my personal space. Margaret took a step back.

She lumbered over to the other wing-back chair and rearranged it to face mine.

I seated myself again and crossed my hands in my lap, trying to look professional and unimposing. She was my client, after all.

After a moment, I said, "These are the facts as I understand them. Helene was poisoned with fentanyl and died on the dinner cruise. Celia was given the same drug. It's used for extreme chronic pain. It's a class II narcotic. Do you know anything about this medicine?"

She shook her head.

I watched her eyes. She didn't fidget or glance around the room. She just stared at me straight on. She didn't look nervous in the least, only sad.

Finally, I said, "It's mostly prescribed to terminally ill cancer patients."

She nodded her understanding.

"Do you know anyone who could have been on fentanyl recently?"

She turned her lips down and shook her head.

"We were all on the cruise, so everyone—you, me, Sara, Evelyn, and our husbands—had access to Helene, including her own husband, Bruce. But only a few people saw Celia on the day she was poisoned—you, me, Bruce, and Evelyn."

Margaret's eyes shifted almost imperceptibly. "What about Alan?"

"No. Not that I know of. He says he was at the office all day. So he didn't have any contact with Celia and also he requested the toxicology screen for Helene from the medical examiner. If he had poisoned her, he wouldn't have pushed for that."

Margaret crossed her legs, leaned back into the chair, and contemplated what I'd said. "I was so sure he had done something with those drinks."

We sat in silence.

"So you say that leaves us with who? Evelyn and Bruce?"

And you!

I watched her nervously swing her foot forward and back, but said nothing.

"Evelyn or Bruce, huh?" she repeated. "It's got to be Bruce. Evelyn had no reason to kill Helene. I mean, I know she was a little bitter about being kicked out of the group, but that's no reason . . . she can't be that petty, right?"

"No. That kind of motive doesn't make sense," I said. "And what about Celia? Why would Evelyn try to poison her own midwife?"

Margaret nodded.

"I understand Bruce may have had access to the fentanyl. His grandmother passed away recently from cancer."

Margaret dipped her head.

"Margaret, did you used to be addicted to pain meds?" I asked.

Her head shot up. "Who told you that?"

"Alan," I admitted.

She jumped out of the chair. "That no good . . . what else did he tell you?"

I shrugged.

She began to pace again. "So that's it, huh? You think I killed her because I'm a recovered addict. I'm recovered, Kate. Recovered."

She stormed out of the room, leaving me sitting in the chair waiting for her. She returned a few minutes later holding a frame that she clutched to her chest.

"I'm sorry for flipping out on you," she said.

I nodded.

"Five years ago, before the kids, I broke my foot skiing. I got addicted to pain meds then. It didn't last very long. About six months, but Alan never let me forget. I've been reflecting on our marriage these last few days here at my mom's. I think back to that time and I think he purposely wanted to get me addicted. It gave him control over me and our life."

She handed me the frame. It was a picture of Margaret, Alan, and a small boy. They were on the beach and Margaret was just starting to show with her second baby.

"This photo was taken less than a year ago. It was our first family vacation. Miami, the same day I met Celia. Look at how ridiculously happy I was. I've been crying myself to sleep hugging that photo every single night since Helene passed away. But no matter how hard I cry, I can't get back to that happy place."

"I'm sorry," I said.

A car pulled up into the driveway. Presumably, it was Margaret's mom back with the kids. I hadn't wanted to leave Margaret alone feeling sad and vulnerable so I was glad to see the car park.

"I should thank you, Kate. A job well done. You got the information I requested. It wasn't what I hoped for but . . ." She rose. "Let me write you a check. We'll call the case closed."

"Don't you want to know who killed Helene?"

Margaret shrugged, her body listless. "What does it matter now? I guess we'll let the cops handle that."

When I got home, all the lights were out. Jim was asleep on the couch with Laurie in his arms. Laurie had her little hands folded on her chest. She looked like a miniature version of a praying monk. I gently picked her up out of Jim's arms. They sighed in unison.

I clutched Laurie to me and kissed her soft cheeks a dozen times. She remained asleep so I set her down in her bassinet and squeezed onto the coach next to Jim.

Still sleeping, he rolled onto his side to make room for me. I kissed his lips. "I love you."

"Glad you're home safe, honey," he murmured. "Laurie and I were waiting up for you . . ."

I smiled. "I see that."

I hugged him. I was sad after leaving Margaret. Her marriage was over and I suspected Sara's was in distress, not to mention that obviously Bruce and Helene's life together had been less than perfect and now she was dead. I felt so fortunate to have my family intact. Tears filled my eyes and I pressed myself against Jim. "Love you forever," I whispered.

His soft sleepy breath filled my ear and the last thing I heard before falling asleep was "Love you, too, honey."

• CHAPTER THIRTY •

Rooting

To Do:

1. Thanksgiving Prep!!!
2. Order turkey.
3. Get pie recipe from Paula.
4. Stuffing? Check online.
5. Potatoes—same old boring mash?
6. Cranberries—canned or fresh?

I woke up with a stiff neck from sleeping too long on the couch with Jim. I hadn't remembered moving to the bedroom, but somehow Jim, Laurie, and I were all safely tucked in.

I stretched my neck and contemplated coffee. Laurie started moving her head from side to side. Rooting. I picked her up and played my favorite game. Kissing her cheek so when she automatically turned toward me, I turned my head and her mouth landed on my cheek. I did this over and over, pretending she was showering me with kisses.

Laurie didn't like the game this morning and let out a howl, telling me she meant serious business.

I squeezed her. "Love my little bunny girl!"

Laurie's cry escalated into a high-pitched wail.

"Okay, I know you want service."

I took her into the nursery, and after changing and feeding her, I put her up on my shoulder and rubbed her back, waiting for the inevitable burp. She was asleep again before I could even place her back into the bassinet.

I slipped on jeans and a sweatshirt, then scribbled a note to Jim. I headed to the café and tried to sort out my feelings.

Last night Margaret had effectively terminated me, but technically I was still working the case for "The Grizzly." I thought about my report to him. Now more than ever he would think Margaret was guilty or at least try and build a case against her—anything to steer attention away from Bruce.

With the toxicology results available now, I thought it was just a matter of time before McNearny arrested Bruce.

I pushed open the door to the café. Kenny was seated at a table near the counter, earphones securely in place and feet drumming out a rhythm.

"Kate! Got time for chess?" He pulled the earphones out and reached for the chess set that was on a nearby bookshelf.

I ordered a decaf latte and perused the pastry case.

How many calories did a biscotti have?

Ooh! They had chocolate-dipped ones today.

I ordered two and put one in a bag to take home to Jim.

I took a seat across from Kenny. "I don't have time for games, Kenny. I'm working on serious business."

"Cool," he said, ignoring me and setting up the board.

"Shouldn't you be rehearsing or something?"

He looked confused. "I was."

I laughed. "You were listening to your iPod drinking a cappuccino. How does that count for rehearsal?"

He looked offended. "No, no. Not just listening. I was visualizing playing!" He continued to set up the chessboard as the barista brought my coffee.

"Yeah? You can visualize yourself playing chess, too, because I just told you I have serious work I need to do." I dipped my biscotti into the latte and ate it.

Kenny nodded thoughtfully as he completed setting up the board. "Okay. On your investigation stuff?"

I nodded.

He pushed the chessboard to me. "Tell me about it."

"Okay." I picked up the white queen, rook, bishop, knight, and a pawn, then selected the counterpieces in black. I grabbed the pair of pawns. "So, Jim and I go on this cruise—"

"Wait. Are you guys the pawns?"

"Yeah." I sipped my latte.

Kenny shook his head. "No, no. Here." He replaced the pawns with the king and queen. "There. You and Jim."

I laughed. "No seriously. I was a pawn."

"Never!"

"Right, I'm not going to argue with you, let's make them all pawns. Except for the victim. We'll give her the respect of being queen."

I laid Queen Helene down.

Kenny made a sad face by sticking his lower lip out and turning it down. "You killed off the best piece right away. I told you, you should be queen."

"This is serious, Kenny."

He sat up. "Right."

I took the matching king representing Bruce and placed him next to Queen Helene. "Husband," I said.

Kenny nodded and frowned, trying to give the respect I was requiring of him.

Then I lined up the four sets of pawns. "These are the couples on the cruise." Then I took the other queen and placed her precariously on the edge of the board. "She'll be Celia, the midwife. She wasn't on the cruise but had an attempt made on her life."

"The price of royalty," Kenny said.

I glared at him. He ducked his head and drank his cappuccino. I sipped from my latte.

Yum.

But it needed a little extra something. I pulled out the second biscotti that I'd been saving for Jim, dipped it in the latte, and ate it.

Much more yummy.

I took one pawn representing Alan and placed him next to Queen Helene. "Affair."

Kenny nodded. "Affair equals motive, right?" He raised his eyebrows and wiggled them up and down to demonstrate how clever he was.

"Not in this case. Long story—just take my word for it."

I replayed the drama as best I could with the chess pieces. Kenny seemed to be following along nicely and it was helping me to review all the facts I knew. I ended by lining up the pieces that had seen Celia on the day she was poisoned. Me, Margaret, Evelyn, and Bruce.

Kenny studied the layout then took the pawn representing Howard and placed it in my lineup.

"What are you doing?" I asked.

"You said Margaret saw them together at the sandwich place."

I froze.

Suddenly the drama before me changed. If Celia was having an affair with Howard, we had a motive for him . . .

No. Not Howard.

Why would he kill his mistress, or Helene for that matter?

Sara.

A motive for Sara, Miss No-Nonsense. What if Sara had known Howard was having an affair but didn't know with whom? Let's say she suspected Helene. Certainly Helene could have been acting suspicious because she *was* having an affair, only not with Howard.

Sara had been on the cruise. They'd had a fight. The wet dress, the spilled drink, it was all starting to add up.

Had she seen Celia that day?

Celia hadn't mentioned seeing Howard or Margaret to me; maybe because she'd been covering up her affair. Had she seen Sara, too, and just not told me?

I stood. "I gotta go. I need to talk to Sara."

Kenny grabbed the chess pieces and threw them into the box. "My work here is done," he said proudly. He popped up and joined me on the walk home.

We said good-bye to each other as we approached our houses. I let myself inside and found Jim in his underwear watching the morning news with Laurie secured in the crook of his arm. I took Laurie from him and nuzzled her. She fixed her blue eyes on me and cooed.

"Did you get me anything?" Jim asked hopefully.

"Uh . . . yeah, I did."

Jim smiled.

"But I ate it."

He laughed. "Look." He indicated the television. "There's a huge protest downtown," he said. "Tons of arrests."

"Since you're not dressed, does that mean you're staying home today? No meetings?"

Jim nodded. "Yeah. It's crazy out there. I'm staying here with my little sasquatch and her mommy."

"I need to run an errand. I want to follow up with Miss No-Nonsense, see where she was on the fifteenth."

Jim's brows furrowed. "All right, but be careful."

"Should I stop on the way and order the turkey?"

Jim smiled. "I'm a step ahead of you. I already preordered it online."

I sat outside Sara's house and contemplated my strategy.

Could I come right out and ask her about Howard?

How sure was I that Celia and he were having an affair? If they weren't and Sara was completely innocent, I'd be sticking my nose where it didn't belong. On the other hand, Celia was still alive. If Sara was plotting something, better to be safe than sorry.

I rang Sara's doorbell. She opened the door and squinted at me.

"Oh, I wasn't expecting you." She had on a bright orange T-shirt and jeans with paint splotches across the front. She stood in the doorway and kept me on the stoop.

"Sorry I didn't call first. Do you have a minute?"

She glanced behind her, into what I knew was the living room. "Just one. Go ahead."

I imagined baby Amanda at her huge play station, flailing around.

"Uh. Yeah. Okay."

Why wasn't she letting me inside the house?

Why was Miss No-Nonsense dressed in a dirty old T-shirt?

"Sara, can you tell me where you were on November fifteenth? Did you happen to see Celia Martin that day?"

I waited for her reaction to Celia's name, but she simply scratched at her chin. "Was that last week? What day? Who's Celia?"

"It was a Tuesday. Celia is a midwife. She did Margaret's birth and now she's helping Evelyn . . ."

Sara scrunched her nose in distaste at the mention of Evelyn's name. "Oh. Yeah. The midwife."

"I understand Howard was the general contractor that remodeled the birthing center."

She frowned and blinked rapidly a few times. "Oh . . . uh . . . uh-huh."

She hadn't known.

Her husband had taken the job on the side and hadn't told her. Even Margaret knew about the job. I guess the mommy group wasn't as close as they had pretended. Venom, lies, and betrayal all around.

Sara composed herself and asked, "How can I help you?"

"Where were you on the fifteenth, Sara? Did you see Celia?"

"No. Why are you asking?"

"Someone poisoned her with the same drug that killed Helene."

Sara swallowed and appeared frozen. "Is she all right?"

She didn't seem to know anything.

I nodded. "Can you tell me where you were on Tuesday morning?"

"Tuesdays are Amanda's swim class. We were at La Petite Grenouille."

That would be easy to check.

I rapped on the doorframe. "Okay. Thank you for your time."

I proceed down the walkway toward my car. As I got in, I noticed she was watching me from the window.

Strange, but was she guilty?

•CHAPTER THIRTY-ONE•

Swimming?

I stood at the front desk with Laurie in my arms and looked at the pools through the glass doors. There was a small wading pool and another larger pool complete with a covered yellow slide.

In the larger pool there seemed to be a toddler class going on. Only three children and one teenager with a bright pink swim cap on. The teenage instructor was assisting the kids to alternately swim through a tunnel. The children were swimming remarkably well given their age and looked adorable with tiny flippers on their feet.

In the wading pool were several moms holding their infants in their arms. They were following the instructions of another teenager, this one with auburn-colored hair. All the moms would hold the infants up in the air and duck them in the water at the same time.

I couldn't hear anything through the glass doors, but

every time the babies resurfaced, their mouths were shaped into giant O's and I'm fairly certain they were screaming their little hearts out.

What about this was supposed to be good for them?

I turned Laurie toward the baby pool. "Does that look fun to you? Do you want to do that?"

Laurie pedaled her little feet.

"Is that a yes?"

From the changing area a slim instructor with wet hair that was pulled back in a ponytail approached us.

"Are you here for the free trial class?" she asked.

"Actually, no." I hesitated. "I . . . uh . . . I wanted to sign up." I smiled.

She frowned and stepped toward the desk. "Are you on the wait list? Did we call you with an opening?" She flipped through a huge black book that was by the phone.

I eyed the book.

Did they mark the attendance there?

"No. I thought I'd just sign up."

She frowned. "You thought you would . . . right." She closed the book with a loud thud. "Why don't you give me your name? Our wait list is quite long. We'll call you if any classes are added."

Still looking at the book, I said, "Right. Or, you know, if anyone drops out or—"

"Our students don't generally *drop out*. Yes, there is the occasional one that moves or has, say, perhaps a medical issue, but frankly speaking, there's not a lot of movement is the existing classes."

I nodded.

"How old is your daughter?" she asked.

"She's two months."

"It's a shame you didn't sign up earlier. We have a mommy and me starting next week." She glanced thoughtfully at the pool. "Have you had a tour?"

I shook my head. "No, but—"

She moved away from the desk. "Come along then."

She led me to the glass doors separating the reception area from the pools. I wished now that I'd brought Paula or Mom along. They would be able to snoop through the book while Laurie and I toured the facility.

As the instructor pushed open the door, the smell of chlorine hit me. I inhaled deeply; somehow the smell made me want to dive in.

I've never considered myself a swimmer, but why should my limitations become Laurie's? Maybe lessons would be good for her.

The instructor told me how the water temperature of both pools was reminiscent of the womb, then recounted the benefits of swimming. By the time she was done, I really wanted a spot in the class.

Odd. I hadn't thought about swimming in such a long time and now in the middle of November it seemed the thing to do.

She led me to the changing rooms. There was an open shower area and several bathroom stalls. Additionally, portable cribs and playpens were set up and scattered throughout the room. The mommy and me class had just finished and two moms holding their towel-wrapped babies followed us into the area.

One mom put her baby into a crib and rummaged around a locker for shampoo. The other mom simply turned on the shower and ducked herself and her baby under it.

My cell phone rang from the depths of my diaper purse.

"I'll let you get that," the instructor said, leaving the room.

I looked around for a dry place to put Laurie and settled on the crib next to the one with the other infant.

As I dug around for my cell phone, one mom said to the other, "So, when do you guys leave for Germany?"

They carried on their conversation as I answered my phone. I didn't catch it in time but read Gary's office number on the caller ID in the missed call window. I waited for the voice mail beep and listened to the message as soon as it came through. It was his secretary looking for my status report.

Darn. I'd have to go home and send him something quick.

As I put away my phone, I heard the mom showering say, "Thank God we're traveling now. Did you know the airline makes you pay for an extra seat if your baby is over two?"

I picked up Laurie and headed out to the reception area. The desk was empty. I looked around, certainly there were still people in the pool area, but the instructor who had given me the tour was nowhere in sight.

"Don't tell anyone," I whispered to Laurie.

I circled around the desk and flipped the book open. I saw where the woman had added my name to the wait list.

Number 187!

Jeez, this place was in demand.

I quickly turned the pages of the book. A computer printout of class rosters was stapled into the pages. I found the Tuesday 10 A.M. class and baby Amanda's name.

There was a neat row of little checkmarks in each graph box representing all the Tuesdays in the past three months.

Perfect attendance.

Miss No-Nonsense and her little sprout had been here at La Petite Grenouille on the morning Celia was poisoned.

I looked up from the book and jumped to find the instructor standing in front of the desk, glaring at me.

"What do you think you're doing!" she demanded.

Shoot!

"Uh. Nothing . . ."

"Are you trying to put your name at the top of the wait list!?"

"What? No! I . . ."

She crossed to behind the desk and advanced on me, causing me to back away from the book. Laurie let out a little whimper.

The woman harrumphed and opened the book to the wait list page. She studied it a moment, then took a pencil from a cup on the desk and erased Laurie's name from the last line.

"Hey! You can't do that!" I said.

"Oh? Can't I?" she asked, pushing the eraser debris from the book with a smug look.

I was blowing Laurie's chance at swim lessons at the premier spot in San Francisco!

"Just because I was snooping a little . . ."

She motioned to the front door. "Thank you for coming by, Mrs. Connolly."

I arrived home in a funk. Jim was online searching for recipes on turkey brines.

"I got Laurie boxed out of swim classes."

"Hmmm. Do you think this one sounds good?" He handed me a printout as I passed Laurie to him.

"I'll have to leave the turkey brining overnight," Jim continued. "Maybe I can use the ice chest again?"

"The hag at the front desk erased our name off the list."

"What hag?"

"I'm telling you. No swim classes for Laurie. We were axed."

Jim looked surprised. "What does she need swim classes for? She's barely awake for five minutes at a time."

"Well, you know, by the time she's ready, we won't be able to take her there. They have a long wait list and now we're not even on it."

"Where?"

"The little frog swim place."

Jim frowned. "Uh-huh. Okay, Kate, do you need to lie down or something?"

"I don't want her to drown."

"I'll teach her how to swim," Jim said.

I sat at the computer as Jim took Laurie into the kitchen to inventory ingredients needed for the brine.

I e-mailed Gary, filling him in on my suspicions about Celia's affair with Howard, and informing him about Sara's alibi. I kept my meeting with Margaret out of the report. At this point she was probably the strongest suspect outside of Bruce, and I feared Gary would use that as leverage.

Was it really appropriate to leave it out? After all, I didn't have any control over who was guilty. I really just wanted justice.

I checked my news update feed. The riots downtown were escalating and hundreds of arrests had been made. Before I logged off, I refreshed my e-mail. A response from Gary had arrived in my inbox.

Kate,

Tail Celia, see if she leads you to Howard. Maybe he's our guy.

G

I sat outside Celia's center in Kenny's van. Jim had agreed to watch Laurie for the afternoon and I was determined to find out one way or another if Celia was seeing Howard.

To kill time, I dialed Paula and recounted for her the swimming story. She was much more sympathetic to Laurie's being blacklisted than Jim had been.

"Where are you now?" she asked.

"Outside the midwife center waiting for her to lead me to her lover, Howard."

Paula laughed.

"What?"

"Is that guy, Howard, attractive?"

"Sort of. Irish guy, light-colored eyes, good bod, you know, construction and all. Why?"

"I guess I imagine her with a sexy Latin guy, like a 'José,' not a 'Howard,' but that's probably because she's Latin and from Miami."

"She's not from Miami, she's from L.A."

"Really? She told me she was from Miami," Paula said.

Suddenly I recalled Margaret telling me that she met Celia in Miami, the same day the photo was taken of her family on the beach.

Why would Celia tell me she was from L.A.? Why lie? Or had it been inadvertent? Lots of people in the Bay Area were transplants, and when asked from where, they didn't give a laundry list of all the places they'd ever lived.

That was probably it. She'd lived in L.A. before or after Miami, no matter.

Miami?

Why did that stick out in my mind?

I recalled the news item I'd read on Google, the missing expectant mom on her way to a midwife . . . in Miami.

"Paula, I need you to look something up for me."

I gave her as much search criteria as I could to find the news story, then hung up, but before I released my phone, it rang.

"Kate! It's Kenny, guess what?"

He sounded as though he'd won the lottery.

"The Opera called. The principal trombonist is sick. I get my chance to perform tonight!"

"That's fantastic!" I said.

"I need my van. I'm sorry. I would take the streetcar, but all my gear is in the van."

That would blow my stakeout.

"Oh. Hey, I have an idea," I said. "Why don't you go over to my place and get my keys from Jim. You can drive out here in my car and we'll swap."

"That works!" Kenny said cheerfully, ringing off.

The San Francisco Opera.

I was proud of him. He deserved it. What a good kid!

I imagined Laurie all grown up and playing in the San Francisco Opera.

What instrument would she play? Maybe the violin?

She did have long fingers. Perhaps the piano.

I put my cell phone away in my diaper purse and rummaged past Laurie's puppy for a piece of gum. For fun I pressed the puppy's ear and listened to Laurie's recorded coos. I listened to the playback about a dozen times.

What in the world was I doing here?

This was ridiculous. I should be home with munchkin and Daddy.

A blue car turned the corner and rolled down the street past me. I strained to get a look at the driver. I watched in the rearview mirror as the car pulled up to the center doors. I was parked down the street, hoping I was far enough to be tucked out of view.

The center doors opened and Celia rushed out to the car.

Could it be Howard?

Come on, come on. I need a break here!

Celia helped the driver out. It was Evelyn! She was hunched over. Celia held her as she rocked back and forth.

Oh my gosh! Evelyn was in labor. She was going to have her baby!

After a few moments Evelyn stood straight up. Celia helped her to the center and looked down the block.

Had she seen the van?

Oh, well. Not like she'd be running off to see Howard now. May as well head home and knock some items off my to-do list.

Wait, Kenny was on his way here. I grabbed my phone to see if I could reach him. If I could catch him before he left, then I wouldn't be stuck here waiting for him.

I dug around my bag for my phone. I dialed Kenny but got his voice mail. I started to text him when I heard a car start.

I looked in my rearview mirror and saw Evelyn's car zooming toward me. Celia was driving.

Wait.

Where was she going in Evelyn's car? What about Evelyn in labor? Maybe Celia was simply reparking the car.

I studied the spot where the car had been. It looked like a legal spot.

My phone rang in my hand. I glanced at the caller ID. Paula.

"Did you find anything?"

"I did!" She was breathless. "I found the story, and then I called the paper and spoke to the writer. She was able to look up the midwife's name for me. Get this. Cecelia Martinez."

• CHAPTER THIRTY-TWO •

Labor

Cecelia Martinez?

What did this mean? I knew her as Celia Martin—certainly that was an alias . . . or was it all a coincidence?

Wait! When I had been at the hospital, the nurse had called her Martinez. Yes! She'd said that.

"Kate. What do you know about that adoption she was arranging?" Paula asked.

My throat felt thick. It was difficult to breathe. "No. They can't be related. The story in Miami is more than a couple years old, right? Bruce and Helene were going to adopt a newborn, Celia's cousin's baby. I saw Helene's plane ticket from SFO to Costa Rica. There were notes about traveling with an infant."

I recalled the moms at La Petite Grenouille this afternoon discussing plane travel. Children over two years old needed their own ticket.

"Wait. What did you say?" Paula asked. "Did you say SFO to Costa Rica?"

"Yeah."

"Why would she be traveling with an infant from SFO? Wouldn't she be traveling there solo and then flying *back* with the baby?"

I needed air. I cracked open the window and felt a breeze hit my face.

"Oh my God! They were going to steal a baby. Celia and Helene were going to steal a baby. I'm sure of it. Only maybe Helene had changed her mind. She canceled the construction plans and was going to leave Bruce. She was going to live with Alan and fight for custody of his children. It's all making sense now!"

Celia was driving Evelyn's car away to hide it. Make it look like Evelyn had never arrived.

Evelyn. Her baby! I had to get to her.

I started the engine and drove down the street to the front of the birthing center. One tire popped the curb but I didn't care, I slammed the transmission into park.

"But you said Celia wasn't on the cruise!" Paula said.

I swung the van door open and reflexively put the strap of the diaper bag on my shoulder. "She wasn't."

"Then she couldn't have slipped something in Helene's drink if she wasn't even there. And then what about poisoning herself? I mean, do you think that was a suicide attempt—"

"No! Her dose wasn't lethal. Galigani told me that—"

Suddenly a hand reached into the van and gripped my hair. So fierce was the grip that it literally launched me out of my seat. My cell phone fell out of my hand. I gripped my bag to me and screamed, "Paula! Call 9-1-1."

A kick found its way to my ribs and I doubled over in excruciating pain.

Had she heard me?

Would Paula call 9-1-1 or would she think the call had simply dropped?

My assaulter screamed, "What the hell do you think you're doing parked in front of my center?"

Celia!

Images of the riots on TV flashed in my mind. All of SFPD would be downtown. Was there anyone available to respond to a 9-1-1 call?

Celia's knee crashed into my face and she seemed to be pushing me back or was I retreating?

Laurie's face filled my mind and I swung the diaper bag as hard as I could into Celia's side. She blocked my blow, grabbing the bag out of my hands and pushing me into the birthing center. I landed on the cool marble floor, out of breath and in pain. She threw the bag at me.

Kenny!

Kenny was on his way!

Out of the corner of my eye I saw Celia's leg move back, gaining momentum for another kick. I rolled out of the way. Her miss only served to infuriate her further; she came at me and drew her leg back for another swipe. This time I was ready. As her leg swung forward, I grabbed it and pulled her off balance.

She struck the floor hard and I scrambled to my feet.

Could I make it out the door and back to the van?

Celia screamed and pushed herself up as I sprinted toward the door. She hurled herself at me, yelling obscenities.

When would Kenny be here?

Fifteen minutes at least. My cell phone was on the street. I had no backup. No weapon, no nothing.

Celia was punching at me and I was scrambling as best as I could to get out of her way.

"The cops are on their way," I bluffed.

"Liar!" she screamed, knocking into me and throwing me off balance. "You're going to ruin everything!"

I fell to the floor. This time she came with me, landing on top of me hard and knocking the wind out of me.

She put her knee between my shoulder blades and pinned my arms behind my hand. "You should have stayed out of it," she said.

Adrenaline shot through me and suddenly I was so furious that I wrung my arms out of her grip and launched myself to my feet. She fell back, momentarily stunned.

Fury boiled up inside me and I flung myself down on her—wrestler style— screaming, "You killed that woman in Miami and took her baby. You sold her baby! You killed her and sold her baby!"

Celia pushed at me repeatedly. "Shut up! Shut up! Shut up!"

"That's how you got the money for this remodel!"

She shoved me into the reception console. A packet that had been on top of the counter went flying. My eyes followed it as it landed on the floor. Patches. It was a bunch of medicine patches.

Her face contorted. "And I'm going to kill you!" she spat. "Just like I killed her!" She dove for the package.

The patches.

The drug had been on the nicotine patches. It had never been in a drink. Celia hadn't needed to be present in order to poison Helene!

Animal instinct overtook me. I pressed against the counter

and propelled myself forward through the air, landing on top of her. I pounded my fist into her face. Blood poured from her nose.

"You broke my nose!" she screamed.

My face was wet and I realized I was crying. "You were following me the other day! Your yellow VW bug. You almost crashed into me!"

My hand stung and my body ached, but I wasn't weeping from the physical pain. I was weeping for fear of my life and grief for the lives lost at the hands of this woman.

Celia twisted to the side and knocked me off her. She scrambled to reach the patches.

I reached the packet before her. "You killed Helene with the patches and you tried to pin it on Bruce by poisoning yourself!"

She slammed her elbow into my side. The packet flew out of my hands as I tried to defend myself against another onslaught.

Celia punched at my face screaming, "You're damn right I killed her. She was backing out. First she wanted Evelyn's baby then she didn't."

Evelyn!

She punched at me again, this time landing a blow to the side of my head.

My vision blurred.

"After all I went through to get things arranged for her," Celia spat. "Then she falls in love with that stupid foot doc—wants his kids instead. And what? I'm supposed to be left high and dry? No. Plenty of buyers for that baby. And like I'm going to let her turn me in?"

She pushed at me. I blocked her.

I heard a voice coming from the birth room.

I had to get to Evelyn. The woman in Miami had not lived to hold her baby. And now Evelyn and her baby's life were on the line.

Celia seemed to momentarily retreat, I struggled to my feet, looking down the hall for Evelyn. When I glanced back at Celia she was clutching the patches in her hand.

Blood streamed from her nose and her smirk both sickened and frightened me.

My eyes locked on the patches, my vision suddenly clear. She peeled one off and dangled it in front of me. "Helene was so addicted to cigarettes I knew she'd use the patches I gave her." She laughed. "Especially when I told her a proper mother couldn't smoke. She'd have done anything to be a good mom even if it meant stealing the kid."

Celia advanced on me, I stepped back.

"I never dreamed she'd use the patches on the night of the cruise. How perfect is that? With me nowhere near her." Her lips curled and she lunged at me. "But then you—"

I thrust my elbow out using her own momentum against her. She cried out as my elbow connected with her broken nose. She fell to her knees. A moan came from the birthing room. I ran down the passage way. Evelyn was lying on a bed in the birthing room, her head rolling from side to side, a ridiculous smile on her face.

"I'm so high," she said.

The first effects of fentanyl were like drinking a couple glasses of wine. Helene had seemed so drunk on the cruise; now I realized it had been the drug.

I rushed to Evelyn, but before I could reach her, Celia rammed her shoulder into my back. I stumbled and fell.

"You're going to die!" she said through her teeth. "You meddling—"

I got to my feet and used my position below her as leverage and head-butted her in the chin with as much force as I could muster.

Fortunately, I have a very hard head.

Hers snapped back and she lost her balance. She stumbled and fell. I heard the door to the center open and Kenny called out.

"Help!" I screamed as I dove toward Evelyn.

"Whoa, whoa," Evelyn kept repeating.

I pulled three patches off her arm.

How much had she absorbed already?

Kenny flew into the room and stopped short, his eyes bulging out of his head.

Poor kid, only seventeen. What did I expect?

Celia let out an ear-piercing scream and attacked me with new fury. Kenny pulled her off me and shoved her to the ground.

Sirens reverberated from down the block. Kenny and I tried to restrain Celia until the EMTs burst through the doors.

"In the back!" I screamed.

Kenny and I were trying to hold Celia down but she was punching and kicking at us with fury. We scrambled out of the way as one EMT grabbed and restrained her. The other EMT ran to Evelyn's side.

I rushed to the EMT by Evelyn. "She's in labor and she's been given fentanyl. This woman"—I pointed at Celia—"was trying to poison her and take her baby."

The EMT frowned, looking at me like I was crazy. He pulled out a stethoscope and placed it on Evelyn's chest.

"You have to get her to the hospital!" I cried.

The EMT continued to evaluate Evelyn.

I felt Kenny's hands on my arms. "Everything will be okay now, Kate."

"They have to pump her stomach!" I screamed.

"She's in active labor," the EMT said to his partner.

I glanced over to the EMT holding Celia. She'd composed herself in their presence, her face a cold hard mask.

She pulled away from the EMT. "I can deliver the baby."

"No!" I screamed. "Call Inspector McNearny! She's killed two people! Call Inspector—"

Evelyn let out a low moan.

Celia rushed to her side.

More sirens sounded from down the street.

The EMT said, "Her heart rate's too low. We're losing her."

More EMTs rushed in. Soon they had Evelyn on a stretcher and into an ambulance with Celia. Kenny and I were ushered to the other ambulance. When we made our way through the lobby of the center, I spotted my diaper bag strewn across the floor. I gathered up my items, including Laurie's purple puppy, which had fallen out.

I remembered that my cell phone was somewhere in the middle of the street. When I asked the EMT if I could go retrieve it, he gave me a look that would freeze over hell.

We were silent on the ride to the hospital. I was examined by a middle-aged physician, who told me my ribs were bruised where Celia had repeatedly kicked me. He taped them up for me and then I was left to wait with Kenny for Inspector McNearny or Jones in the waiting room.

Please, God, let then send Jones. Please send Jones!

My understanding was that Celia was having her nose set, and given my accusations, she would be held in a separate waiting room.

Suddenly my hand flew to Kenny's knee. "The Opera! Oh my God! What time do you have to be there?"

Kenny looked at the giant white clock on the wall and smiled. "Half an hour ago."

I grabbed his shoulders. "Kenny! I'm so sorry."

"It's okay, Kate. Helping you catch a murderer is much more exciting than—"

"Don't say it. You should be at the Opera right now. I'm so sorry I dragged you into this."

He waved me off. "Nah. This is a much cooler story for my friends."

We waited in silence. Kenny pulled out his phone and started texting. "Are you already bragging?" I asked.

He laughed.

I thought about Evelyn. We hadn't seen her since they'd rushed her out of the center. When I arrived at the hospital, I'd asked a nurse about her, but she'd been grim-faced and told me she didn't know the status of the mother or child.

I thought of Evelyn's little son, "the biter." Where was he tonight? Probably with his nanny. Poor little guy, he needed to have his mommy live.

Please God, let them be okay.

I dug into my diaper purse and pulled out Laurie's puppy. Her toothless grin flashed in my mind. I pressed the puppy's ear to hear her little coo.

Instead of Laurie's coo, my voice came out of the recorder:

"The cops are on their way."

My jaw dropped and I glanced at Kenny.

"Liar! You're going to ruin everything! You should have stayed out of it."

Kenny squeezed my arm.

"You killed that woman in Miami and took her baby. You sold her baby! You killed her and sold her baby!"

"Shut up! Shut up! Shut up!"

"That's how you got the money for this remodel!"

"And I'm going to kill you! Just like I killed her!"

Kenny jumped up. "You got her on tape! You got her on tape!"

The door to the waiting room swung open slightly and I could see Jones's cropped hair.

Yea! It was Jones! No McNearny!

Jones pushed the door open and walked into the room. The door swung closed behind him only to reopen as McNearny followed him into the room, a tired expression on his face. "Got who on tape?"

My hands were shaking as I replayed the tape for Jones and McNearny.

McNearny listened, a stoic expression on his face.

They took statements from Kenny and me and confiscated Laurie's little puppy.

"Any word on Evelyn and her baby?" I asked.

McNearny and Jones exchanged looks. Jones hung his head.

McNearny's lips formed a straight line. "They delivered the baby by cesarean. She's going to be fine."

My heart stopped. "And Evelyn? What about Evelyn?"

"They don't know yet, Connolly," McNearny said. "It's not looking good."

• CHAPTER THIRTY-THREE •

Thanksgiving

To Do:

1. Cook!!!

I awoke to the phone ringing. I was immediately annoyed. It was bad enough that I'd gotten to bed at midnight only to be woken up every few hours by Laurie's hunger cries, but now that both of us were sound asleep, to have the shrill sound rupture my dreams was the limit!

"Hello?"

"Kid! You got a write-up in the paper!" Galigani said.

Suddenly being woken up wasn't so bad.

"I did?"

I swung my feet off the bed and stopped short. Every part of my body ached. There were bruises up and down my legs, and my ribs were stiff where the doctor had taped them.

"Nice big spread, but it's mostly about your client, The Grizzly," Galigani said. "He does mention you, though. At the very end. Almost like small print."

Time to let go of any media darling dreams.

"It's a good thing I didn't get involved for the glory," I said.

"Yeah, because they misspelled your name, too." Galigani laughed.

I snorted. "Geez. No good deed goes unpunished!"

"What time is dinner?"

The smell of pumpkin pie filled the house. The wind whipped through our chimney as Jim was preparing a fire. He crumpled some newspaper and stacked the logs against each other in an upright triangle. I finished setting the table and lit the candles.

Some heat started to kick out from the fireplace and the house was getting cozy. I played my new Ricky Martin CD, and Laurie snoozed in her bassinet. The doorbell sounded. It was Galigani and Mom standing on my front stoop. Galigani had brought the stuffing and Mom had made the potatoes.

I helped Galigani take everything to the kitchen while Mom woke Laurie.

We sat down at the table and said prayers. Mom was sitting across from me with Laurie in her lap. Jim was at the head of the table and Galigani sat opposite him.

Jim carved the turkey and laid out a delectable platter, alternating the white and dark meat.

He passed the platter to me. "I'm most thankful for my wife and daughter."

I selected a piece of dark meat and put it on my plate.

"I'm most thankful for my lovely peanut, her father, my mother, and my boss."

I passed the platter to Galigani.

"I'm most thankful to be with such wonderful company tonight and thankful a murderer is behind bars because of our efforts," Galigani said. "Kid, I'm sure glad you insisted I sponsor you!"

"Wait," Mom said. "I insisted you sponsor Kate. I'm the insister!"

"Yes, you are, Mom," Jim said.

"Here's to justice!" Mom said, holding up her wineglass. Jim followed suit and we all drank to the toast.

Galigani served himself some turkey and passed the tray to Mom.

Mom said, "I'm most thankful that Jim got the turkey in the brine before the EMTs interrupted him with a call about Kate!"

Galigani laughed. I gagged on my wine.

"God, Mom! Aren't you thankful for Laurie?"

"Of course I am! I'm thankful for all of you! *And* I'm especially thankful that my bunions aren't bothering me tonight!"

Jim snickered into his napkin.

"And another thing I'm extremely thankful for is that Paula sent the pumpkin pie! It smells delicious!"

I frowned. "How do you know she sent the pie?"

Mom laughed. "Well, I know you didn't make it and Jim doesn't bake."

"Will you pass the potatoes, Vera?" Galigani asked.

Mom handed him the potatoes, and after he served himself, the bowl made its way around the table.

I served myself some stuffing, then shoveled a spoonful of mashed potatoes onto my plate. I poured gravy over the turkey and potatoes then reached for the cranberries. Canned.

Who had time to make fresh with a newborn and a new career on their hands?

I cut into my turkey and savored my first bite. It was deliciously moist.

We made small talk during dinner. My thoughts kept drifting back to Evelyn. I was still waiting to hear from someone at the hospital. I'd been calling all day to check on her status, but no one had given me any information.

I thought about the case against Celia. The Grizzly had told me that any criminal defense attorney worth his weight would get that recording disallowed, but he'd promised not to take the case.

I'd spoken with Bruce in the morning. He'd been stunned by the news of the fake adoption but grateful for the update. Of course, with the cops arresting Celia, it meant he was off the hook. He could start rebuilding his life after losing Helene. He vowed that he would help the police build their case against her and wouldn't rest until she was convicted.

I'd also phoned Margaret, feeling like she was owed some closure. To my surprise she was up to speed having already spoken with Miss No-nonsense. It turned out Howard confessed his affair after receiving a call from McNearny. Margaret was distraught about Evelyn and promised to call me if she had any news before I did.

We finished dinner, then Jim and I cleared the plates to ready the table for dessert. In the kitchen I turned on the coffeemaker.

Jim leaned into me. "I love you, Kate. This is the best Thanksgiving ever because you're my wife and we have Laurie."

Tears sprang to my eyes and I hugged him. "I'm so worried about Evelyn. That's a family that might lose their mommy tonight."

Jim held me. "You can't think that way, honey. They saved the baby. I'm sure they're thankful about that. All we can do now is pray."

We held each other in silence. After a moment we heard Mom call from the dining room, "Where's my pumpkin pie?"

I brought out Paula's magnificent pie and served it at the table with a generous scope of vanilla ice cream on the side. When it was ready, Jim poured coffee and splashed a little Irish Crème into each cup.

As I sat down to dig into my pie, the phone rang. Jim and I looked at each other expectantly.

"Let it go," Mom said. "Whoever it is can call back."

I jumped up. "I can't. It might be—"

"Kate? It's Evelyn. Thank you."